A n… …ll and Earth

Dolan Cummings

Lockdown Press

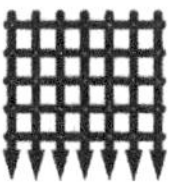

The characters and events portrayed in this book are fictitious. Any similarity to real persons, living or dead, is coincidental and not intended by the author.

ISBN: 978-1-5272-6708-4

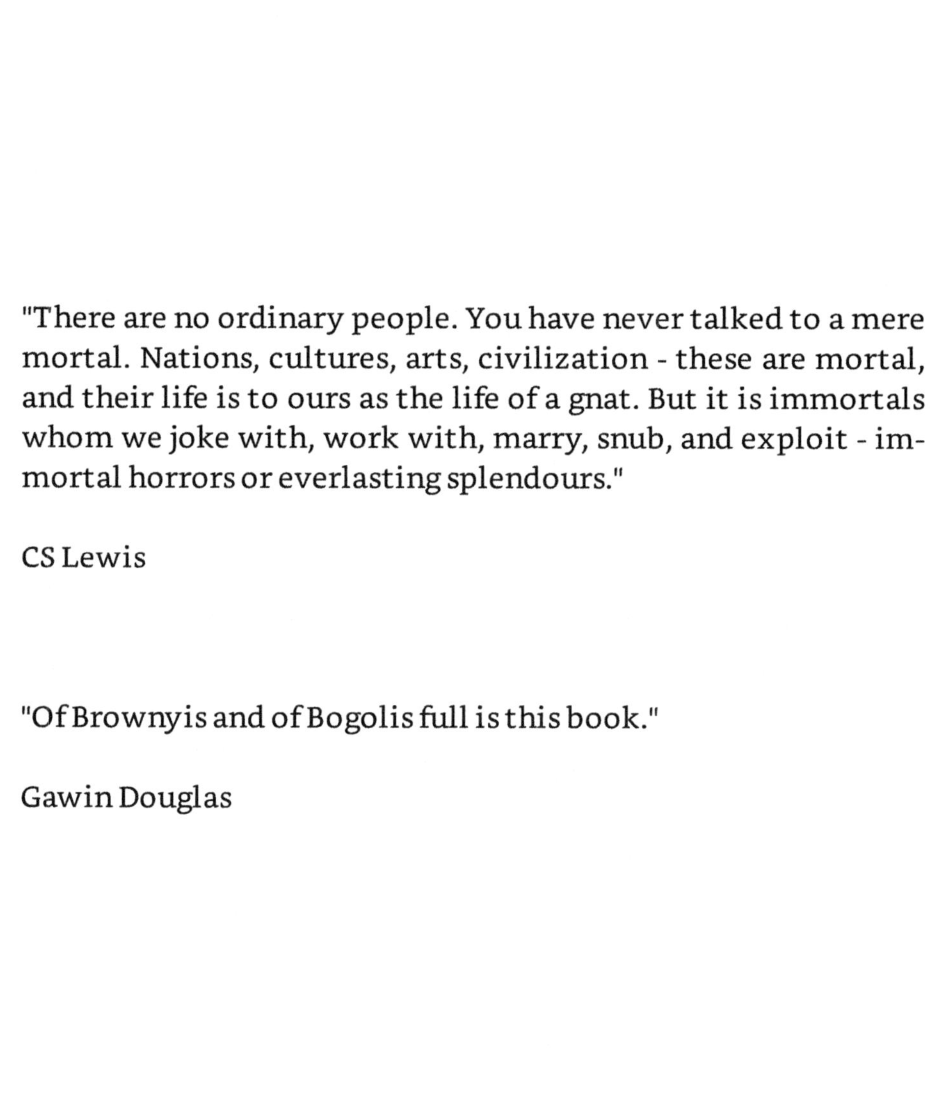

"There are no ordinary people. You have never talked to a mere mortal. Nations, cultures, arts, civilization - these are mortal, and their life is to ours as the life of a gnat. But it is immortals whom we joke with, work with, marry, snub, and exploit - immortal horrors or everlasting splendours."

CS Lewis

"Of Brownyis and of Bogolis full is this book."

Gawin Douglas

CONTENTS

PROLOGUE: ALEXANDER'S HAT

When Alexander was married to Laura, he had been untroubled by demons. Looking back now, he remembered those years as an altogether simpler and more innocent time. But really he knew that was an illusion, or at least an exaggeration, and one he could sustain only by blocking out certain memories, and in particular the memory of the night he had stumbled on something very much closer to the truth.

In those days, when the shift ended at a social hour and everyone packed up in a good mood, whether heading straight home or going for a pint, Alexander always went for a pint, and never just a pint. He enjoyed those pints, enjoyed the company of his police colleagues, even if he did not always let on. He enjoyed getting drunk, and did not think about going home, where he had no doubt his sulky sullen dame would be nursing her wrath to keep it warm. Not that she shouted at him, or called him a skellum, or a blethering, blustering, drunken blellum. She merely reminded him that he always regretted overdoing it, which was perfectly true. It was the same if he was away from Glasgow on a case. He'd find some dive to drink in, roping in a colleague when he could or otherwise drinking alone. Laura told him she felt like an American TV cop's wife, only she worried not that he would be shot, but instead found passed out in an alley. The only thing Alexander knew better than Laura was just how close he had come to that, but he felt he had a licence to ignore even the wisest counsel when it came from his own wife.

One winter's evening, a case had taken him to Ayr (a town unsurpassed for honest men and bonnie lassies), and he found himself comfortably planted in a local hostelry with his friend Johnny Souter. The weather outside was foul, but that just made his situation all the cosier. Alexander and Johnny had worked together only briefly some years ago, but they had always enjoyed a drink together, and they grew closer with every pint and every one of Johnny's increasingly outlandish stories. Alexander also discovered warm feelings towards a certain barmaid, who rewarded him with generous smiles amid the general bonhomie of the busy pub, where laughter and even songs drowned out the sound of the raging storm outside. Time flew, as if in a hurry to make Alexander late, but he was enjoying himself far too much to notice: he was feeling victorious, happy and glorious, never mind the rain over us.

Pleasure like that never lasts, of course. Like cut flowers, it fades and dies as surely as it blossoms. Like snow falling on a river, its colour melts to nothing. Like the northern lights, it flickers away before you can point to where it last moved. Like a rainbow, it is barely noticed before it is gone. Time and tide wait for no man, not even DCI Alexander. The unhappy hour came when he had to leave for the last train, pulling on his old woollen Rangers hat and taking to the night in weather the like of which he hoped never to see again. The wind blew like a bastard. The rain bounced hard off the pavement. And it was dark: thunder rumbled deep and long, but no lightning breached the darkness. Morgan was still a baby then, at home in bed, but even she would have seen that the Devil had business in hand that night.

Alexander had no desire to spend any longer than necessary outdoors on such a night, so when he saw an unlocked bicycle propped against a wall, he decided to requisition it, leaving a note to say its owner would find it at the station. Then he set off unsteadily. And in the wrong direction. After a few minutes, he did register that it seemed to be taking longer than expected to reach the station, but he put that down to the weather, or the whisky, and continued charging south, away from the station and indeed out of the town. In his confusion, he clung both to his trusty blue bonnet and to the conviction that he must persist on his now semi-rural path, resolve seeming wiser than prevarication. He warded off his fears of the bogieman by crooning a ditty or two, drowning out the spooky cries of owls or worse.

Now he recognised to the side of the road the scene of the crime he had come to investigate earlier that day, a detective being a detective even when defective. But Alexander rode on past where the travelling salesman had been found smothered in the snow, past the birches and the mighty boulder he had noticed before. What he did not know was that this had been the site of another incident some years before, when a drunken lad called Charlie had broken his neck. Or that a short distance through the gorse lay a cairn where shooters had once found a murdered child. Or indeed that nearby was a hawthorn looming over an old well, from which one Mrs Mungo had hanged herself.

He could hear the roar of the River Doon some distance ahead of him, though, swollen as it was by the storm. And now there was lightning, flashing across the sky as the thunder rolled. But he needed no illumination to see the ruins of Alloway Kirk looming through the trees, as the old church seemed almost in a blaze, light beams glancing through every gap. As he drew nearer, he heard what sounded like a wild party. 'Just kids,' he told himself reflexively, but he did not believe it for a second. Given the storm and the general menace of the night, even the coolest of sceptics could not have helped fearing something far less innocent than a drug-fuelled rave.

But Alexander was drunk, and the bolder for it. And, after all, in those days he did not believe in demons and the like, not really. Leaving the road to approach the church from cover, he struggled to get the bike through the undergrowth, but as he ventured closer and peered through a glassless window, what he saw and heard was uncanny to say the least. It was a dance, all right, but no 'kids' were in attendance. The sinister figures he saw before him could only be witches and warlocks. They whirled about the ruins, not to electronic dance music, but to old-fashioned hornpipes, jigs, strathspeys and reels, which put life and mettle in their heels. But Alexander's attention was drawn to an alcove to one side, where a huge, shaggy black dog sat playing the bagpipes. He recognised the beast instantly as Old Nick, the Devil himself in canine guise. It was not at all a suitable guise in which to play the pipes, of course, but it was just like the Devil to think that was funny. And the music he made, like the cry of the proverbial tortured cat, rang through the ruins to shake what remained of the roof.

Frozen to the spot, DCI Alexander took in the whole scene. There were coffins arrayed around the dancers, open to reveal the dead within, each of whom by some devilish magic held a up lamp in its cold, dead hands. By their light he could see on the church's holy table what he assumed to be the bones of a long-dead murderer, since they were still in gibbet irons, next to another museum-worthy adult corpse, mouth agape like a hanged man. Then two dead babies, no bigger than a man's hand. Historic or more recent, he could not say. In addition, he noticed five blood-rusted tomahawks and five gore-encrusted scimitars, adding an exotic air to proceedings. The other artefacts included a strip of cloth and a knife. Alexander could not have known that the former had been a garter used to strangle a baby, while the knife had been used to cut the throat of the murderer's own father, whose grey hairs still clung to it. And there was more, unspeakable except as a solemn warning. In each corner of the ruined kirk lay three lawyers' tongues turned inside out so you could see the lies inside, and three rotten clerics' hearts. Alexander took it all in as a detective should, before his attention was drawn back to the devilish dance itself.

Satan played louder and faster by the minute, and the

dancers flew about the ruins gleefully: reeling, setting, crossing and linking, fast and furious. Evidently it was hot work, because soon the increasingly sweaty dancers began to raise a stink, and the witches stripped off their rags to dance in their underwear. Alexander could not help wishing he'd been at least half right about this being a rave. The prospect of watching comely teenage girls cavort in snow-white pants was certainly more alluring than the spectacle of these old hags in greasy greys. Fortunately or otherwise, his loins remained in check as he watched these withered mares hurl themselves about the place.

Then the detective spotted an outlier. There was one winsome wench joining the coven just that evening. Her fame as a witch was ahead of her: rumours would haunt the Carrick shore for years to come of livestock meeting unnatural deaths, crops failing and boats sinking at sea thanks to her malignant influence. But tonight she bewitched only with her fine looks. Alexander fancied she resembled the barmaid he'd noticed earlier, but maybe he just found it convenient retrospectively to rationalise his lust that way. She had stripped to a sorely scanty slip, no doubt her best, selected for the occasion. Unknown to Alexander or anyone else in attendance, it had been a gift from the girl's dear old granny, who would no doubt have shuddered to think she'd spent her modest riches on eye-catching garb for a dance of witches.

If words could describe how the girl pranced and frolicked, perhaps the reader would be as transfixed as was Alexander, as he watched this strong and supple youth display herself in all her physicality. He stood, bewitched indeed, consuming her with his very eyes. Even Satan was smitten, and fidgeted at the sight of her, rocking backwards and forwards and panting like the dog he was that night. She feinted this way, and threw herself another, till Alexander lost all reason and uttered - surely not that loud? - '*Phwoar*!'

In an instant, all was dark.

Alexander had scarcely planted his stolen bike back on the road when the hellish legion sallied forth as one from the ruins. Like wasps buzzing angrily from their byke to attack an intruder, like wild animals in pursuit of their prey, the witches went after Alexander, with many an eldritch screech and holler.

Alexander was sure he was toast. He did at last think of Laura, but only to grieve her impending widowhood. He pedalled as fast as his legs would take him towards the roar of the Doon, banking on the superstition that witches cannot cross running water. Superstition, ha! But before he could make the keystone of the old bridge, he felt the slightest touch from behind. The young witch had sped far ahead of the others to catch him, and leaping into the air, caught hold of his hat. A last desperate burst of energy brought Alexander over the keystone to safety, but his old Rangers bonnet was his toll.

Whoever reads this true crime tale
Must learn its lesson without fail.
When tempted to go on the pish,
Or lusting after some young dish,
Take time to reconsider that.
Remember Alexander's hat.

But it was just a hat, after all. For a long time after that night, Alexander felt he had got away with something. Now, he was not so sure. Increasingly, he had begun to feel more like he had brought something with him. That same obstinate recklessness that had taken him to Alloway Kirk and almost left him there, a fresh trophy for the unholy table. He had got away *with that*. Survived unchastened. Saved from everything but himself.

He had avoided coming to this conclusion before now by telling himself the episode had never happened, or rather both believing it and not believing it. That in itself was a kind of recklessness, a refusal of intellectual commitment one way or the other, as if it did not matter. That episode at Alloway Kirk, and his response to it, had revealed a flaw in his own character. Oh, no doubt there were many more, many worse. But this reckless, careless strain was undeniable, revealing itself in his very reluctance to confront it. It was as if he did not care what happened to him in this life. Let alone eternity.

CHAPTER 1: DARK WOODS

Alexander stood hesitating at his bedroom door, peering through the darkness at his bed. The darkness was filled with unknown horrors. His bed was his only safe haven. With as much dignity as he could summon, he darted through the room and leapt back into bed and sighed in bemused relief. Safe. He supposed they thought this was funny, driving a grown man to behave like a daft wee boy having bad dreams. But that was the rule. As long as he stayed in bed, they left him alone and he was unafraid.

His nocturnal visit to the toilet had been an act of defiance. He had known they would come. There had been a distant laugh as he'd opened his bedroom door, a shadow racing across the ceiling in the hall, and then mysterious jostling to make him splash the floor as he peed. He had avoided looking in the mirror, where he knew he'd have seen his own face smiling back at him with a malicious grin; once had been enough. Their purpose, clearly, was to terrorise him. And having succeeded before, they could do so at will using only modest means. Alexander was literally afraid of his own shadow.

Indeed, perhaps best of all, from the demons' point of view, was that Alexander now attributed to them all kinds of things that were probably accidental or innocuous: he mislaid his mug, the bread went prematurely mouldy, a fuse blew. Demons? Who knew?

There were other rules, though. The demons only bothered Alexander when he was home alone. When he had his six-year-old daughter Morgan, or if his girlfriend Karen stayed over, nothing happened and he was not even afraid. In fact, Alexander's complete lack of fear for his loved ones caused him to doubt the reality of the demons altogether. If he really believed something objective was menacing him, how was it that he had no qualms about exposing his daughter or his lover to this danger? He didn't know, and thus went from being convinced he was being persecuted by demons when he spent nights at home alone to dismissing the whole thing as a delusion the rest of the time. There was a kind of comfort in those rules, then: not so much because they kept the demons at bay as because their very existence made Alexander suspect the demons only existed in his imagination.

Certainly he was untroubled by demons when he was at work. In fact, if he had allowed himself to believe in demons in his professional capacity, his work would have been very different. Alexander was in charge of a special unit dedicated to 'occult crimes'. The unit's work was premised on the assumption that the occult was a matter of superstition rather than actual supernatural occurrences. Unlike the infamous South African anti-occult police unit, none of the detectives believed in the supernatural – well, you know, not really, not most of the time – but nor could they afford to indulge their polis common sense by dismissing the occult as outlandish or irrelevant. That meant following procedure while remaining imaginatively open to the uncanny.

The unit had been initiated a few years before - and Alexander promoted to Detective Chief Inspector in charge - to take on a case of child murder in which the victim had been completely drained of blood. Inevitably it had become known as 'the vampire case', and inspired something of a moral panic, since it coincided with a fad for various, mostly harmless, occult practices. The unit never did solve that child murder, but it had taken on a series of other seemingly uncanny cases and discovered prosaically criminal explanations for all of them. Alexander liked to think of it as the Scooby Doo unit.

Just a few months ago, as the year 2000 had approached, the unit had even been responsible for investigating a case related to the so-called Millennium Bug. It had been feared that when the clocks ticked from 23.59 on 31 December 1999 to 00.00 on 1 January 2000, computers and other electronics whose calendars had thoughtlessly been programmed with two rather than four-digit years would fail to cope as 99 reverted to 00. Systems would shut down, planes would fall from the sky, anarchy would ensue. Alexander's unit had been called in when this fear had been seized on by a local religious sect, which spammed the world with promises of apocalypse and explicitly referred to the unit's original child murder case as a sign of the end of days. Having ruled out any material connection with the murder, Alexander and his colleagues had issued a statement that actually used the cranky character of the sect's pronouncements to dispel fears about the Millennium Bug more generally. The emails had been no more than jeremiads - literally - they had quoted from the Book of Jeremiah: '*Wherefore a lion out of the forest shall slay them, and a wolf of the evenings shall spoil them, a leopard shall watch over their cities: every one that goeth out thence shall be torn in pieces: because their transgressions are many, and their backslidings are increased.*' Then 2000 arrived and all was well.

The Millennium Bug scare would soon seem even more naive, innocent even, in the wake of the 9/11 terror attacks of 2001. But the story that follows took place before all that. Before counterterrorism became an organising principle for police work. And before a man could point to an enemy in a cave or in an internet chatroom and tell himself that *there* was evil. Of course, the pretence that evil springs from over *there* would not last long. Evil cannot in good faith be held at arm's length indefinitely. It creeps back to its real source and home: the human soul. The problem faced by Alexander, however, was not locating evil; he was inundated with precisely those criminal cases - many of them pathetically domestic - that were explicitly described as evil. The hard part was making sense of it.

Happily, comprehending evil was not actually Alexander's job. That was solving cases. Overall, the unit's remit had expanded slightly since its inception, partly as a result of its success. Alexander had managed to overcome early attempts to limit it to 'genuinely occult' cases by pointing out there was no such thing. He and his colleagues took on cases with a sinister hue, occult or otherwise - often these involved sex crimes, which always proceed from the dark side of human nature - and they solved them, or tried to, by refusing to be distracted by the darkness. Alexander was content to do his job by establishing the guilt of the guilty; as much as he struggled to understand it, he was blissfully unencumbered by any *fascination* with evil.

So, as far as he was concerned, work was good. In fact, because Alexander only experienced spiritual attacks when alone, company - whether domestic or professional - became a kind of refuge. While he refused to seek out company just for comfort – he didn't linger at work, and made a point of spending as many nights alone as before the attacks began – he no longer treasured solitude as he always had done till now. Or more accurately, he no longer felt the benefit of having time away from other human beings, because that time was no longer his own.

Still, a renewed enthusiasm for company was perhaps a good thing, given that Alexander's allegedly sullen tendencies had been a point of contention with Karen both professionally and personally. Karen was both Alexander's junior colleague and his consequently semi-secret girlfriend, and the double dose of dour was a bit much for her.

At work, Alexander's methods were necessarily introspective at times, as well as collaborative at others, but it did make a difference when he seemed pleased to see his colleagues. And in fact he likes his colleagues, not just Karen, and enjoyed the accidental bonhomie than ensued when he smiled at them, even if he only smiled at them because he was relieved to be in company other than that of his tormenting demons. It was immediately after such an episode, joking with the team about the dress sense of a suspect who'd just been convicted in an important case, that the rules changed.

Alexander opened the door to the briefing room, where he often sat alone to gather his thoughts, and the next instant he was breathless with terror. Three huge animals glared back at him: on the table stood a spotted leopard; on the floor, a lion raised itself up towards him, but worst of all was a hungry-looking wolf that made him shake with terror. Alexander shut the door as if doing so would make the animals go away. Perhaps it would.

When he opened the door again, the animals had indeed gone. Alexander's relief was tempered by two thoughts. First, this attack had come at work. Were the gloves now off? Would he be plagued by fear wherever he was? Secondly, these animals were straight out of the Biblical prophecy he'd made such light of in the Millennium Bug case. Maybe that was a good thing; the idea had been put into his head *as* an idea, and now it had given form to some inner anxiety. A vision of some completely novel and unknown horror would have been more worrying; it would have suggested something on the outside trying to get in.

On the other hand, what if it meant the prophesy were true? What would that even mean? Alexander marched boldly into the room and sat down to think.

Alexander had first been referred to Dr Bakshi after a routine psychological assessment at work: he'd been told he should talk to someone about his stress. He suspected this had been engineered by the Chief Super, his immediate boss, after one too many disagreements. Not that it was malicious or underhand: the Chief Super no doubt believed Alexander's occasional dissent was a cry for help; he was like that. And a special unit like Alexander's unsettled the usual chain of command, so the boss probably felt the need to assert himself for the sake of it, even if only by subtly undermining Alexander's authority.

Reluctantly, though, Alexander found himself enjoying his weekly sessions. It was nice to have someone to talk to about whatever happened to be on his mind, and Dr Bakshi seemed a sympathetic woman. He never seriously considered bringing up his spiritual attacks, though. You don't go to a witch doctor to talk about how your feelings of inadequacy are rooted in your childhood, so why trouble a psychotherapist with your demons? Still, this apparent change to the rules weighed heavily on him, and he wondered if he could broach it somehow.

At his last appointment, he had instead discussed his alleged 'wandering eye', something Karen had been complaining about. 'I really don't think it's a sexual thing at all,' he'd insisted. 'I mean, if you take cleavage, that's really an aesthetic response. The eye is drawn by the curve of the breast, just like looking at a painting. Don't you think?' He motioned with his head, following an imaginary curve downwards.

Dr Bakshi would not be drawn.

'Or, I don't know, sometimes it's a chicken and egg thing. I swear sometimes what catches my eye is a woman's hand tugging down her dress or whatever, and then it looks like she's doing it because I'm looking.' He laughed at himself. 'Oh, I'm sure that's well documented subconscious behaviour, isn't it? Women attract attention just so they can repel it?'

'If you say so.'

Alexander smiled to himself as he rehearsed this conversation in his mind, but his enjoyment of the memory could not stave off the question of what he would talk about this time. The vision of the animals was the only thing he could think about, and the thought was terrifying. Did it mean he could expect torments at work, interference with investigations? Did it mean Karen and Morgan were no longer off limits, either in his flat or anywhere else? He thought of rushing to his ex-wife's house to protect Morgan, but something told him this would have been missing the point.

Even as he doubted it, he drew reassurance from the feeling that there *was* a point. That would mean his unconscious was trying to tell him something. There was a mystery to solve. The demons were not real.

But in Alexander's experience, such reassuring thoughts were to be treated with caution. Children who tell themselves their loved ones are safe as long as they don't step on the cracks know deep down they are playing a silly game. In the real world, the danger is not that you step on a crack and something awful happens, but that something awful happens regardless of where you put your feet. What if the supernatural were no less terrifyingly real than anything else? It was when he doubted whether the demons' rules had been any more than a cruel joke that Alexander was truly afraid.

'Let's talk about superstition,' he said to Dr Bakshi that evening.

'Are you superstitious?'

'Not in the conventional sense: horoscopes, shoes on tables, that kind of thing. But yes, I think I am, in a more ordinary way. I have rituals, ways of doing things, like a lot of people. We get unsettled by even trivial deviations from the scripts we set ourselves. Isn't that a kind of superstition?'

'Perhaps it is. Can you give me an example?'

Here was one Alexander had prepared earlier: 'In the canteen at work, there's a young woman who serves hot drinks. I always smile at her when I go there for coffee on morning shifts, and she always smiles back. Only the other day she didn't. She barely made eye contact. And that bothered me all day.'

'Perhaps she was just in a bad mood.'

'Clearly.'

'Maybe it had nothing to do with you. Maybe she'd had a fight with her boyfriend.'

'What makes you think she has a boyfriend?'

'Why not? Are you jealous?'

Alexander laughed. 'Not especially. But if she'd had a fight with a boyfriend, you're right: it was nothing to do with me. That's a relief in a way, but also kind of annoying.'

'You do know the world doesn't revolve around you, Alexander?' Dr Bakshi asked, more probingly than accusingly.

'You sound like my ex-wife,' Alexander said, enjoying the cliché far too much. 'But, no - sorry - I mean that's what I meant by superstition. Expectations about the world. As if we can control the world through our own wee rituals, by obeying certain rules...'

'"*A* boyfriend",' she interrupted

'Huh?'

'Just before, you said "if she'd had fight with *a* boyfriend". I'd said, "*her* boyfriend". Do you see the difference?'

'You don't want to discuss my theory about superstition?'

'One thing at a time. You brought up this example of something that upset you, so I think we should get to the bottom of it.'

'OK, so "*a* boyfriend" diminishes the significance of the relationship, suggests something fleeting rather than an established relationship, right? Meaning I prefer to think of all desirable women as available to me?'

'Do you?'

Alexander arrived home and wished he'd arranged to see Karen that night. He had implied that his session with Dr Bakshi meant he was too busy, but there was no reason they could not have met for a drink afterwards, and Karen knew that: she had merely accepted it as an excuse. Registered it as an excuse. Stuff like that is not good for a relationship. Alexander would have a drink anyway, of course. He took a can of lager from the fridge and took his usual place on the sofa, reaching for the TV remote control. There was the usual triple explosion, as the TV spluttered on, he punctured the beer can open and leant to one side to release a fart. Did he like to think of all desirable women as available to him? Well, who could resist?

The local news was reporting an arson attack on a car dealership. Probably gang-related, they said. Alexander winced. That could mean anything from the Mafia to a bunch of wee neds – why did people have to be so sloppy? Most likely the dealer was involved with drugs or nightclubs, and owed money to some hard man. Nothing to do with bloody 'Tongs ya bass' anyway. Anyway, no occult connection, which was always a relief. He perked up when the football news came on. Rangers were 18 points clear at the top of the table and it was only a matter of time before they clinched the title. Alexander had a good feeling about their prospects in Europe next season too. Onwards and upwards.

The rules had been a cruel joke, he decided when the football news was over. He flicked absently through the channels as he pondered what the demons wanted. Not that demons could be expected to have comprehensible motives, of course – police work had shown him that human beings were odd enough, never mind unnatural spirits – perhaps the Devil only knew what this was about.

It had been some time since Alexander had last spoken to Satan, who had used to visit him regularly. In fact, Alexander was no more certain about whether these visits had been real or imaginary than he was about the demons, but some of the conversations he'd had had been helpful in developing his thoughts about the unit, and sometimes life in general. He reflected for a moment that the Desolate One's place in his life had more or less been taken over by Dr Bakshi. Still, he missed their chats. And he was somehow sure that the Devil was not responsible for his torment. He thought of Agent Starling in *The Silence of the Lambs*, confident that Hannibal the Cannibal would not hunt her down, because, 'he would consider it rude'.

He called Karen, partly to check she wasn't upset with him. He couldn't rule out the possibility that he was also calling partly because he was afraid of the demons, and wanted to hear her voice.

'You don't call for chats.'

'No, I suppose I don't.'

Whisky, then. It dulled his anxiety about the strange shadow figures creeping about behind the TV screen. And now he could sort of blame Karen for his resort to drink.

CHAPTER 2: SWEPT ALONG

It occurred to Alexander that his life was not as he had planned it. He had not, in fact, planned it. His career was conventional, in a good way. He had always, nearly always, wanted to be a detective, and he had followed the time-honoured (and non-negotiable) pattern of serving in uniform before climbing the ladder. Sure, he'd taken the time to go to university first, and not to study anything especially relevant to his chosen career, not at least in terms most people would recognise. Theology is relevant to anything to which you choose to think of it as being relevant. But other than that, his career was as conventional and predictable as any other professional's – time served, talent shown, promotion earned in accordance with one or the other. Regardless of the success or otherwise of the unit, he would one day retire with a pension.

Alexander's home life was not like that. He had married; a nurse, at that. And they had had a child, more or less planned. Just the one, though, before divorce had loomed with all the expectedness of promotion and none of the sense of progress. It just happened, they had told themselves, even as they had made it happen. Now he lived in a rented flat, had his daughter to stay intermittently, the schedule improvised according to two interweaving and unpredictable shift patterns. And he had

Karen. That had been predictable, perhaps, but unplanned and without a plan. They had chemistry, they had proximity, they had been swept along until now. And when you're being swept along, now never comes.

Somewhere at the fringes of his consciousness, Alexander worried that he was supposed to be leading a different life altogether, not necessarily with a different cast of characters, but almost certainly with a different kind of male lead.

Karen had been planning all day to have a bath in the evening. Alexander's flat, where she had spent the previous night, did not have a bath. It had a standalone shower, which had its uses, but soaking was not one of them. As she stepped into the tub, she winked at herself in the mirror that covered the wall alongside. She was looking good, after all. F-I-T. She sank back into the soapy, steamy water and raised a leg so she could admire it, turning it this way and that. Who could resist that firm, elegant leg? Nobody. And she had two.

After her bath she stood in front of her bedroom mirror, contemplating her hair. She'd had it cut just a few days ago, but in a style she had not changed all her adult life. She liked it still – it made her feel like her – but wondered if it were not somehow wrong to keep the same hairstyle for so long. Stupid gender thing, she supposed; not the sort of thing men bother about.

Still, she could still remember the moment when she had assumed responsibility for her own hair, wresting the privilege from her mother at around the same time she'd been given her own set of house keys. She'd had it cut all of a centimetre shorter than had been her mother's preference, just to satisfy herself that she could. Karen did not believe in taking such things too far, and the style she had eventually settled on was unremarkable. Does one want one's hair to be remarkable? Karen did not, not really. Alexander had once made her blush by whispering with a twinkle in his eye that her hair was her second-best physical feature, and leaving it at that. He was a clever bastard like that. She picked up her brush and brushed her hair wearily but systematically, an end-of-day ritual as old as the style itself.

When she had finished, she put the brush down and began practising her repertoire of facial expressions. Unlike her hairstyle, her expressions had changed over the years, not dramatically but subtly, in response to changing circumstances and requirements. She had little use now for the coquettish smile she had once been so pleased with. Instead, she liked to experiment with authoritative expressions of various kinds. She had often been complimented on her 'polis face', which her friends told her was right scary. But she was also cultivating a more 'substantial' face that she felt was in keeping with her years and accomplishments. Not that Karen was all serious these days. She also had the carefree laugh of a woman old enough not to worry about her facial expressions. The trick was not to make it *too* carefree.

Unknown to Karen, it had been her carefully controlled face that had first aroused Alexander's passion for her. On an early date, she had greeted him with a smile – not the coquettish one, but an apparently warmer one that was in fact so deliberate and careful that it moved Alexander much more than a merely spontaneously smile. It had told him that she cared, just a little too much for the casual circumstances, but he had been thirsty for that kind of affection.

Much later, though, he had complained about another of Karen's faces.

'Would you stop making that face?'

'What face?'

'That "listening" face.'

'You want me to stop listening?'

'No, I want you to stop doing the "listening" face.'

Evidently the listening face made Alexander nervous, as if he were expected to say something. She didn't stop doing it.

Karen had once thought of becoming an actress, or at least realised she might have a talent for it. Reading plays out loud at school, the other kids had read their parts in an unintentionally comical monotone. Karen read with feeling, trying to inhabit the character and express something of what she was reading. She'd enjoyed it. The other kids had said she was mental. But she remembered the shiver of anticipation that would go round the room every time her lines were coming up.

She had opted instead for a career in the police partly because she wanted a secure career path, partly because she wanted to bring criminals to justice, and partly because she liked telling people what to do. Actually, that last part was just Karen's wee joke; in any case, it did not seem to be a big part of the job. It was the justice part that kept her motivated, even if the pickings were lean.

Alexander slept badly till dawn, when he fell into a deep sleep. When he woke it was almost noon. It was an overcast Good Friday and he had nowhere to be, so he fretted aimlessly till he was interrupted by an email from an author of his acquaintance. He said he had a tip that would be of interest to Alexander's unit, and might even involve a bit of an adventure. Alexander respected the author, and had even found himself half-consciously emulating one of his characters – a hardboiled detective who had featured in a sort of postmodern *bildungsroman* – but he was sceptical about the offer of help. The author was no polis, and Alexander no adventurer.

The author replied immediately to Alexander's non-committal response by explaining that he had been approached by a someone from the detective's past, a woman he could not name, but who was now extremely well-connected and wished to extend a hand of friendship. Alexander was intrigued, obviously, but also irritated by the author's refusal to name a name. He made a brief mental roll call of women he had known one way or another, but only one raised a flicker of excitement to match the intrigue. Leanne McGlone?

Leanne had been a sixteen-year-old schoolgirl when she'd got caught up in a murder case a few years before. Originally her boyfriend had been charged, but the killer had almost certainly been another boy who was subsequently killed too, again almost certainly by Leanne's sister, who had subsequently disappeared. At the time, Alexander had been in the midst of a premature midlife crisis that coincided (ha!) with the breakdown of his marriage, and he had fallen in love with the girl. Unfortunate as it seemed at the time, it had probably been just as well that this had led not to a scandalous affair, but instead to a rather touching friendship. Leanne babysat Morgan and, in their snatched moments together, she and Alexander discussed life in general and Leanne's future in particular. This turned out to be as a musician and composer. Alexander had even taken Morgan to see her perform in New York. As Leanne's fledgling career had taken off in the States, they had kept in touch by email, and while it had now been more than a year since he had heard from her, she hardly needed the author's help to contact Alexander if she wanted to. So was his mysterious woman not Leanne? Who else? He had no idea.

As dusk approached that very day, the author's instructions took Alexander to a street corner in an unfamiliar part of Glasgow's East End. As the instructions had indicated, there indeed stood a pub, the Hope. It appeared to be abandoned. But when Alexander pressed his ear to the plywood hoarding he heard familiar pub sounds within. He wandered along the street looking for a way round the back. A couple of doors down was an open close. He went in and found the back door similarly unsecured. Out the back and over two brick walls, he found the pub's fire exit door ajar and in he went.

As he entered the bar, a few drinkers glanced at him, but they didn't seem that interested, and nor did they seem interesting. Given the lack of a proper entrance, Alexander surmised surreally that they had been regular drinkers who had simply never left when the pub shut down. Their nondescript appearance was somehow affirmed by a prominent poster: 'No Football Colours'.

Alexander approached the bar, and the barman scowled. 'We're closed. Go and drink somewhere else.'

'I'm not here by choice, 'Alexander said. 'I was sent. And I was told to order a rare malt.' He read haltingly from a scrap of paper. 'Lascia-togne-speraigh?'

The barman eyed him suspiciously, but reached for a bottle. He poured the whisky carelessly into a tumbler and set it on the bar.

For a 'rare malt' it didn't look or smell like something to be savoured, so Alexander threw it back like a TV detective would, ready to follow the motion with the obligatory grimace. But before he could even feel the heat of a rough shot, he was immediately overwhelmed by nausea, his vision turned scarlet and he passed out.

He came to still on his feet and looked around him: everything looked the same but worse, uglier somehow, and devoid of grace. The light was garish, the décor vile and the people ugly as sin, drinking joylessly to stave off hangovers. He looked inside himself and saw only fear and despair. What was the point of doing this, of doing anything? He didn't care. Worse than that, he realised he'd made a mistake; he was terrified of some unspecified thing. No, he was just terrified; there was no object. What had he done? But wait. He understood. He was in Hell, but only as a visitor. He pulled himself together: he didn't have to feel good about it, but would go through the motions as necessary.

He recognised a recently deceased murderer of his acquaintance among a group seemingly queueing for the toilets, but they were all too agitated and impatient to notice Alexander. A sign on the wall indicated there was another room downstairs; Alexander ignored a 'Private Function' notice and descended purposefully, only stumbling a little halfway down. There was a function room, but it was empty. Passing through it, Alexander found himself in a corridor along which the queue he had seen upstairs snaked from another staircase towards the toilets. There was a skylight in the ceiling above, but it had been completely blacked out. He flashed his warrant card to skip the queue and went straight in to find a row of confession boxes instead of toilet cubicles. The last confessant's booth was empty, so he took his place and said nothing.

'You're not supposed to be here,' said a voice from behind

the screen. But before Alexander had a chance to respond, the voice added, 'Still, what have you got?'

'The usual, I suppose.'

The voice hesitated. 'Well you can follow the others to the next level down.'

With that, the confession box became a lift, in the unproblematic way such things happen in dreams. Alexander felt himself descending until the lift stopped without a jolt, and the doors opened.

He stepped out into a corridor where he felt a powerful draught that grew into a strong wind and soon overpowered him. He lost his footing and was blown tumbling along the corridor until he was simply whirling through space with no idea which way was up, down, or anywise. A stray heel crashed into his mouth, alerting him to the fact he was not alone. Several figures, in fact, flew haphazardly alongside him, some faster than others, so the company kept changing, and Alexander had to twist and turn as best he could to avoid further collisions. Not just several, in fact; innumerable bodies tumbled around him. But a few were unmistakable.

A face whirled by with a beautiful nose that could only be Cleopatra's, the passionate queen towing Mark Antony after her. Tristan and Isolde span past grasping after one another like a dog chasing its tail. Alexander narrowly avoided crashing into Romeo and Juliet, Troilus and Criseyde, countless others he could not name. The detective also noticed a few same-sex couples and made a mental note. Others had seemingly come uncoupled: Semiramis, not recognised by Alexander, but the original sexual revolutionary, who had abolished morality in ancient Assyria; Paris, who chose love over wisdom and power, and seemed still to be searching for it; Anna Karenina, Lady Chatterley, Heathcliff, Casanova, another Casanova. Some caught hold of others for a few seconds or longer, all tumbling helplessly through space, driven by the mad, mysterious wind.

But Alexander's attention was caught by a figure that looked like Karen. Not that he mistook her for Karen – no such horror – but this woman had Karen's look. It was the look that had first attracted him to Karen, a certain self-assurance, perhaps – or was it an unembarrassed vulnerability? – captured in a particular style. Brunette, demurely feminine, but with a hint of defiant independence. She even had the same elegantly unremarkable hairstyle. Alexander felt a twinge of lust and the wind seemed to speed up, but, with a tantalising flash of leg, the woman was gone.

Before long, Alexander recognised another passing figure – another handsome young woman – and reached out for her, more from curiosity than excitement.

'Ms Rimini?' he enquired, clasping her ankle.

'Do I know you?' she replied, momentarily turning her attention from the young man with whom she was entangled.

'I arrested your husband,' Alexander explained.

'Aha!' she called to her paramour, 'This is the detective who arrested your brother.'

'There's a place below for that murdering bastard,' the young man shouted to Alexander, wriggling in the wind to get a look at the detective.

Alexander didn't doubt it, but was more interested in the lovers' own story. Francesca Rimini had been the wife of a prominent Glasgow ice cream magnate who caught her in bed with his younger brother Paolo and killed them both on the spot.

'Your story is tragic,' he told them, 'but what made you take the risk?'

The pair sighed in unison: 'Amore, amore, amore!'

Francesca continued tearfully, almost winsomely, 'He bought me a book, the romantic fool. What could be more innocent than a book? Second-hand at that!' She gazed longingly at her lover as the three hurtled through space. 'But when we read together about Lancelot and Guinevere, their doomed love, their reckless passion... And then we caught one another's eye, well something gave. Call it a rush of blood, if you like. The rest is history.'

At that, Alexander lost hold of Francesca's ankle and the

unhappy pair sped away from him. Perhaps he took another accidental blow to the head from another doomed lover, because suddenly he passed out and dropped like a corpse from the windy thoroughfare.

He regained consciousness to find himself in bed with Karen, or rather all over the bed with Karen, in the throes of passion, ecstatic. Before long it was over and the lovers collapsed in a triumphant heap.

'God, we're good,' Karen said.

CHAPTER 3: PORTION CONTROL

Morgan stuck out her tongue. This was becoming a habit; or the return of a habit Alexander had thought she'd grown out of. He knew Morgan was lying, but she wouldn't back down. The six-year-old was defiantly unrepentant.

'Who else ate them?' he demanded. 'One of your imaginary friends?'

'Maybe it was *your* imaginary friends.'

That unnerved him. Who was to say the demons hadn't eaten Morgan's entire Easter egg haul in one day just to get her into trouble and sow discord? But Alexander could tell when people were lying, most of all his own daughter. 'Don't be cheeky,' he said sharply.

She stuck out her tongue again.

Morgan's mother, Alexander's ex-wife Laura, had dropped her off at his place that morning, Easter Saturday, despairing at their daughter's increasingly bad behaviour. Detective Dad had told her he'd get to the bottom of it, but already he suspected the bottom of it was human nature. 'Well, you'll get no more chocolate till you confess,' he said firmly.

'That's not fair!' Morgan shouted.

He gave her a look and she ran in tears to her room.

After a weekend of domestic stalemate interrupted only by biblical epics, Alexander returned to work on Monday, police work being no respecter of bank holidays. DC McGrain handed him a gift-wrapped box that had come for him. He guessed from the shape and weight that it was a bottle. 'Are you going to share it?' McGrain added with a grin.

'Nah,' said Alexander, taking the gift to the relative privacy of his cubicle. 'I'm feeling greedy.'

As Alexander had suspected, the tipple turned out to be Lasciatognesperaigh, presumably a gift from the author. He pondered whether it would be wise to drink it in the office, and decided against it, not liking to imagine how that would work out. So late in the afternoon, he poured some of the damnable malt into a flask and went out for a walk. At what seemed a safe distance from police HQ, at a quiet spot under a motorway flyover, he took a swig. Immediately it began to rain heavily. The sky darkened and Alexander was soon in the midst of a hailstorm so violent and blustery that the motorway above him afforded little if any shelter. 'Bloody Hell,' he muttered, pulling his raincoat tighter about himself in a vain effort to resist the sudden chill.

Now a cacophony of barks and howls alerted Alexander to the horror that surrounded him. The dark, drenched terrain about him was strewn with sorry sinners, who were being savaged by wild dogs. One such beast leapt at Alexander, dripping foul-smelling slaver over him before he managed to hurl it to his side, where it landed on a prone, helpless fat man and bit greedily into his face. All around him, Alexander realised, similarly corpulent sinners suffered the same fate, blood streaming from their wounds only to be washed away by the lashing rain. Meanwhile, even the dogs' fierce barks and howls could not drown out the racket made by the giant hailstones battering into the ground and ricocheting painfully off the poor sinners, Alexander included.

'Hey, pal! Pal! Remember me?' A fat guy in a Rangers scarf had escaped canine attention long enough to get up and hobble towards Alexander. He was shirtless under that scarf, and his pale, blubbery torso had been ripped by the savage dogs, leaving several strips of flesh hanging loose, looking much like the processed cheese strings Morgan enjoyed so much.

'Sorry, no, I don't think I do,' Alexander replied, looking away squeamishly. 'Though maybe you look a bit different now.'

'Aye, fair point. But I mind you fae the Govan stand at Ibrox. They used to call me Porky, for obvious reasons.' A scrawny hound leapt at him and hungrily tore off the man's loose-hanging flesh with its teeth. Porky howled in pain and then added through an agonised wince, 'I should've listened.'

Alexander felt bad for his fellow Rangers supporter: there was no point lingering on the man's obvious gluttony and his punishment for it. 'Can you still follow football in here?'

'No point. There's nae buzz when you know what's gonnae happen. Like watching a fuckin' car crash.'

'What?' Alexander was bemused, but he decided to humour the apparently prophetic Porky. 'You can see the future?'

'Aye, and as far as I can see, the future's green and white. I blame superbia, invidia an' avarizia,' Porky said, shaking his head.

It sounded bad, but Alexander hadn't heard of what he supposed was a trio of trouble-making Italian players. He changed the subject, asking Porky what if anything he knew about his friend the author, also a regular at Ibrox and the surrounding bars.

'That writer? He's a worse sinner than me. If he's deid, you'll find him deeper into this place. Remember me to the boys, anyway.' With that, Porky sat down wearily, stealing a last glance at Alexander as he rejoined his glutinous pals and their hungry best friends.

Alexander did not think the author was dead, but there was clearly a lot he did not understand. He took a last, doleful look of his own at the carnage, and then turned away: the rain had stopped, and the day brightened as he walked back towards HQ. He passed a Greggs, and bought a couple of pies, which he scoffed greedily, perfectly aware of the irony or whatever. Then he felt an urge to see Dr Bakshi, but his next appointment was two days away. He decided instead to have another dram after catching up with his colleagues. Hell was proving sort of therapeutic.

It was already dusk when Alexander reached an appropriately seedy part of the city some way from HQ and took a sip from his flask, but as the whisky went down he felt the atmosphere change and the sky darkened further. His attention was drawn to a flickering light above a doorway a couple of hundred yards up the street: it looked like a nightclub, though not one he had ever noticed before. As he approached, he noticed a bouncer at the door, and soon recognised him as a notorious but long dead loan shark known as Bluto. On recognising Alexander, he blurted incomprehensibly, distorting his vowels just for badness, as members of Glasgow's criminal classes were wont to do. He made as if to block the policeman's entrance, but Alexander brushed him aside wordlessly and descended into the club.

Inside, he found his way to a balcony overlooking a vast subterranean dance floor, where a Hellish roller disco was in progress. The noise was deafening, and Alexander strained to make out what was happening, as the scene was illuminated only by strobes and coloured lasers shooting in all directions.

The floor was teeming with roller-skated figures hurtling this way and that, regularly colliding and exchanging abuse. Nearly all were dressed in suits, and Alexander couldn't make out any faces, even when the sinners drew near beneath him, as they all seemed pretty much interchangeable. It was only his years of experience as a detective that allowed him to distinguish certain types. There were lots of bankers and the like, fund managers, insurance people, possibly some civil servants? In fact, many of the sinners gave off a distinctly public sector vibe. All were brandishing bits of paper, some tossing them around, others snatching paper out of the air. 'How can you justify this salary, you leech?,' shouted a woman in a trouser suit, crashing into a pinstriped fat man and thrusting a sheet of paper in his face.

'It's in my contract, you tight bitch!' he returned, spinning off at speed before colliding with a local government manager, who was squatting over his skates as if shitting, or perhaps trying to hold it in.

Alexander winced, but stretched himself over the balcony to try to make out more. There was more screeching about white elephants, risk management, earmarks, budget guarantees and financial casinos. One way or another, spenders or hoarders, these people had clearly been obsessed with money.

Suddenly, one of the skaters managed to leap from the dance floor and grab onto the balcony rail. 'Pal, do you have life insurance?' he shouted to Alexander. 'Home insurance? Is your phone insured? I can get you a good deal. Honest.'

But the insurance salesman was swept from the balcony when a blast of wind ripped through the crowd, tearing the paper from the sinners' hands and knocking several of them off their skates. 'Rollover!' they began to shout. 'Here it comes! Rollover, Rollover!' And here it came: a giant flaming ball emerged from somewhere beneath Alexander's feet, and crashed into, and then over, the sinners. Some in fact seemed to stick to the ball, to be carried full circle and crushed again. When the giant flaming ball plastered with sinners reached the far side of the dance floor it divided into two balls, and each rolled off around the perimeter in opposite directions, crushing and absorbing yet more sinners before reconverging and disappearing back under the balcony, leaving charred sinners flattened all over the dance floor.

There was a moment's silence, and then more wind. Now the air was filled with more bits of paper, swirling violently in the wind as they fell from the ceiling, as if from the mortal world above. Instantly the sinners were back on their skates. Chasing one another around the dance floor, they snatched at the papers, some stuffing them into their jackets only to have them torn out by others, while others still seemed to be trying to burn bits of paper in the few dying flames left by the giant flaming ball. All the while they shouted furious abuse at one another. Alexander turned to leave, bemused. He had never had much interest in economics.

Stopping to use the toilet on his way out of the club, Alexander did remember something the author had written that touched on the subject. It was a short story about a butcher, a brewer and a baker, inspired by Adam Smith's famous observation that such businesspeople supply the public not out of benevolence, but from regard to their own interest. In the story, the butcher was struggling to compete with a rival who had set up on the same street, and their price war was intensified by a new fashion for vegetarianism in the town. The brewer had to contend not only with rival brewers, but also with a pincer movement caused by changing demographics, with traditional beer drinkers being replaced by wine-drinking gentrifiers and teetotal Muslims. Meanwhile the baker was losing business because he refused to cater to an emerging market for obscenely decorated cakes for hen parties and stag dos.

The declining fortunes of all three were mirrored by the rise of new businesses better suited to the circumstances, in particular an all-in-one catering business owned and run by a brash young woman who was convinced she could read the market like a book. She quickly got rich sure enough, but just as quickly the business failed as the result of overcapitalisation. The butcher made something of a comeback, but the brewer and the baker both went out of business, and the story had ended with the three of them silently playing cards in a former barber's turned community enterprise hub.

CHAPTER 4: A LOSS OF PERSPECTIVE

Having left the nightclub, Alexander decided to walk for a while along the nearby Forth and Clyde Canal. There was a full moon, and he was able to see far in both directions along the path that lined the bank, but observed nothing but a scrawny fox darting from his view. Then he looked down at the water, near-black polis blue in the strange light. He took a fresh swig of the magic medicine before looking up at the moon and the stars. The sky was beautiful, but any gathering reverie was aborted by the sound of the water bubbling below him. Looking down, Alexander saw something he hadn't noticed before: there was an outlet beneath his feet, channelling a lively little stream of water under the path. He looked behind him and to his left at what had appeared before to be a grassy wasteland. Now it looked more like a bog, sodden with water from the canal. He approached, intent on seeing what he probably didn't want to see.

'You fool!' someone shouted, not to Alexander but to his companion. Now the detective could make out figures moving in the darkness, knee-deep and naked in the freezing bog. He could feel the wrath in the air before he realised they were fighting. Muddy figures wrestled furiously, landing kicks and punches whenever they could get a limb free, along with liberal insults. Straight ahead of him two naked men were trading head butts, or rather, repeatedly smashing their heads together with an elegant symmetry that made it impossible to say who was butting whom. To their right, a naked woman was biting lumps out of anyone who came near her, until she took a kick to the head and flopped noisily into the bog. Furious conflict raged all around. And the language. Shocking.

Once he'd taken in the general scene, Alexander strained to make out in more detail what was going on. He tried to home in on particular scuffles, matching angry words with their owners. Then he recognised one of the sinners as a recently deceased newspaper columnist. She was being harried by two detractors, keen to tell her that something she'd written had been deeply fucking offensive. She gave as good as she got, kicking out violently as she spat, 'Blog away, losers!'

'Fascist scum!' one of them replied.

'Controversialist!' shouted the other. And now they were at each other.

Alexander looked up again at the sky, allowing the cacophony to swirl about him. Amid the expletives came a few repeated epithets, but by far the most common was 'bigot'.

Looking more closely at the surface of the water a few feet from him, Alexander noticed a steady stream of bubbles rising from below, a pattern repeated elsewhere as far as he could see. Leaning closer, he thought he could hear music. Reluctantly, he got to his knees and pressed his ear to the surface of the freezing water. It was unmistakable: a miserable dirge of some kind filled the bog. Then he recognised it as 'The Flower of Scotland'. Alexander had always hated that hymn to sullenness, much preferring the jauntier 'Scotland the Brave'. In any case, the water resonated with gloomy self-righteousness and self-pity, gurgling to the surface in stinking bubbles, presumably from the throats of miserable sinners below. Apart from the bubbles, and the occasional wave or splash from furious fighting, the bog was utterly stagnant. Alexander stood up and wiped the slimy, acid water from the side of his face.

Alexander's next few days were taken up with case work, mostly mundane and if anything unusually banal until, towards the end of the week, it became clear that something was going on. As per standard operating procedure, the unit had been notified early on about a series of incidents in Glasgow schools, because of several red flag factors: the involvement of young people, copycat behaviour and the potential for unhelpful media interest. And very soon, the sum was greater than the parts.

The first incident was at a primary school in the West End on the first day back after the Easter break, when, the teachers all agreed, the kids had been unusually hyper. One teacher reported what she called an epidemic of lies: it had started in fun, when a girl told the class she'd met Tutankhamun's mummy while on holiday in Egypt. The others had tried to outdo her with even more fantastic holiday stories, and at first the teacher had encouraged it, but then it turned nasty. One girl said another's father was a known paedophile and was going to prison, and a flurry of allegations and counter-allegations followed. The teacher shouted at the class to stop their silliness, but unusually there were unmoved by her anger, responding instead with outrage that she would not believe their lies. She lost control, and ran from the classroom in a panic, returning with the deputy head to find the class in silence. The children flatly and unanimously denied anything had happened.

In another class, a fight broke out when one boy accused another of stealing a bag of crisps, and the whole class had rounded on the accused, a fat boy, goading him with vicious taunts till he started kicking furiously at them before suffering a seizure of some kind and collapsing. He recovered when removed to a quiet room, but it later transpired that when left there alone there for just a moment he had stolen money from his teacher's purse.

Then at lunch time, a group of nine and ten-year-olds from the school had left the premises, in defiance of the rules, and caused havoc in a local shop, abusing the owner and customers, and blatantly stealing sweets and other seemingly random bits and pieces. On their return to the school, they too flatly denied any wrongdoing, and later even refused, furiously, to recognise themselves in CCTV footage from the shop.

Without any links anyone had so far been able to establish, the behaviour had spread. At afternoon break at a nearby secondary school, two boys fought over a lottery ticket they found in the playground, and things escalated when other claimants weighed in. A computer studies teacher brought the altercation to an end by snatching the ticket and theatrically eating it in front of the angry children. The parents of another pupil had since claimed that the ticket had been hers, and what's more that her numbers – the same every week – had come up in the Wednesday night draw. This had yet to be proven, but the teacher and the school were being threatened with a lawsuit.

At two further schools, slightly further afield but still in the West End, scandals had emerged concerning bullying, racist and homophobic respectively. Such incidents were not unusual, and nor was it uncommon for more to be made of them than might have been thought reasonable. The scandal was that these incidents involved teachers, not pupils. One teacher at a Catholic primary had thrown a banana at a colleague, apparently not maliciously, and perhaps not even registering it might be construed as a racist banana since the colleague in question was black. This was after all a staff room and not a football stadium, where bananas were obviously racist. But a third colleague, not even in range, had recoiled in shock. He made a formal complaint and went to the press.

The other incident had been in a private secondary: a secretary reported a male English teacher for suggesting a disproportionate number of female gym teachers were lesbians. He responded that since he was gay he couldn't possibly have meant it offensively, and made a counter-complaint alleging the secretary had been motivated by prejudices of her own. The lesbian-looking gym teacher who had probably prompted the comment in the first place was so far staying out of it. But a group of sixth-years had got wind of the matter and started an online campaign group.

Each incident on its own was unfortunate. Taken together, and occurring in such proximity, they were uncanny. Karen described it as being like the set-up for a novel, and Alexander wondered what the author would make of it. But the author had been impossible to contact since setting Alexander on his path to Hell.

A normal CID unit would have ignored the weird school incidents, but that was precisely why they had been referred to Alexander's unit. The wrong kind of common sense would make the connection all too readily: the kind of common sense, that is, that prevails in the media. An unofficial role of the unit, and the justification for having a dedicated press officer in Morag, was to contain uncanny stories, to demystify disturbing incidents and prevent media mischief-making. The danger of keeping a step ahead of the press, of course, is that you can end up doing their job for them. More than once in the past, Alexander had found himself providing the link between an otherwise mundane case and the rumours of something more sinister.

Reviewing the school incidents, he missed DI Knox PhD etc, the unit's psychological profiler and general voice of reason. She had taken an academic sabbatical to write a book, and gone all the way to Australia to escape distractions, so he supposed she would not welcome an email. She was staying with Alexander's old friend Steph, another former colleague, who had emigrated there for good, joining the local police. No one had seen that romance coming. Alexander felt doubly deprived of wise counsel, even if Steph lacked the letters after his name.

'I don't even know what "reasonable" means sometimes,' said Dr Bakshi. She was messing with Alexander's head.

He had always been sceptical about psychotherapy, or psychoanalysis or whatever it was, not because he doubted its scientific credentials (though he did), but because he doubted the ability of science itself to explain what went on in his head. Dr Bakshi was a proper psychiatrist, she had told him: a real doctor as well as a psychotherapist, that is, and Alexander enjoyed bringing up other complaints she might be able to help with; she retaliated by telling him, whatever the problem, that he needed to cut down on drinking. His only real physical complaint in fact was chronic indigestion, and he suspected that was just as beyond scientific reason as his mental disturbance – or anyone else's.

And now Dr Bakshi was joining in with his scepticism, objecting to Alexander's own withering diagnosis of the teachers who were due to strike the following day in protest at the behaviour of their pupils. Things had escalated since the spate of incidents last week, most of all at the primary school where they'd begun. The teachers were calling for several children to be suspended, and the one-day strike was meant to increase pressure on the reluctant school authorities. Alexander thought the teachers were suffering from a collective neurosis; Dr Bakshi demurred.

Certainly misbehaviour had become a serious problem at the school. The biggest problem was lying. It wasn't just the usual 'it wisnae me', though there was plenty of that. The children were constantly making things up, accusing one another, and their teachers, of anything from stealing a pencil case to murdering half a dozen prostitutes. And they refused to back down, even when taken aside or sent to the head teacher – making ordinary discipline impossible. Teachers with decades of experience seemed to have lost their authority overnight. Their adult presence was no longer magical. The children stuck resolutely to their stories, however absurd, even demanding to speak to the police when they were not believed. A handful of children were particularly bad, shouting outrageous lies from the playground to passers-by, and lashing out violently when challenged. These were the ones the teachers wanted suspended, or expelled – or executed, at least one of the teachers had been heard to mutter.

Alexander sympathised, of course. But he saw the teachers' behaviour as a continuation of the children's, rather than a sensible response to it. It was not reasonable, he insisted, to strike over the behaviour of primary school children.

'It's important to you that people behave reasonably, isn't it?' Dr Bakshi said.

'Of course. Isn't it important to everyone?'

'Presumably the teachers think they are behaving reasonably. Responding to an unreasonable situation.'

'No doubt,' Alexander conceded, 'but having a reason for doing something doesn't make it reasonable.'

He was thinking of so many cases he had worked on over the years. Why did they do it? Deprived circumstances, bad parents, just bloody malice? People acted unreasonably; that was plain enough. Why were the teachers going on strike? Because their kids were behaving badly; because they didn't feel supported by management; because bombing the school would have been disproportionate. Why did the chicken cross the road?

'Aren't you making a *moral* judgement now?' Dr Bakshi asked.

'Well it's not a clinical assessment.'

'No.'

Anyway, Dr Bakshi wanted to know how Alexander felt their sessions were going. She said it was fine to discuss whatever was on Alexander's mind, but he wasn't there just to vent, but to make progress on a journey of sorts.

'Where am I supposed to end up?'

'That's what we're here to find out.'

That evening, Alexander drank alone at home. He was not morose, but contemplative, mentally burdened. He had meant to read, but instead found himself standing and staring vacantly in various parts of the flat. At the kitchen sink, as Alexander gazed absent-mindedly out at the communal middens, something in the sky caught his eye. A bird, he thought. He followed the little shape with his eye and realised it was not a bird. It was a bat. He couldn't help smiling at the sight of it circling the back court as if it owned the place, revelling in the twilight, freshly liberated from its sun-imposed curfew, dancing just for badness in the embers of the day.

CHAPTER 5: STALEMATE AT THE GATES OF HELL

Early the next morning, Alexander set out the unit's new priorities at a team meeting. As ever, there was a backlog of cases that might never be solved. But the newest involved a series of recent burglaries of places of worship. Ceremonial objects had been taken from each, suggesting something ominous in the offing. Then there was the mutilation of a pair of cats; something very similar had happened last year, but the perpetrator was now in jail for assaulting a person, so Alexander was afraid they were dealing with a copycat (that always made the occult unit detectives nervous, however trivial the crime). There were also some suspicious bits of vandalism to investigate, and various possibly sulphurous online threats – everyday stuff for the unit.

The immediate task at hand, however, was to check on the primary school whose teachers were now on strike. After the team meeting, Karen and Alexander sat in a surveillance car across the street from the troubled school. A pair of uniforms had been considered adequate 'crowd control' for the striking teachers' picket, and indeed things appeared to be very good natured. But it wasn't public order the detectives were worried about, at least not in any immediate sense. The good thing about the strike, at least from the teachers' point of view, was that the misbehaving kids had been kept out of school for the day. That might not have been such a good thing for anyone else, of course. Alexander had had a quiet word with the senior officer responsible for patrols in the area that day, reminding her that the liberated delinquents were unlikely to be 'at home' all day. But so far, the school had been the focal point of bad behaviour, and Alexander wanted to be there, just in case.

Karen waved to a couple of the teachers she recognised, and they waved back. Alexander gave her a disapproving look, but she laughed it off; this was hardly a covert operation. He hadn't told Karen about his visits to Hell, and he was sufficiently moody in normal circumstances that she hadn't noticed any change in his demeanour. Anyway, it was hard to see exactly what *that* had to do with *this*. But besides the unanticipated whatever looming over the school, there was not much other than *that* on Alexander's mind, so it was hard to make conversation.

Presently a TV news crew arrived. Alexander's stomach registered its disapproval, and he called Morag to update her so she could prepare a press brief. Karen attempted a reassuring look. This was a quirky story – teachers striking over their kids' bad behaviour – but the media would be looking for angles. What was the bigger story behind all this? Kids out of control? Teachers losing the plot? The whole world going to Hell in a handcart? It would depend on what else they got hold of. Despite his disdain for the striking teachers, Alexander's preference was for a simple 'kids today' line, he told Morag. Everyone was comfortable with that cliché.

'What's the worst-case scenario?' Karen replied, not getting what he was so anxious about.

Alexander showed her a number of newspaper stories he'd saved from over the past week. There were three about the strike, and some of the incidents that had led to it. There were two more about the lottery ticket controversy; the parents were now suing the teacher who'd eaten the ticket, though it remained unclear how credible their case was. Nothing about the incidents involving teachers, but there was something else: 'Concern over teen Ouija board craze' read the headline. This was about a school in Falkirk, but it was an online version of the game and probably being played by kids in Glasgow too. A Church of Scotland minister with kids at the Falkirk school had contacted the local paper after the head teacher had failed to take his warnings seriously. Alexander could see this one taking off.

Today passed without incident, however, and in the evening Alexander felt drawn back to the canal, where he was disturbed to find the Hellish bog still there without the need for a dram. Angry sinners were still raging away. He felt his phone vibrate and took it out to see that it was flashing. Then he saw a flash in the distance, as if in response to the flash of his phone. He realised it was coming from a boat speeding towards him along the canal. It was a police motor boat piloted by the legendarily bad-tempered, and long dead, Sergeant McGinty of the marine policing unit.

'You, ya prick, you'll get what's coming,' the surly boatman shouted gleefully as he drew near, turning the boat to let Alexander board. Evidently he took him for a damned spirit. With the big and very much alive detective aboard, though, the boat sat noticeably deeper in the water, causing McGinty to swear as furiously at the semi-submerged sinners he had to dodge as they set off. Alexander didn't bother asking where they were going; he had the general idea. The bog sprawled on either side of the canal without regard for the geography of the city, so that Alexander saw about him nothing but Hellish desolation. In the distance, though, an imposing building, presumably their destination. What looked like minarets protruded at intervals, glowing like red-hot pokers against the dull sky.

Before they could reach it, a pair of filthy hands grasped the side of the boat, and a muddy figure hauled himself partly out of the water to address Alexander. 'What are you doing here?' he demanded.

'Just passing through,' Alexander replied. 'And who might you be?'

'A poor bastard, that's who,' the sinner replied, welling up. 'If you only knew the suffering. And it's not my fault. Everything I did wrong was a cry for help.' It was pathetic.

Suddenly Alexander was filled with an appreciation of ultimate justice. The idea of punishment rather than excuses for a wasted and destructive life pleased him immensely. He adjusted his position in the boat so he could stamp on the damned man's fingers, sending him back into the mire of his making. Moments later Alexander saw him torn apart by raging sinners shouting, 'Get Bilko!'. The flying body parts then dropped back into the bog where they grudgingly reassembled themselves.

Alexander's attention was drawn by horrific screams from up ahead. The boat was arriving at its towering destination. The building had all the architectural charm of HMP Barlinnie, and inspired in Alexander the dull terror of a convict arriving there for the first time. The canal became a moat surrounding the iron-clad citadel, and Sergeant McGinty steered slowly round before shouting to Alexander, 'Oot!' They had arrived at the entrance. The detective stepped out of the boat onto a narrow strip of land before a vast pair of gates. He looked up with terror as demons quickly gathered in fury over the gates: some reached over from behind, others perched on top, still others hovered above, all staring down at Alexander with outraged contempt. 'Who. The fuck. Is that?'

Until now Alexander had only had a vague sense of what demons were. Those who'd tormented him in his flat at night had never appeared to him in person. Indeed they had seemed more metaphorical than personal; they'd been easily conflated with his own fears and anxieties, his own 'demons'. But now he was looking up at unmistakably literal demons: these were fallen angels, and their angelic qualities scared him even more than their demonic corruption. They were bigger than men, more powerful, winged, authoritative. And their palpable personal animus was more terrifying than any animal menace. And soon there were more than a thousand of them. The gates remained firmly shut.

Alexander turned back towards the moat, but McGinty was gone. What could he do? He took out his phone and called the author, from whom he had heard nothing since his first visit to Hell. 'For fuck's sake,' he whispered determinedly between his teeth as he listened to the author's phone ring, '*Answer the phone*'. On Alexander's second attempt, the author answered.

'The thing is,' he explained, 'I'm inside the citadel, and I can't get out. So it's just a case of getting them to let you in, and then I can guide you safely the rest of the way.'

'And how am I supposed to do that?'

The author paused. 'Put one of them on.'

Alexander rolled his eyes in disbelief, but he had no choice. He held the phone high above his head and shouted, 'If one of you will speak to my friend the author, he will explain my presence here.'

There was a brief commotion among the fallen angels, and then one swooped and snatched the phone.

Alexander heard only the demonic side of the conversation: 'No. ..No. ..Well, he can find his own way back. ..Tough. ..No. ..No. ..No.' The demon tossed the phone to the ground, and returned to the top of the gates. Alexander picked it up, 'Are you still there?'

'Yes. Don't worry.'

'Well if I can't get in, can I go back?'

'There's no need for that. They don't have the authority to keep you out. I just need to... Hang on.' He seemed to be talking to someone at his end. 'It's not up to you. Do you know who authorised this? ..Do you know the kind of trouble you'll be in? ..Don't give me that! ..For fuck's sake!' Then to Alexander, 'Listen, don't worry. They're just trying it on. Don't worry: your passage has been arranged on the highest authority. It's just... Hang on.'

Alexander hung on, trying not to look at the demons,

who were not getting any less menacing. He wondered what the author had meant by the highest authority. Satan? If his meetings with the Devil had not in fact been figments of his imagination, perhaps his old friend was behind all this after all. For all Alexander's doubts, Satan had always seemed very real. But he'd never frightened Alexander like his minions up on the gate did now. The Devil had made him nervous, certainly, especially the time he'd mentioned in passing how he'd watched his 'rival' call the disciples, clearly resentful of his pull. But he'd always seemed genuinely interested in discussing ideas, learning about Alexander's work and so on, not like he'd been after his soul or whatever. These demons, by contrast, were heart-stoppingly terrifying.

CHAPTER 6: HERETICS

The author's voice returned. He sounded cross, not at Alexander, but in frustration at the situation. It seemed the demons were insistent that Alexander would not be allowed into the citadel, whoever commanded it.

'It's a battle of wills,' the author said. 'But don't worry – I'll just have to break down their resistance. Otherwise...' He paused. 'I'm 99 per cent confident. I mean, she said... It's just taking a bit longer than anticipated.'

'How did you get in there in the first place?' Alexander asked.

'That's a long story,' replied the author, but Alexander lost interest, and his breath, when he glanced up.

Never mind the demons on the gate – at the top of the tower, three monstrous female figures looked down at him. They were a mockery of femininity, like the wrong end of a hen night (an unwelcome reminder of Alexander's time in uniform). The three harridans screeched and hissed mercilessly, and when Alexander recovered from his initial shock he realised that the hissing came from their hair, not in fact hair at all but writhing snakes, while their faces and bodies were stained with blood. Alexander gasped in horror, maybe even groaned in despair.

His phone was still clasped to his ear. 'Are you still there?' he asked the author when he had his breath back, desperate for reassurance.

'Yes, what's happening?'

'Three... like Medusa,' Alexander stuttered.

'The Furies,' the author explained, 'vengeance made flesh. Their names are Grudgia, Naggie and Revengina, and they will not let anything go.'

The Furies beat and tore at themselves as they shrieked, 'Medusa! Come! We'll turn this one to stone to make up for Theseus.'

'Oh, *now* it's Medusa,' Alexander said, keeping the author in the picture.

'Don't look!' the author shouted urgently. 'Turn away, keep your eyes shut tight. You've seen *Clash of the Titans*, haven't you?'

Alexander complied, slightly annoyed that this was indeed the main cultural reference he had to work with here. Then, after a minute, 'There's a camera on my mobile. Should I use it to see what's happening?'

'Put the phone away, and put your hands over your eyes to make sure they're shut tight. Seriously, if you catch sight of Medusa, it's over. I can't help you.'

There's a lesson there, reader.

Alexander squatted with his back to the Furies and his hands firmly over his eyes, clasped shut. He wondered how he'd ever know the coast was clear, if indeed it ever would be, but before long his thoughts were interrupted by an almighty whooshing noise in the distance, accompanied by a sudden change in the air pressure and a cooling breeze: something awesome seemed to be sweeping over the water towards him. A storm, a tsunami. Keeping one hand over his eyes, he reached for his phone. 'Are you still there?'

'Yes.'

'Something's coming.'

'I know. It's safe to look: the monsters are diving under their duvets now.' He sounded more than a little relieved. 'What do you see, big man?'

'The damned are going mental! All over the bog, they're scrabbling to the edges, getting out the way of...' Alexander couldn't speak when he saw the figure approaching across the bog. At a distance he seemed incredibly tall, but as he drew closer, seemingly skating over the surface of the water, it was clear he defied perspective; he didn't belong here. He waved the stinking air from his face as he approached, and generally seemed supremely pissed off. 'Keep out of his way,' the author advised. Alexander did just that.

'Who are you trying to impress, you worthless losers?' the intruder shouted at the demons, as he flicked a little wand contemptuously at the gate, opening it instantly. 'Why do you insist on challenging what cannot be challenged? How many times do you have to be told?' Then he turned impatiently and left as he had arrived, not even looking at Alexander.

Alexander quickly entered the citadel, resisting the temptation to strut and provoke the demons now cowering by the gate or off to the Devil knew where. Inside he found a vast graveyard, alive with misery. Tombs of various sizes were scattered about, but unlike the sleepy sepulchres found on Earth, these were on fire, and glowed red hot. Their lids were propped open or lay by their sides, while screams of agony came from within to echo about the place. The fear Alexander had felt in the presence of the demons at the gate began to return. Then: 'Boo!', a voice from behind him, causing him to jump. It was the author.

'Sorry about the trouble on the door,' he said, when Alexander had calmed down. 'But I can take you from here, and answer any questions you might have.'

Alexander had a few questions all right, and had to struggle not to say something uncivil. 'You can start by telling me what's going on here. Who's in the tombs?'

'Heretics,' the author said with a wink. 'Every sect and school of thought who got it wrong – there's a tomb for each, and as many within as followed that particular heresy. Some are pretty darn full, I can tell you. And some burn hotter than others, but I'm not sure if that's to do with numbers or the degree of heresy, assuming that's even a thing. Anyway, follow me.'

Alexander followed the author as he started purposefully along a narrow path. 'This is more how I imagined Hell,' he said, looking around at the burning tombs.

'Yes, that's right. It's a bit more "as advertised" in here,' said the author.

'Only, shouldn't there be demons with tridents to keep people in?'

'That really isn't necessary,' the author said. He pointed to a large nearby tomb: 'This one holds materialists, for example, and they refuse to come out on the grounds that they no longer exist. Dogma is its own punishment, you know.'

Alexander strained to see into the tomb as they passed, but could only see screaming flames. Then the author invited Alexander to peer into another enormous, smoke-filled mausoleum. Inside, he could see sinners beating themselves with whips and chains. 'They think if they keep at it for long enough they'll be let out,' the author explained.

'Anyway,' he continued, gesturing ahead towards the other tombs, 'soon enough one or other of these sinners will talk to you, and you can get some answers.'

Alexander was bemused, and began to demand answers from the author about what he was doing here, berating him like a suspect in the interrogation room, but he was soon distracted right enough.

'Ho! Is that a Glasgow accent?' came an older man's voice from somewhere behind them. It startled Alexander, perhaps especially because the voice was not only friendly but urbane. ‘Hold on - let's chat a while. I mean... Would I be wrong to go further,' he added something new and ever-so-slightly camp to his voice, 'and say you talk like a Glesga polis?'

Instinctively, Alexander had moved away from the voice, and closer to the author, but his guide pushed him back. 'Look, over in that tomb. He's sitting up to talk to you.'

Alexander turned and saw there was indeed a sinner sitting upright in a smouldering sarcophagus, like a B-movie vampire. He was a big man, or had been. Alexander moved closer and recognised him. It was a former Chief Constable, from before Alexander's time, but known to him by reputation.

'Farrell?'

'Guilty as charged,' said Farrell with the practised charm necessary for a response like that. 'And who might you be? A man of rank?'

'DCI Alexander. I run a special unit.'

'Oh aye,' Farrell said enquiringly.

'Our job is to debunk supposedly occult crimes and various other sensitive cases.'

At this, Farrell began laughing uproariously. '*Debunking* is it? ..I like it,' he got out between chortles. Before he could go on, his merriment was interrupted: a head appeared next to him in the same tomb – a sinner of lesser stature it seemed, perhaps raised up on his knees.

'Is my son with you?' the second sinner demanded of Alexander, even as he looked behind him at the author. 'If you're clever enough to find your way down here before your time, tell me where my boy is. Is that him with you?'

The detective recognised this one too, as the father of a former schoolmate he'd later had convicted for making a death threat. 'No, that's not Greg,' he told him. 'That's my guide the author, and I wouldn't be here without him, but I don't think Greg would have appreciated his work.'

'Would have? Past tense? Are you saying Greg's dead?'

Alexander was slow to reply this time, confused ever since Porky's prophecy about what the damned did or didn't know about the world – as far as *he* knew, Greg was still alive - and the disconsolate sinner sank back into the flames.

Farrell resumed his fun at Alexander's expense without acknowledging his tomb-mate. 'You realise that unit was my idea, do you?'

'What was?'

'Your unit. I came up with the idea years ago, proposed it several times: a special unit to deal with occult crimes. The need was obvious, but there was always resistance – cowardice about the whole thing. I made detailed plans anyway, because I knew something would come along and swing it. Spooky child murder, was it?'

'That's right. Maybe ten years after your... retirement.'

'And did you "debunk" that?'

'No. That case is still open.'

'That's police work, my friend. But anyway, the purpose of the unit was never to "debunk" anything, and I expect you know that. The purpose of the unit is to fight evil.'

'A noble aspiration, no doubt,' Alexander said, glad of the opportunity to rehearse a debate he'd had often enough in his own head, 'but not a practical one for policemen. The language of good and evil is counterproductive, I've found. Never mind fighting evil; I've been fighting since day one to stop the unit doing more harm than good.'

Farrell shrugged. 'You'll have many more fights over good and evil in the years to come, and you'll lose as many as you win. I can tell you that. But evil isn't going to fight itself, is it?'

Alexander thought about replying, but decided to change the subject instead. 'Explain this to me, then. You damned know the future of the mortal world? But not the present?'

'Something like a bad dream – distant events are clear to us, but knowledge fades as they draw near. In the end we'll see nothing.'

'Then do me a favour and tell that man his son is still alive, as far as I know; I didn't answer because I was confused.'

Farrell ignored him.

'Are there others down there with you?' Alexander added, anxious to learn as much as he could.

'Millions,' replied Farrell. 'Among them are politicians, priests... I could name names you might know, but I'm not here for your entertainment.'

The author whispered that they should continue on their path, but Alexander was still thinking about the damned's knowledge of the future. Porky had suggested that what he saw of the future was bleak for Rangers, but Alexander knew how fickle fortune could be in football - as in police work - and for now at least, his team was on top. He turned back to Farrell and said: 'You won't be aware, of course, that Rangers are running away with the league again.'

'If that's true it pains me more than these flames,' Farrell replied haughtily, and disappeared into the tomb. He had been a Celtic supporter, which might once upon a time have been considered a minor heresy in itself for a polis. ('How did that happen?' people had joked when he'd been made Chief Constable.) But of course, things are never that straightforward. Alexander himself was no stranger to the nuances of religion in Glasgow, having been the only Rangers supporter at a private Catholic school. He and Greg, in fact, had been the only two Prods in their year; Greg had supported Celtic, though.

The author gestured for Alexander to follow him. 'Well?'

Alexander shrugged. 'What exactly was his heresy? Do you know?'

'I believe that particular tomb holds Manicheans, loosely defined: those who are wedded to an overly black and white view of things.'

That made sense. Alexander certainly disagreed with Farrell's philosophy of policing. He did not believe that police work was about fighting evil; for him it was a far more prosaic matter of holding people to account when they failed to abide by laws everyone implicitly affirms. He felt strongly enough about it that Farrell's Manichean approach did seem 'heretical' to him, but his own 'orthodoxy' was not something that had been passed down to him, least of all through his training as a police officer, which had been procedural rather than philosophical. It felt more like something he had intuited his way towards. Maybe he was wrong. And as he pondered what Farrell had said about the unit, and the battle between good and evil, suddenly Alexander felt dismay, and started babbling to the author.

He explained that had always told himself that whatever ambiguities surrounded the 'occult unit', he could control the narrative by sticking to solid criminal investigation work and refusing to indulge media speculation about anything more sinister. But he had often suspected that the unit had been so ill-conceived from the start that it could not help but fuel such speculation, even lending perfectly mundane cases an occult flavour simply by taking them on. And if Farrell was right, that had been half the point. It was less a case of Alexander struggling to correct misperceptions of the unit than struggling against what it had originally been conceived to be.

The author raised his finger to silence Alexander's fretting. 'That's all very interesting, but I don't think it's exactly why you're here.'

'So are you going to tell me at last?'

'Not now. You'll get the whole picture from the woman who asked me to guide you,' he muttered.

Alexander rolled his eyes. The mysterious woman again, who apparently wanted him to understand something about heresy.

Apparently there was a lot of it about. He looked around at the countless tombs and mausoleums filled with sinners who had staked their souls on the wrong ideas. Several were trying to crawl their way out of another large tomb, but each time one made progress, the others would drag them back in, furiously condemning them as they did so. At yet another mausoleum, one or more sinners would intermittently run out triumphantly, only to stop uncertainly, as if they had wandered into the kitchen and couldn't remember why, before wandering back in for more of whatever punishment awaited them. At yet another, sinners in bath towels eagerly filled a huge tub with water, apparently preparing to wash themselves. Only both the tub and the vessels they were using to fill it were covered in holes, so the water poured out as fast as they could pour it in. Alexander wondered how they did not lose heart, but evidently their heretical belief in the imminent cleansing power of the bath was replenished just as mysteriously as the water that dripped through their vessels. It was almost as if they cared more for the filling of the bath than for the prospect of washing in it. It was a very strange spectacle.

'Don't just look at the bigger tombs with multiple inhabitants,' the author told Alexander. 'Not all the heretics belonged to a particular sect or school of thought.' He pointed to a vast field covered in individual but identical flaming tombs spreading off as far into the distance as the eye could see: 'Those ones imagined themselves to be free thinkers.'

CHAPTER 7: THE GEOGRAPHY OF HELL

Then Alexander tripped over a stone and hit the ground. Actually, he could not be sure the author had not pushed him. Recovering himself, however, he realised he was in the Glasgow Necropolis at twilight, and the author was nowhere to be seen. He sat for a moment on the stone that had felled him, and looked around at the familiar gravestones and monuments with an eerie unfamiliarity. City merchants, mostly - pious or otherwise. But pride of place went to the statue of John Knox, who stood on a pillar towering over the other monuments, his back to Celtic Park, which lurked in the distance looking like anything but Paradise.

A pigeon swooped down and landed by Alexander; a scrawny thing, one leg mangled, its feathers mangy. 'What do you want?' Alexander demanded. The pigeon shrugged and wandered off. Alexander dusted himself down and made for home, quickening his pace only slightly as he crossed the Bridge of Sighs in the direction of the setting sun, and making the gate just as it was being closed. 'Night,' the park ranger said amiably as he let him through, but Alexander was afraid to look him in the eye.

The next morning, he emailed Leanne McGlone. He did not ask outright whether she was the mysterious woman who had used the author to summon him to Hell for some as yet undisclosed purpose. That would have been gauche. Instead he asked how she was. He asked about her career, if there were any new recordings of her music he could buy. He told her Morgan was doing well and was learning the glockenspiel. He said work was as interesting as ever. He said Karen said hi. It all seemed perfectly natural, but if Leanne were behind his visits to Hell, surely this would prompt her to come out and say something. He hit send and spent the next several minutes waiting for a reply, which he knew was ridiculous, especially given the time difference with the States. Eventually, he snapped out of it and returned his attention to work, and the series of religious burglaries.

There was a clear pattern: in each case, on consecutive nights, a place of worship had been broken into with minimal damage, and without either setting off alarms or showing up on cctv. Many items of value had been left, while a single religious artefact had been taken from each place. A communion cup from a Catholic church, a prayer mat from a mosque, a kirpan from a gurdwara, and just last night, a Torah pointer from a synagogue. Apart from the burglary part, it was like a school project. But Alexander suspected a more sophisticated motive, and doubted whether schoolkids could even have pulled off such tidy break-ins.

In any case, the project was incomplete. Alexander wondered if the culprit would now target a Protestant church, or even go for more than one denomination, but even these days, it would hardly be practical to keep all the Protestant churches in Glasgow under watch. The same might not be true of Hindu and Buddhist temples, but frankly he could not justify committing the resources even to do that. After all, this was hardly the crime of the century. He was more worried about the burglaries being interpreted as religious hate crimes and sparking a media panic, so he decided not even to issue a warning. He would simply wait and see.

He did not have to wait long. It turned out there had been

a fire last night in a house in the south side, and having put it out, fire fighters had identified the cause as a candle that had fallen from what appeared to be a makeshift shrine. All four missing artefacts were in it, along with many more. Alexander went to the scene and immediately suffered a spine-chilling attack of déjà vu. The shrine reminded him of the holy table at Alloway Kirk all those years ago, cluttered with occult bric-à-brac. He tried not to think about that as he investigated further. The fire had been stopped before it could do too much damage, and the religious artefacts were mostly unharmed. But the artefacts were not only religious. The shrine also contained the remains of two football scarves, some pop CDs and a stash of pornography. A uniform told Alexander that the sole occupant of the house, and presumably the devotee of the shrine, was in hospital being treated for smoke inhalation.

Alexander went to the hospital and was told that the patient was well enough to be interviewed. As soon as he set eyes on him, however, he was struck with the same terror he had felt at the gates of Hell. The patient was not a man, but a demon. Apparently no one else had noticed. And all right, he *looked* like a man, presumably a man he had possessed. He lacked the monstrous size of the demons in Hell, and had no wings or other such mock angelic accoutrements. But Alexander saw what others could not - he saw the evil spirit that occupied this human shell - and he sensed that the demon knew it. That grin told Alexander that malice was not a human invention. What could he do? He fled.

It was easy enough to make his excuses to the hospital staff, but now he had a criminal case in which the prime suspect was not a subject of Her Majesty but a minion of Beelzebub. Even if it were not absurd, it was *impossible* for Alexander to interview the demon and build a case against it. Impossible. Demons were surely outside his jurisdiction. He would have to let the case drop. What else could he do?

In the course of his work with the unit, Alexander had encountered two or three men who had claimed to be exorcists, one an actual Catholic priest, the others self-appointed, but none had struck him as particularly convincing. Even if he had believed in demons, which he had not. Did not. Anyway, he was not going to call in an exorcist.

In fact, he had discussed one case involving a supposed exorcism with Satan himself, back when the Evil One had been wont to visit him. The Devil had been very dismissive of the whole business, and Alexander had asked if there were not a difference between random charlatans and proper, accredited exorcists.

Satan had snorted: 'Accredited? They're the biggest charlatans of all.' Then he had mimed someone holding a crucifix in one hand and a certificate in the other. 'Look, I've got a thertificate,' he whined in a camply nasal voice, 'you've got to do what I thay.' Then, returning to himself: 'I don't fucking think so.'

That evening, Alexander had Morgan over for tea. He was both happy to be able to spend time with her and worried about her. Not because he feared she was endangered by demons. Even after his close encounters both in Hell and on Earth that very day, and the resulting escalation of his own terror, he felt no danger to anyone else. Morgan was safe, for now at least. But Laura had told him her behaviour was becoming a problem, both at home and at school. Morgan had never confessed to binge-eating the chocolate eggs and still reacted with outrage if the accusation was repeated, so her parents had let it lie, so to speak.

But the lies continued. Both routine lies and more scandalous ones that made Alexander think nervously about the school incidents, which were also ongoing, though not so much at Morgan's own school. That was why her behaviour stood out. And in fact it was not anything so terribly bad, so much as a general insolence that infuriated her teacher and every other adult with whom she came into contact. She followed instructions only grudgingly and ungraciously; she deferred to no one, and she complained about everything. Alexander had said he would talk to her.

The six-year-old slouched at the table like a teenager, which looked wrong in so many ways. And there was no awkward build up to the father-daughter chat. Morgan went on the offensive. 'Don't want peas.'

'You like peas,' Alexander said. The peas were a token garnish for fish fingers and potato waffles; hardly an affront to the most childish palate. But he did insist on telling her she liked them. He was training her to like them.

'No, I don't.'

'And you know your Mum and I like you to eat greens. They're good for you.'

'So should I eat them because they're good for me, or because you tell me to?'

Alexander resisted the temptation to roll his eyes. Or indeed to feel pride at his daughter's philosophical bent. 'Both. We tell you to eat them because they're good for you.'

'How do I know that?'

'Because...' he began in anger, before recovering himself. 'Look, I could show you dozens of peer-reviewed scientific papers setting out the evidence in great detail. But unfortunately, you wouldn't be able to understand them. So you'll just have to take my word for it. Or better still, just do as you're bloody told regardless.'

'I'm telling you swore.'

Alexander sat down next to her and looked her in the eye. 'Morgan, I'm your Daddy and I love you. That's why you have to do as I tell you. Don't you understand that?'

She shrugged, but he had got to her. 'Just four peas.'

He gave her eight.

He hoped spending quality time with her for the rest of the evening would do more good than a stern talking to, so they played games until it was time to take her back to her mother's. As soon as he'd dropped her, he was filled once again with terror about the demon he had seen earlier. The swiftly setting sun did not lift his spirits.

Reluctantly, but resolvedly, he went back to the Necropolis with the whisky flask and sat on a bench to ponder the situation while he waited for his curiosity to trump his fear. But once again, he did not need to drink the whisky. The author emerged from behind a large tomb whose inscription was illegible. He was wearing a park ranger's uniform. 'Don't get up,' he said, and joined Alexander on the bench. 'We'll have to wait here for a bit.'

'Why's that?'

The author sniffed the air, prompting Alexander to do the same. He almost retched: there was a violent stench brewing. 'What *is* that?'

The author let that stand as a rhetorical question. 'We'll sit here till you get used to it. Then we can move on.'

'Good. The perfect opportunity for you to start giving me some answers about this place.'

The author smiled, 'That's just what I was thinking. How have you found it so far?'

Alexander hesitated. He could have said facetiously that his time in Hell had been pretty Hellish, but that was not really true. He had often been afraid, of course, especially on his approach to the citadel. He had felt like a convict approaching Barlinnie, but he had experienced the simile as such, which is different, he supposed, from what a convict actually feels. Maybe a convict feels like he is being dragged into Hell, but he is not. And as for one of the damned who really is being dragged into Hell? That would be like nothing on Earth. And while Alexander really was in Hell, the difference was that he could return to Earth. Because was not dead and not under sentence. At least not yet. And so his visits had been less terrifying than intriguing. 'It's given me plenty to think about,' he told the author.

'And you're adjusting all right when you return to life above?'

'I suppose. Some of the transitions are bit messy.'

'Sorry about that. Really, I should have had you in, through the whole place and out in one go, but I wanted to give you time to digest what you see here, and to think about it in terms of your own life.'

Then Alexander said what he had been afraid even to think. 'As long as I'm not taking Hell back with me? I'm starting to worry I've become a human Hellmouth.'

The author decided to give the *Buffy the Vampire Slayer* reference a pass. 'Why?'

For some reason - guilt? - Alexander did not want to mention the demon in the hospital. 'Well, there's some really disturbing stuff coming up at work. And after the first few times, I haven't even had to drink the whisky to return to Hell.'

'Wait. You've drunk it more than once?'

'You sent me the bottle.'

'No, I didn't.'

'Then who did?' Demons?

'Just don't drink any more. The very fact that you were sent more shows you've had more than enough already.'

Alexander had not properly thought about the rules concerning his demonic attacks since visiting Hell itself. The demon's appearance in the hospital, and more importantly at the centre of a case, was in flagrant violation of the rules as Alexander had understood them. And if demons had indeed sent him the whisky at work, that too. But then perhaps he had changed things by visiting Hell. He could no longer quarantine his superstitions from the rest of his life, his work. And if the whisky was not some kind of Hell key at his own disposal, he would have to trust the author - and not accept any more drinks from strangers. He worried about the damage that extra dose might have done.

'What happens if you have *too* much?' he asked the author.

'You're worrying needlessly about being a human Hellmouth,' the author replied, realising Alexander was still worried about this 'disturbing stuff' at work. 'There are no physical portals in and out of Hell any more than Hell exists geographically as part of the Earth. You've seen that it doesn't work like that. And you certainly don't have to worry about taking evil out of Hell back to Earth. The direction of travel is quite the opposite, I assure you. Anyway, for you, at least, Hell is not a place, but a journey of sorts.'

'You sound like my therapist,' Alexander said.

'Touché.'

The author went on to explain that the geography of Hell was not primarily physical but conceptual. With each descent, Alexander was being drawn deeper into the idea of Hell, which is to say the nature of sin. He might find it helpful to think of it with reference to his studies at university, where he had surely read Aristotle's Ethics. 'Remember Aristotle's distinction between mere incontinence and actual malice or 'mad bestiality'? What were those sinners in the 'upper' parts of Hell guilty of? Falling in love? Having an appetite? Thrift and generosity, passion and melancholy? Those aren't sins in themselves. It's the ridiculous excess that's sinful, the lack of control. And, by the way, lacking that kind of energy all together is no better – think of the bloodless creatures you saw in the Hope.'

'But surely their fate is less awful? They suffer boredom rather than the physical torture inflicted on the incontinent.'

'Pff. If you want to rank the eternal punishments in terms of desirability, feel free. One way or another, everyone down here gets what they deserve.'

The author then revealed that there were three more broad categories of sinners for Alexander to see, and said he would explain now what each was about, so the detective would understand when he got to them. All the sinners from now on were guilty of malicious sin; they had deliberately caused harm either by violence or fraud. The latter was more complicated as well as being further down, so the author came first to violence. In this first category there were three subdivisions, and so Alexander would find three distinct sets of sinners: those who committed violence against others, those who had inflicted violence on themselves, and a third kind that the author himself was still struggling to understand.

Violence here was to be understood not only in the sense of physical force, but also in the sense of violation, even effrontery. Violence against others included not only murder or assault, but also the deliberate destruction or extortion of a person's property, reputation or happiness. In the case of violence against oneself, it meant not only suicide or self-harm, but also squandering one's time on drink or drugs, gambling away one's wealth, or generally ruining one's own life. The final kind of violence seemed to involve the deliberate perversion of morality and disdain for natural goodness. Alexander would understand that better when he saw it.

After violence, they would come to fraud, which is deliberate by definition, and itself divided into two broad categories. First, they would encounter those who had deceived people who had no particular reason to trust them beyond the basic human expectation of honest dealing. Liars, conmen, tricksters, embezzlers and bullshitters would be nestled together. Next, and finally, Alexander and the author would come to those who had betrayed a particular trust. Traitors were the worst sinners of all.

This did not seem obvious to Alexander. 'I see the logic, now you've set it out for me,' he told the author, 'but I can't say I get it as a moral system. I mean, where does Hitler come in? Surely mass murderers are worse than traitors, not to mention liars and conmen?'

'Again with the ranking,' said the author. 'Keep an eye out for Hitler below and see if you think he's been let off lightly. What you need to understand is that Hell is not just a prison for monsters. It's where ordinary human beings meet with just punishment for their sins, history-making or otherwise.'

Alexander mulled this over, thinking about the meaning of sin as Aristotle and Aquinas slowly came back to him. Then he asked, 'What about usury? Where does that fit in? Because to be honest I've never really understood what the problem is, in principle, I mean.'

The author smiled. 'Nor has anyone else if you ask me.'

Historically, it was obvious why people had resented moneylenders, even – especially – when they needed them. Certainly, loan sharks were guilty of exploiting people in desperate circumstances. But the charging of interest was not in itself sinful. Why should it be? Significantly, Aristotle dealt with usury in his Physics and his Politics rather than his Ethics. But the author explained that the final and worst group of violent sinners, guilty of what he had called deliberate perversion of morality, would include those who used spurious means to extract wealth from its producers while contributing nothing to the world.

There was something else Alexander wanted to ask about these perverse sins they were soon to come to, but he hesitated, and instead asked something else. 'What about you?' he asked the author. 'I found you with the heretics, so...?'

'Well, yes,' the author replied, 'but luckily I'm not dead yet, so I'm free to guide you out of here.'

'So you're just visiting like me?'

'Not exactly visiting, but I don't belong here either, I hope. I'm only appearing here for your benefit, so think of me as a kind of tour guide.'

Then he said that now Alexander was used to the smell, it was time to descend and see the violent sinners.

CHAPTER 8: MURDER POLIS

The author led Alexander around the tomb from behind which he had emerged. Looking downhill at where the city ought to have been, Alexander saw instead a desolate valley. He and the author stood above the valley at the brink of an impossibly steep slope. There was a way down, a gentler slope comprised of rubble, but the path was guarded by a monstrous creature, half-man, half-bull.

'The Minotaur?' Alexander hazarded.

'That's the one,' said the author. 'You know the story, I suppose, and won't wonder why he's here. He was born of bestiality in the more current sense, and fed on young men and women. He's not human, so I don't think he counts as a sinner, but he certainly serves as an illustration of what we've been discussing.'

Seeing the intruders, the beast took his cue and began raving wildly, skipping and hopping about and biting at itself like violent rage personified.

The author shouted to it, 'Calm down. He's not a hero come to torment you, just an observer come to see the punishments beyond.'

The Minotaur responded by intensifying its rage, lost for words, lost for purpose, dedicated only to perverse fury.

'I'll keep him distracted whole you make a run for it,' the

author told Alexander, who duly clambered past the beast and down the craggy path, stumbling noisily and sending stones clattering this way and that. The author followed more serenely.

Alexander was deep in thought when they reached the bottom of the slope.

'You're probably wondering how this path was created,' the author said. 'Apparently it was a landslide caused by an earthquake. And that earthquake is the only historical event that's ever happened in Hell, or at least part of that event. They call it the Great Escape.'

'Someone escaped from Hell? Who?'

'Nobody here really knows. Some say it was a few chancers who took advantage of the earthquake, but that makes no sense to me. The damned aren't imprisoned here physically, but psychologically fixed for eternity. They don't even want to escape.'

'What about us? Was it someone visiting like we are?'

The author shrugged. 'Then it wouldn't be an escape, would it? It would have to have been someone actually *condemned* to Hell, who somehow beat the system. It's a mystery to me.'

'Anyway, look at the river,' he said, pointing to the floor of the valley where a dark river snaked into the distance in both directions. 'It's blood. And in it those who in life were violent against others simmer for eternity.'

Alexander took in the scene, before asking, 'What blind cupidity, what driving frenzy, spurs us on in our short lives, only to offer us up to ravenous eternity?' The author decided it was a rhetorical question.

The river of blood curved like a moat around what looked like a dense wood on the other side, but before they got close enough to see the violent sinners, they heard a dull roar in the distance, which soon grew louder. Coming towards them was a line of Hell's Angels, racing along the bank of the river on now-deafening motorbikes. As they approached, three riders broke off from the line to confront the intruders. They wielded sawn-off shotguns, and one shouted, 'What are you in for? Stop where youse are and tell us or I'll shoot.'

The author took charge. 'We'll talk to Chiron,' he shouted back, 'not you, heid-the-baw.' He turned to Alexander to explain, 'That's Nessus. He tried to rape the wife of Hercules. The one in the middle with the huge beard is Chiron, more of an intellectual. The other one's Pholus... He's the other one. Anyway, thousands of these Angels ride along the riverbank to steward the damned.'

He led Alexander towards their welcoming party, and as they approached, Chiron produced a comb from his jacket and used it to tug at his overgrown beard so he could get his words out. 'See how that one's kicking stones about?' he said to his companions. 'He's a living mortal here in person.'

'That's right,' said the author, boldly standing in front of Chiron's revving vehicle. 'He's alive, and that's why I'm here to guide him. And believe me: he's not here for the fun of it, but strictly on business.' He stepped even closer to Chiron, so Alexander could not hear him over the engine. 'I was given this mission by another sort of angel altogether, so we'll stay out of your business. Only understand what kind of power brings us to this bloody racetrack of yours, and have one of your riders give the mortal a lift to the ford and across.'

Chiron leaned over to Nessus: 'Head back with our guests, then, and see they're not harmed by our brothers.'

Nessus span his bike around, then, inviting Alexander to ride pillion. As soon as his passenger was in place, the Angel sped off back along the bank of the river, and the author was forced to float blatantly alongside.

Now Alexander could see the damned boiling in the rushing blood, in as deep as their now permanently raised eyebrows. 'Those ones are murderous tyrants,' Nessus said. 'The 20th century ones are just coming up.'

Alexander looked to the author, who gestured to the effect that Nessus was as reliable a guide as he for now. He was surprised at how gratified he found himself to see Hitler as promised, or at least that unmistakable fringe, along with many of his Nazi henchmen; many more tyrants he didn't recognise. Watching them scream hot, bubbly screams of agony as they boiled head to foot in scalding blood, a mere snapshot of their eternal fate, he had to concede that Hitler and his fellow mass murderers did not seem to have got off lightly after all.

As they sped along, they passed sinners only neck deep, then shoulder deep and so on. 'War criminals, serial killers, certain sorts of terrorists,' Nessus said breezily as they passed. Then around the waist-deep mark: 'Marauders, rapists – the child abusers boil upside down – assorted thugs, saboteurs and hooligans.'

Alexander recognised a number of the damned: a vicious gangster he'd known, an arsonist he'd put away, and so on, but they were moving far too fast for him to try to speak to any of them.

Then another line of Hell's Angels appeared in the distance, ten or twelve of them, racing towards Nessus and firing intermittently into the river of blood, whooping and hollering as they did so.

'Who's that with you?' one of them called to Nessus as they approached.

'Fuck knows,' he answered as they passed. 'I'm running an errand for Chiron.'

The Angels' guffaws faded only with the roars of their motors and the bangs of their soon distant gunfire.

'Alexander,' said Alexander.

'Whatever. Whoever you are, without my protection they'd have shot you as an escapee.'

'Do the damned often try to escape?'

'No. Because we keep them in their places by shooting at them.'

Alexander snuck a glance at the author, who was smiling wryly.

At length they came to a point at which the sinners were

merely paddling in the boiling blood, though that seemed of little comfort to them. Here, Nessus was able to ride across to the other side, explaining as he did so that from here the river got deeper again till it wound its way back to the tyrants. Once safely over the river, Alexander dismounted and thanked Nessus, who sped off again without a word.

Alexander's phone was ringing. 'Take it,' said the author, sitting himself on a rock. 'Might be important.'

It was. Murder.

The author clapped his hands impatiently and Alexander found himself on Buchanan Street in the early hours of the morning, where a small army of officers buzzed around the crime scene. It was immediately obvious why he'd been called. More than a murder, it was like something out of a horror movie. The victim was a teenage girl in a white dress that was now drenched in blood. She'd been hunted through the city centre at midnight by a gang of teenage boys, who had then stabbed her to death in front of numerous terrified bystanders. Two of the killers had already been arrested, and good-quality cctv footage meant it would not be difficult to identify the rest. Alexander understood immediately that his job was more complicated, in two ways.

Within 24 hours, all 14 assailants were in custody. They ranged from 15 to 19 years old and all were initially charged with murder. Not all had inflicted wounds, however. Before handing the case over to the lawyers, detectives would have to determine whether there was evidence to support the murder charges for all 14, or whether a clear distinction could be made between the killers and others guilty of lesser offences. It was a controversial legal issue, and ultimately a decision for the Crown, but the unit's input would be crucial.

The second problem for Alexander, bluntly, was political containment. The victim had been a teenage girl. She'd been subjected to a brutal and sustained attack in the middle of the city. There was no obvious motive, and it seemed likely that the attack had been more or less random. This made it an especially terrifying crime. It would not be enough for the unit to secure convictions for the killers: they would have to do it in such as way as to restore faith in public safety, which meant decisively allaying all fears of murderous teen gangs real and imagined.

Alexander interviewed each of the assailants and at first got similar and consistent stories from each. The 'gang' was actually no such thing. The 14 comprised two groups of four and two of three; none knew the other groups. Each had been drinking in a park or street in a different part of the city before heading into town on an adventurous whim. All of those involved had been carrying blades, out of neddish habit rather than in anticipation of anything in particular.

Each individual reported the same thing: all of a sudden, they'd started a chase, following the others in their group without knowing whom or what they were after, or indeed was after them. Then they'd become aware of strangers joining the chase - strangers the like of whom they'd expected to find themselves chasing or being chased by, but each individual took a cue from his pals and carried on in pursuit of whatever they *all* were chasing. Finally they'd seen the girl in the white dress fleeing onto Buchanan Street and bolted after her. Each assailant insisted someone else had been first to take hold of the victim, though none could say who exactly. Each of those who had actually stabbed the girl remembered a feeling of horror – 'that sinking feeling', as one put it – and a grim inevitability: 'The knife went in'.

The case was at once heart-sinkingly familiar and unlike any Alexander had encountered before. It was not unusual at all for murders to seem almost accidental, at least to the perpetrators, and especially when knives were involved. But usually there was some kind of context that made sense of things. A fight, a confrontation over something, some intent to harm even if it fell short of intent to commit murder. In this case, the killers' feet had led them in pursuit of mischief, and their hands had shed innocent blood without their brains apparently becoming engaged at any stage. There was nothing to link any of the attackers with the victim, nor any apparent reason for her to have been targeted. One of the officers who had gone over the cctv footage described them as being 'like things possessed'. That sent a chill down Alexander's spine.

He concluded anyway that there was a clear case for prosecuting all 14 assailants for murder, since all had acted in concert in the very immediate run-up to the girl's killing, even if not all had got as far as plunging in a blade. He had sent far less legally clear-cut cases to the Procurator Fiscal with every moral confidence that the suspects were as guilty as sin. This time, he had to admit to himself at least that even if it was clear *how* it had happened, he did not in fact understand *what* had happened. So he simply did his job and passed the case on for lawyers to argue over.

At least, he had done the first part of his job, the technical CID part. Then he sat down with Morag to write a press statement that would sound as reassuring as possible, and rubbish the wilder media speculation about violent gangs, the possible involvement of drugs and worse; there had even been florid rhetoric about 'blood sacrifice'. The good news was that all 14 suspects were in custody. There was no disguising the brutal nature of the murder, however, so all they could do was stress that it was shocking because it was so exceptional. Glasgow remained a very safe city. But as Alexander and Morag were struggling to make that the core message without seeming to downplay the murder itself, they were interrupted by Karen, who wanted as a matter of urgency to let them both know about a very different new case.

Actually, it was not a criminal case at all. A colleague had called Karen because she didn't know what else to do. A fifth year girl at a school in the south side had written an essay in defence of the Nazi Holocaust. *Nobody* knew what to do about it. It was a well-written and historically informed essay, and would have been given a very good mark – except that it was a defence of the Nazi Holocaust. The girl's teacher had been shocked and disturbed. She'd spoken to her one-to-one to gauge her motivations: the girl seemed to have written it sincerely, not simply as an adolescent provocation. There had been no shrill appeals to freedom of speech or accusations of politically correct brainwashing. She had just calmly explained that she had thought about this a lot – the class had been discussing Holocaust denial – and decided it was hypocritical of Nazi sympathisers to deny the Holocaust, when surely they should be defending it, so she'd thought she would give that a go. Her poor teacher hadn't known where to start responding to that.

The head teacher had called in the girl's parents, then, and they'd been suitably appalled and embarrassed; they were 'not a Nazi family'. They'd wanted to know if she would be suspended, but the head assured them nothing like that would happen. He was concerned about the girl herself. Her behaviour had never been a problem, and she was never abusive to ethnic minority classmates, but this was too disturbing to ignore. Was she really a Nazi sympathiser? The parents had no idea. They had all agreed to keep an eye on her, but what to do about the essay? After agonising over it, the teacher had proposed to award a decent but not stellar mark, interpreting the essay as an experiment in form, like counter-factual history, 'counter-moral history', perhaps. But the head forbade it, fearing what would happen if the papers got wind of it. They had decided instead to stick the essay in a proverbial drawer and hope she didn't do it again. But now the troublesome piece of writing had appeared on the not-so-proverbial internet. The police community liaison officer had been called in when its author was beaten up in the playground by a girl who had decided anti-Nazism was as good a cause as any. She knew DCI Alexander's unit had been involved in the earlier school incidents, and called Karen for advice.

If the story were picked up by the media, which was now likely, a connection would certainly be made with those previous school incidents. These had died down at the school whose teachers had gone on strike, but there were now blogs devoted to recording bad behaviour in other Glasgow schools.

Karen had been monitoring these and had established that most of the worst reported incidents were fabrications, including two alleged rapes. Still, there was an atmosphere of crisis, and people had begun to speculate about 'something in the water' or variations on that theme: dietary factors, vaccines, websites – including the oujia board game Alexander had been worried about. But the reason Karen had interrupted Alexander and Morag was more specific. The girl who had written that essay was the younger sister of one of the knife killers, while another was in the same year group as her at the school. It was the coincidence from Hell.

CHAPTER 9: WASTED LIVES

That night, Karen lay awake in bed, imagining herself making witty remarks in a variety of circumstances. It was a favourite game, albeit one of which she was not entirely conscious. Occasionally, she would find a real-life opportunity to use one of the bon mots she had rehearsed in her mind like this, and usually they went down well, but the reception was never as satisfying as it had been in her mind. There were a handful of people at work, her mother, the girls in the local shop, whose imaginary rapt responses she particularly enjoyed. Alexander was present in these whimsies only to be impressed by Karen's ability to make other people laugh out loud with her cleverness.

On this occasion, the game served also to distract attention from a more pressing matter. Karen was pregnant. Actually, not yet one hundred percent sure, but more or less resigned to it. Needless to say, it was unplanned. Ever since the possibility had occurred to her, and over the course of the few days she had waited for her delayed period before taking a test, she had taken it for granted that, if she were in fact pregnant, she would have an abortion. Now that she had taken the test, however, she felt the decision no longer made itself: it was hers to make, one way or the other.

It would hardly be practical to have a baby at this stage in her life. She was less exercised by abstract questions of career versus motherhood than the simple question of what she would do with the thing when she was at work. Her mother would not be laughing out loud if Karen presented her with a baby to look after all day. Then there was the still uncertain status of her relationship with Alexander. They were not even living together. And he already had a daughter from a previous marriage. While Karen got on fine with Morgan, there was nothing maternal in her dealings with the child. Whatever Alexander wanted from her, it did not seem to be another chance at family life. And after all, Karen had neither done anything to push their relationship in that direction, nor harboured any desire to do so. Things were fine as they were. Except now she was pregnant. So, abortion? No brainer.

Karen's newly emerging qualms about the matter did not concern the life of the unborn child so much as the shape of her own life. It was not that pregnancy interfered with her plans, but precisely that it revealed her lack of a plan. She had allowed the comforting structure of a police career to substitute for any kind of structure in her life overall. Now the universe was calling her bluff: 'Well, if it's all the same to you, here. Look after this'. A determined career woman would have had the ruthlessness to say, 'No, thanks'. Karen was thrown into uncertainty.

When she was younger, she had of course thought about the prospect of motherhood, presumably in marriage. If you'd asked her, she would have thought it likely that she would one day have children. Only now did this begin to seem absurdly passive. When a classmate at school had 'fallen' pregnant, it had been easy to see pregnancy as something that just happened to you, and that you either embraced or rejected depending on circumstances. But now it occurred to Karen that her friends and acquaintances who had actually gone on to have children had *not* done so by accident or on a whim. In some cases, they were the ones who had been pretty bloody ruthless.

Even as Karen regretted her naivety, she found herself

nostalgic for the youth that had made it possible. As a teenager, she had been excited by the infinite possibilities ahead of her, by her own limitless potential to make herself. She could do anything. She could be anyone. It was not that she did not have some pretty specific ideas about who and what. By her late teens, she knew she wanted to be a police detective, a brilliant and cool police detective at that. She worked hard at school and did what needed to be done practically to make that happen, the first part at least. But there was so much other stuff she could do or not do. The possibilities for a brilliant, cool police detective were still endless. Only now, she was increasingly conscious that making decisions is not the only way to close off other possibilities. Time will do that all by itself.

Karen stared at her bedroom ceiling. If she left this one to time, in less than a year she would be a mother. The mother of Alexander's second child.

Alexander had left the office late that evening, just in time to make last orders on the way home. When the barman actually called last orders, Alexander ordered his third pint. He was a fast walker, he reasoned. He smiled to himself.

'What you laughing at?' snarled a man next to him at the bar.

'What? Nothing.'

'Fuckin' prick,' said the man, and thrust his glass at Alexander's face.

The pain came from the force of the blow, and for a moment it was only the taste and sensation of rushing blood that told him he'd been cut. He wasn't down, but still on his feet, and he contemplated taking a swing at his assailant, who had turned to make an exit. He grabbed the man's shoulder, pulling him back, but when the thug turned to face Alexander, the big polis let go in terror. That face was not human: it was a demon. The creature snarled contemptuously and walked off, leaving Alexander stunned as well as bloodied.

He looked around what had been a busy pub. Everyone else was dead, lying in pools of blood that seeped into one another to cover the floor. Great gashes had been torn through their bodies as well as their faces, so horrific that Alexander couldn't bear to look. He pressed a bar towel against his own wound and stumbled over the human debris to follow the demon into the street; he assumed that if it had wanted to kill him, he'd already be dead.

Once outside, he realised that he was in Hell. The streets were deserted and an unearthly pallor hung in the air. The author was sitting at a bus stop across the street. When he saw Alexander, he rose and beckoned him over.

'Let's see,' he said, peeling back Alexander's makeshift bandage. 'Nasty,' he grimaced, 'but not deep. You're lucky it's just one laceration. Just keep a bit of pressure on for now.'

'But what the fuck...' Alexander began with some pain, which made him rethink his intended rant of bewilderment to focus on a more urgent question. 'Are those people really dead?'

The author hesitated for a moment, perhaps only guessing at what had happened. 'Probably not. Whatever that demon did happened here in Hell, so either they were already dead or they're really still where you left them.'

'I wasn't conscious of leaving.'

The author shrugged apologetically, and gestured towards the public park behind him. 'This is more or less where we left off,' he said, climbing onto the park railing. 'Can you manage?'

Alexander shrugged and followed the author over the railing, struggling to keep the bandage pressed to his face as he did so. The park was in fact a large wood, thick with knotted branches and foliage more brown than green.

'This is where the suicides and squanderers end up,' the author explained. 'What can you hear?'

Now he was paying attention, Alexander heard awful moans and sobs all around, but he couldn't see any sinners.

'I believe I know what you're thinking,' the author said.

Alexander looked at the author, wondering what he was supposed to be thinking. His first thought had been that there must be sinners hidden in the thickets, but from the way the author was looking at him, he surmised that wasn't the case.

'Snap one of the branches and you'll soon twig,' the author punned.

Alexander pulled at a branch of a thorny bush and broke it.

'Aeiyaah bastard! What d'you do that for!' the bush cried out in pain. The words spurted along with blood from where Alexander had snapped the twig. 'We were people once, you know. Show some compassion for fuck's sake.'

Alexander stepped back from the aggrieved shrub, letting the twig drop to the ground. The blood was an unwelcome reminder of his own now-throbbing injury. He looked to the author for guidance.

The author addressed the bush: 'Sorry about that, but he wouldn't have believed me otherwise. Why don't you tell him about yourself? He'll be returning to the mortal world, so he can make up for your injury by remembering you to friends there.'

The bush seemed pleased with that. It explained that it – he – had been a senior civil servant who'd been caught up in a corruption scandal. He'd been absolutely innocent, but jealous colleagues had schemed against him to make sure he was implicated, leading to a criminal conviction and a jail sentence. Unable to live with the disdain of the world, he'd turned all his rage against himself and committed suicide by battering his head against the walls of his cell.

When the bush had finished its tale, the author encouraged Alexander to take the opportunity to ask more if he wanted, but he gestured that his face still throbbed painfully, so again the author spoke on his behalf, asking the ligneous sinner to say more about the fate he shared with the rest of the wood.

In response, he acknowledged the poetic justice that those who had used their human bodies against themselves to end their lives were rewarded in Hell with the inanimate bodies of plants. When they arrived in Hell they fell into this place like seeds tossed onto the soil, and sprouted into miserable vegetation like him, unable to do anything but grow foliage to be grazed painfully by Harpies. Alexander looked up and around nervously, but no Harpies seemed to be about.

Instead, a great crashing sound. Something was tearing violently through the wood. Two naked figures burst into view, apparently fleeing unseen enemies. The one in front appeared to be goading his pursuers, holding out his arms invitingly as he skipped athletically through the undergrowth. The other, much slower, shouted admiringly, 'Just like your famous run up the left flank in that cup final!' Perhaps having exhausted his breath, the slower man then lunged at a bush, clasping on as if trying to merge with it. Too late: a pack of black dogs emerged from the thickets and fell on the hopeless sinner, tearing him to bits and carrying them off in their slavering jaws while still other dogs pursued the first sinner out of sight.

With the dogs safely away, the author led Alexander to the now bloody bush. 'Why'd you try to hide in me, you wanker?' it was crying after the dog's dinner. 'Am I to blame for your dirty habits?'

The author asked the bush what it was talking about.

'He was a compulsive masturbator – wasted his life alone in his bedroom.'

'And who's the other one?'

'Maybe you'd have recognised him if he'd made more of his talents', the bush said. 'He was a promising young footballer at one time – had his moments of glory as a rookie. But he pissed it away, thought he could drink like his mates of a night and still perform on the pitch. Just wouldn't put the work in.'

Alexander recognised the description, and tried to remember a name, before realising this now dead footballer's career had probably been before his time. But even just during his own time following football, there had been countless examples. The next time someone asked whatever happened to so-and-so, he'd know the answer.

'And yourself,' the author asked the bush.

'Just a suicide. What's there to say?'

Alexander came to in casualty in the early hours of the morning. Apparently he'd passed out immediately after the doctor had finished stitching his face. He had no memory of getting to the hospital, but he was told he'd been picked up by an ambulance after being assaulted in the pub. A couple of uniformed colleagues were waiting for him, but they had to tell him more than he could tell them: it had been an apparently unprovoked attack at the bar – a glass in the face out of nothing – leaving everyone in the pub stunned as the assailant had run off. Nobody else had been harmed, so it was possible Alexander had been targeted in connection with a case? The descriptions they had from witnesses were not promising. Alexander pawed his bandage, trying to gauge the extent of the injury. It would leave a scar, he was told. Then Karen arrived.

Alexander felt the warmth of her affection, but nothing hysterical. Karen was tough, and he admired the way she took possession of the situation. She took him to her place where he was soon deep asleep thanks to pain-killers, while she returned to her own sleepless ponderings.

The following day Alexander had an appointment with Dr Bakshi. She offered her sympathy, and asked if he wanted to talk about what had happened. He must have made too much of explaining why he had been in the pub alone, though, because before he could go on, she seized on it. Did he want to talk about his drinking habits? Of course, he did not. But he did have thoughts on the subject of drinking in general.

Alexander had seen alcoholism in many forms during his time as a polis, among his colleagues as well as 'customers'. Without doubt, the worst of it was the alcoholism of the deprived: of poor, hopeless losers for whom alcohol was both solace and suicide. Glasgow had more than its share of people who died before their time thanks to booze, and wasted what time they had in a drunken haze, supplemented by whatever other rubbish they could get hold of. Drunken lives cut short: it was a double death.

But Alexander had also known so-called high-functioning drunks, in fact better described as just-high-enough-functioning. They were content to waste only the parts of their lives that were fully theirs to waste, sabotaging the possibility of achieving any more than was required of them, whether at work or at home. Of course, sometimes they lost control and could not even manage that - jobs were lost, marriages ruined - but that was not the point. It was bad enough to waste your own potential to be more than you were.

Of course, none of this was about alcohol itself. People found all kinds of inventive ways to destroy themselves. Alexander was endlessly irritated by the official preoccupation with how much people drank, measured in spurious units. As a real doctor, Dr Bakshi must know it was all nonsense, even before you considered the recommended *number* of units. 'You know what I think?' he asked her. 'I think instead of asking people how much they drink, doctors should ask how much they *enjoy* it. Does drinking make your life better or worse? Is it something you associate with moments of happiness, good company and relaxation? Or with misery, self-pity and despair?'

'Which is it for you?' she asked.

CHAPTER 10: AGAINST NATURE

Alexander met the author as arranged at an abandoned building site on the outskirts of the city. The site had been cleared for a planned housing and commercial development that had never come to fruition. There were suspicions that the whole thing had been a non-starter, based on the promise of investment that was never forthcoming. In any case, it was now an expanse of coarse dirt, made desert-like by the unseasonal heat. When Alexander crept through a gap in the fence to join the author inside, unseasonal turned to unnatural; they were in fiery Hell.

Now Alexander could see sinners all around them, stretching into the distance, far beyond the extent of the Earthly site, though it was impossible to see exactly how far in the smoky gloom. A few lay helplessly on the sand, crying out in pain as great flakes of burning ash fell on them from the sky. Others sat huddled together in groups, each trying vainly to shelter behind the others from the fiery snow. But the greatest number of sinners simply wandered without rest, this way and that, frantically beating and flapping the flames from their bodies, unable to leave themselves alone. When the fire reached the ground, it ignited the sand, adding to the agony of all. And still it fell from above. Alexander had not experienced heat anything like this since a visit to India many years before, but the suffering of the sinners was like nothing he had ever seen.

He knew those burning on the sand were guilty of the third kind of violence, not against others, not against themselves, but something else that was apparently worse. He pointed to one prostrate sinner who refused to cry out in pain, but merely scowled at the sky. Seeing that he had attracted his attention, the sinner called out to Alexander, 'I'm as unrepentant in death as I was in life!'

Alexander looked at the author. 'Unrepentant about what, do you suppose?'

'Who knows? His unrepentance is all that's left. Let's go.'

The author led Alexander along the perimeter of the site, where they were able to avoid the falling ash and the hot sand, until they came to a concrete channel that emerged from under ground and ran as far into the gloom as the eye could see. Alexander followed the author onto the channel's raised wall and looked down to see a great stream of blood rushing inwards from the perimeter. He turned to the author. 'Is this from the river we saw before?'

'That's right,' said the author, 'It runs all the way through Hell one way or another, but I won't bore you with the details.'

A vapour rose from the bloody stream that seemed to repel the burning ash that fell on either side, providing Alexander and the author with a safe path, so they set off along the wall.

After some time, they saw a band of sinners coming in the other direction along the wall, but on the plain below them. The sinners looked up, squinting at the unexpected travellers. Then one of them came closer and reached out to Alexander, grabbing his ankle. 'What a marvel!' he exclaimed.

Alexander peered down at the damned soul's scorched face until suddenly he recognised him. 'Is it Dr Brown? Here?'

'Yes, it's me!' said Alexander's late university tutor, brushing fresh flames from himself. 'Do you mind if I walk back with you a while?'

'Of course not - please do. In fact, I'm happy to sit with you for a bit, if my guide here doesn't mind.'

'Thanks, but that's against the rules. If any of us pauses for just a second, we have to lie down for a hundred years without brushing off the fire.'

That made Alexander shudder, not because of the unthinkable prospect of lying in a Hell within Hell for a century, but because of the mention of rules.

'Please keep walking,' Dr Brown said, 'I'll tag along at your feet, and then catch up with the others.'

Alexander crouched as he walked, feeling that it was improper to be towering over his former teacher. Besides, he almost felt the need to whisper his question: 'So there are *rules* here, in addition to the general torment?'

'Oh yes,' answered Dr Brown. 'Not entirely *consistent* rules, of course, but certainly we are expected to conform to certain expectations, and there are consequences if we stray, or try to. In fact, the very thought of it is an added torment for those of us who are inclined to speculate about such things. What you might think of as mere superstition on Earth really comes to life here in Hell.'

Alexander walked on in silence.

'Anyway, what are you doing here still breathing, and who's your guide?' Dr Brown asked.

'Some kind of mid-life crisis,' Alexander speculated, half-joking. 'This is a friend of mine who's helping me work out my issues. We're getting there.'

'I always thought you'd do well in life,' said Dr Brown, 'When I heard you'd joined the police, I knew you'd make something special of it if you only kept true to yourself. And if I hadn't died so early I'd have liked to help you fulfil your potential.'

Alexander would have liked that. Perhaps if he'd had someone like Dr Brown to talk to about things, he would not be stuck sparring with Dr Bakshi, or indeed being dragged through Hell by the author. He was curious about Dr Brown's sin, but reluctant to ask for fear of giving offence, so he asked instead who his companions were.

'We were all academics and writers in my group,' Dr Brown told him, but he sensed Alexander's true meaning. 'More particularly, we made a virtue of our own curiosity, esteeming it higher than its proper object. We flattered ourselves that there was something intellectual about the pursuit of novelty and the thrill of sophistication.'

Whatever else this might mean, Alexander did remember rumours at university about routine adultery among some of the faculty, seemingly driven less by simple lust - which would have seen Dr Brown's associates blowing about with the likes of Francesca and Paolo - than a wilful transgressiveness arising from existential boredom.

'I know things now,' Dr Brown continued, 'things I wish I didn't. I saw things in life I wish I'd never seen, but now they are part of me. I know it must be hard for a police detective, but if you'll learn from me, do try to guard your innocence. I mean, especially in your job. People will always want to bring you down to their level, but you'll never achieve what you were meant to if you're surrounded by filth. ..If you'll pardon the expression.'

Alexander laughed, and thanked Dr Brown for his advice. 'You know,' he added, 'I still think of you from time to time, whenever I really think about anything. It was you who taught me how to think about eternity, or at least to try. So I'll make note of your advice, and if I ever meet the mysterious woman who's summoned me here, I'll talk it over with her along with the rest of what I've learned.' With that, he looked suspiciously at his guide, and the author nodded ambiguously.

'Do that,' said Dr Brown, 'I have to go. That dust in the distance tells me there's another group coming, and I can't mix with them.' With that, he turned and ran to catch up with his companions. Dr Brown ran with a sense of purpose that reminded Alexander of the self-discipline he had once admired in his teacher, but of course his purpose now was nothing more than to rejoin his fellow sinners.

After walking a little further along the wall with the author, Alexander could hear what sounded like a waterfall, presumably the point where the channel ended and the river of blood fell to the next level. Before he and the author could approach any further, three sinners broke from a group passing in the distance, calling out to Alexander.

'Look over here, at us!' they shouted excitedly as they drew near, each shouting over the others, but with enough repetition that Alexander got their meaning. When they reached the wall beneath his feet, they linked arms to form a circle so they could continue their tormented motion, wheeling around like wrestlers struggling for advantage, each twisting his neck to face the visitor as much as he could.

The author turned to Alexander and said, 'Be sure to treat these with the contempt they deserve. That one is the Marquis de Sade.'

'We may look like ordinary sinners, scorched and covered in ashes like this,' said one of them, who might have been the Marquis de Sade, 'But we're better than that. We deserve better than this!'

Alexander exchanged a look with the author.

The sinners went on to explain that they were *all* quite famous, actually; no doubt Alexander had heard of them. Above all, they were *creative* men, intelligent enough to disdain the shallow morality of the dreary masses. They had walked on the wild side, explored secret pleasures and generally been fabulous. What small-minded way of thinking could hold them worthy of punishment for that?

The author gestured to Alexander that it was time to move on.

'So,' Alexander said as they walked, 'What was that about, then? Sadism?'

The author looked disappointed at Alexander's literalism. 'The Marquis was above all a pornographer,' he explained. 'All that talk of pushing boundaries is just a glamorous gloss on transgression for the sake of it. It's not creative at all, but parasitic on the very morality it disdains.'

This emboldened Alexander to bring up something else he had wondered about when the author had first explained the geography of Hell. This place had to do with unnatural perversion. A generation ago that would have meant homosexuality. So?

The author invited Alexander to think it through for himself as they walked.

The detective recalled having seen gay couples earlier, punished for mere lust rather than 'violence'. Perhaps homosexual people *per se* were no more guilty or innocent than anyone else, which indeed seemed intuitive to him. It also occurred to him, though, that there was an ambiguity about the very idea of gayness, a lack of clarity about what it meant. It would be disingenuous to pretend it had never implied any more than a sexual preference for people of the same sex.

He remembered a controversy several years before about what if anything the police should do about gay men meeting for sex in parks. The politically correct view had been that the practice was a response to oppression: social censure and even persecution made it difficult to form normal relationships, resulting in a secretive subculture of anonymous promiscuity, which had perhaps even outlived the oppression that had given rise to it. No doubt there was something in that. But as a student of human nature, Alexander could not believe that, at least for some of those indulging, some of the time, the sordidness was not part of the appeal. After all, there were plenty of straight people who also got a kick out of walking on the wild side, as it were. Maybe one day, most gay people would 'marry' one another, have children one way or another and get divorced like everyone else. Maybe there would always be some for whom all that would defeat the purpose.

Before Alexander could develop the thought further, his guide told him they had to hurry, and led him on till the sound of the bloody waterfall was too deafening for him to think anyway. They soon reached the end of the concrete channel, where the rushing blood crashed into the blackness below. The author frisked himself, and coming up short, asked the detective for something hard and solid to throw over the edge. Alexander reached in his pockets. He had his phone, but that would be a pain to replace. He was also carrying handcuffs. Heavier; better, he supposed. But as he handed them over to the author, he could not help thinking of an American TV cop being asked to hand over his shield and his gun, the symbols of his office. Not that his handcuffs would be any good to him down here. If he could not arrest a demon sitting on a hospital bed, he was certainly not going try in here in Hell, least of all by force.

The author hurled the handcuffs some distance from the edge into the abyss, watching their trajectory carefully. Alexander supposed this was meant to attract the attention of someone or something.

'I know what to expect,' the author said, 'but you have no idea what's coming. There are some things so unbelievable I'd be embarrassed to describe them to anyone in a position to doubt me. But you'll see for yourself soon enough.' Then an enormous figure emerged from the bloody depths, and launched itself into the air above them. Alexander was certain it was coming for him, and fainted with fright.

It was evening when he awoke on his sofa at home, apparently having dozed off. Karen was reading on the armchair, but looked over when she saw him stir. 'Sleeping Beauty awakes?' she said.

He grumbled an acknowledgement and sat up.

Karen explained that she had let herself in and decided not to wake him because he had looked so sweet. He made a face.

She had come over with the intention of talking to Alexander about her pregnancy. Their pregnancy, in fact. Indeed, she had decided quite deliberately to think of it that way. Step one, as she saw it, in the deliberation process about what she, they, would actually do about it. Had she been sure that she wanted to have an abortion, she would not have felt the need to inform

Alexander. They were not married, they had never discussed children, and Alexander knew she was on the pill. He probably also knew the pill was not a hundred percent effective, but that was not the sort of thing she expected him to think about. He had no reason to believe or expect that should Karen become accidentally pregnant as a result of sex that was never intended to bring forth issue, she would check in with him before dealing with it. It would have been none of his business.

Perhaps the same would have been true even if she'd decided to have the baby. The involvement of his sperm did not entitle him to a veto. But they did have a relationship. And Karen had no intention of becoming a single mother. If she was going to have a baby, it would be Alexander's in more than a biological sense. So it made sense to talk to him about it. Which was why she was here. But here indeed she was, on Alexander's armchair, looking at him on the sofa, and not in fact talking to him at all.

He got up to go to the loo, and she closed her book. She would have preferred to have had a decision of her own to present to Alexander. By definition, considering the foregoing, that would have been a decision to have the baby. And yet she had reached no such decision. She felt a bit pathetic.

The prospect of a baby had unsettled Karen precisely because it did not now seem unthinkable. It felt less like the road to catastrophe than an opportunity to rethink her life. It would be hugely disruptive of her career, yes, but her career was not the be all and end all of her existence. Or she did not want it to be, she was now realising, perhaps for the first time. She could have a baby and be a mother too. Her career would survive, after all; it was not the stone age. It might be nice to have another focus in her life, another priority. To put her career in its place.

Karen loved police work. That was just true and she was not going to apologise for it. It was also true that she had fallen in love with Alexander because she admired him as a polis, the kind of polis she had wanted to be. But since then, she had discovered there was more to him than that. In fact, he was really quite a strange person, but now she loved that about him too. And she liked the idea that she too could be a strange person in her own right. Not just a polis, not just Alexander's concubine... Now she laughed at herself, as she realised she was conceiving of motherhood and effectively marriage as a form of independence. And yet, that was precisely how it did seem to her.

In any case, she now felt it had been wrong of her to put her career at the centre of her being. It meant she had allowed bureaucratic routine to seep around the edges of her vocation and occupy almost every spare inch of her subjectivity. If Alexander had not been her boss as well as her lover, their relationship would have been unthinkable. But perhaps she would serve her vocation better by distinguishing between it and herself. Maybe having a baby would be a blessing in more than the conventional sense. Maybe it would be churlish to reject that blessing just because it had been thrust on her, so to speak, rather than sought after.

When Alexander returned, she did not feel ready to bring the matter up. She decided instead to give him the work news. That day, Karen had visited the school where the girl had written the essay in defence of the Holocaust. It had now been widely reported, and the girl had been taken out of school for her own safety after receiving death threats. Yes, for writing an essay. There seemed to be an atmosphere of heightened fervour all round. It had also been noted that the girl's brother was one of the young men charged with the brutal city centre murder. State of the nation articles were appearing. But the important news was a suggestion that the killers had been acting under some kind of hypnosis.

A computer studies teacher at the school had found websites about hypnosis in the internet history of several pupils, including one of those accused of the murder. Clearly they had been circulating links. Most of the material seemed harmless – 'learn to hypnotise your friends' stuff – but there were also creepier sites about using hypnosis to seduce women, and even self-hypnosis for psychic thrills, 'more trippy than any drug'.

But then the jackpot: a website promising to channel the power of a demon into anyone brave enough enter into a trance and summon it. This had been viewed by the accused boy and one other: his 'Nazi' classmate.

This would have to be investigated. As implausible as it seemed that 14 young men had been possessed by a demon and driven to murder the girl – or even that they had convinced themselves that they had – the case was sufficiently hard to explain in ordinary terms that this outlandish possibility – at least the latter version – was no less plausible than any other. And clearly, there was something of a fad for hypnotism among the school pupils. The next step would be to discover if the other accused youths had shown similar interests. Their lawyers would eat it up.

To cheer Alexander up, Karen told him a funny story one of the teachers had told her when they had discussed ongoing behavioural problems. It concerned a third-year boy who was notoriously cheeky, and who had been sent out of his sex education lesson on two consecutive weeks. The first time had been for interrupting the teacher, who had just told the class there is nothing dirty about sex, by shouting: 'There is if you're doing it right!'

His classmates had fallen about laughing, puncturing the atmosphere of non-judgemental worthiness, and the teacher had lacked the humour to ride it out, so out the boy was sent. In the next week's lesson, the class had discussed pornography, and the question had arisen of whether it is degrading to women. The same boy called out: 'It is if it's any good!'

Alexander was very taken with this, as Karen had known he would be. Both were variations on the same old joke: old but good, good because it was true. Loath as she was to sound like a feminist, though, she asked whether he didn't think there was something a little sad about the second version? He agreed, and they discussed what made it different.

The first version rested on the childish sense that there is something inherently dirty about sex – because of the involvement of 'rude' parts of the body – a sense that never really leaves us, and is surely part of the appeal of sex for adults. Sex is naughty, in the sense of fun, even when we understand that it is perfectly natural and quite hygienic, most of the time. The excitement of transgression survives our realisation that sex in itself is not transgressive at all, even when you are doing it really, really well. Call that 'innocent naughtiness'. The truth of the second version of the joke is darker. The appeal of pornography is fundamentally transgressive in a way young children who giggle about sex cannot consciously understand. Its degradation of women – or more precisely of the particular women involved – is what makes it what it is.

Alexander thought back to the Marquis de Sade and his friends in Hell, then more uncomfortably to the demon's shrine. It had included pornography among various religious artefacts. Was that some kind of joke? A demonic satire? Was it comparing religion to pornography or pornography to religion? He decided he would ask the author what he thought.

CHAPTER 11: THE THIRD KIND OF VIOLENCE LAID BARE

At last, Alexander had a reply from Leanne. She was thrilled to hear from him, she said, and sorry for having been out of touch so long. She said hi to Karen and sent her love to Morgan. Her career was going well, but was not without his frustrations, as she knew he would appreciate. She would post him a CD of her latest recording.

Nothing about the author, nothing about Hell. Just an odd reference to all Leanne's own family being well 'as far as I know, lol'. Alexander realised this was a cryptic query about her sister Adele, who had disappeared after (allegedly) murdering the suspect in the case that had brought Leanne into his life. He should have known his approach out of the blue would have made Leanne think of her sister, and been more sensitive. After all, technically, he was still responsible for bringing her to justice, a fact they had managed to downplay as their friendship had blossomed, mainly because there were no leads on Adele's whereabout beyond the fact that she had flown to New York, putting her pursuit well out of Alexander's hands. The American authorities had been notified, but nothing had ever come up. Hearing from Alexander now, though, Leanne must have wondered if that had changed.

He replied quickly just to say he'd not heard from Leanne's family but hoped they were well, and to keep in touch anyway. He looked forward to the CD. And, still, if not Leanne, he had no idea who this mysterious woman could be.

The demon shrine case, or cases, remained unsolved. The fire had been deemed accidental and was no longer police business. The flat's owner was an absentee landlord, who reported that his sole tenant had disappeared after the fire. The tenant had checked himself out of hospital shortly after Alexander had fled, and been neither seen nor heard of since. And while the stolen goods found at the flat were still being held as evidence, Alexander had effectively dropped the burglary cases. Now, he decided to have another look, both because 'dropping' cases was not really done, and in hope of some kind of enlightenment.

The various religious artefacts combined to give off a kind of occult vibe, which Alexander assumed had been the demon's intention. The non-religious additions were not hard to decode. Football was often described as a religion, not least in Glasgow: the singed Rangers and Celtic scarves smelled like bad conceptual art. The pop CDs were equally obvious: one was Madonna, another occult-flavoured goth metal, but even the bushy-tailed boy band no doubt inspired rapt devotion among its target audience. Pop music as idolatry: very droll. That left the pornography.

Alexander flicked through the magazines. There was nothing unexpected or particularly shocking: just nude or semi-nude models striking the usual repertoire of obscene poses. Almost liturgical if you chose to think of it that way, but he managed not to get too intrigued. There were also videos, though. Two looked professionally produced, with covers promising hardcore action, but the third was unmarked, inspiring a vague dread. Alexander's heart was heavy as he took it to the AV room. He thought of Dr Brown warning him to guard his innocence. That was no doubt wise counsel, but it was wisdom that had been gained at the expense of Dr Brown's own innocence, wisdom Alexander could not understand.

A girl on a sofa. Blushing at the camera as someone behind it asks her to undress, slowly. She complies, awkwardly. Men appear from the wings. Two, three, four. Already undressed from the waist down. Alexander found himself reflecting on the strangeness of 'heterosexual' pornography. Most heterosexual men would rather not be in the same room as another man's erection. And yet here were four men in close proximity, primed and hardly able to ignore one another. They presumably did not consider this remotely 'gay', or perhaps they did not care. They played it cool, as if what they were doing were normal.

It is unfashionable in the modern world to admit to being shocked by anything, but Alexander was honest enough with himself to know that he was shocked by pornography. He knew it went on, he had seen it before, but watching this woman undress for the camera and stoop to fellate these men in high definition, he was amazed. What the Hell was she thinking? Did she have a family? Anyone who cared about her? By what process had she come to the conclusion that this was a good idea? Money was not a satisfactory answer, because most women would not, did not, do this kind of thing for money. And it only raised the further question of why people were willing to pay to watch this. It was not sexual gratification; if anything it was the opposite: the inflammation of an itch. He suspected the pleasure lay in contemplating the very question that is suppressed by the suggestion that money is explanation enough. It was a horribly fascinating question. Why was this woman doing this? It was mind-boggling.

Alexander made himself imagine the woman was his sister, his friend, Karen. Leanne. Morgan. It would be unbearable. What could have happened to her to make her do this? To make herself a sexual plaything to be defiled like this? Could she possibly be on good terms with her parents? Could they know? Could she think it did not matter? Did she have or intend to have children? Did she think they would thank her for the advantages paid for by this performance when their friends found the vintage footage of their mother online? Now she was on all fours on the sofa, one man entering her from behind, another at her mouth, the others lingering, groping, waiting their turn. Was she so spectacularly deluded that she thought this was all right? Or just utterly defeated? He imagined knowing this woman, loving her as apparently no one did. And then seeing her like this. It was heart-rending.

The ensemble ran through every manoeuvre in the pornographic liturgy. The woman was spared nothing. Held nothing back. And there was no suggestion of coercion. There was no doubt that things were being done to her, but she was willingly subjecting herself to it all, seemingly enjoying the attention, and the knowledge that beyond the studio, her performance would be watched by yet more men. Innumerable, pitiless, passionless eyes. She expressed her pleasure not with fake groans and a theatrically tortured expression, but more subtly, almost cheekily. She was not deluded in the sense that she thought this was just fun sex, or defeated in the sense that she was oblivious or careless of what was happening. She seemed to know exactly what she was doing. And finally, as the men sprayed her face and body with their issue, as if sealing her ruin, she winked knowingly at the camera. She wanted to be treated this way, or was doing an excellent job pretending. Either way, why? It was stomach-churning.

Mind-boggling, heart-rending, stomach-churning. You can see where this is going. Alexander could not help but feel the erotic charge the film had been produced to elicit. He watched till the end, trying to watch as a detective rather than a man, a fascinated sinner. He told himself this was about money, but he knew that was at best half an answer, and to the wrong question. He thought again of Dr Brown, who knew things he wished he did not.

In any case, there was nothing illegal about the film. The 'actors' all seemed safely of age and there were no innocent animals involved. He realised that he had been afraid of seeing the Buchanan Street murder victim, or the perpetrators in the porn, but no such horror. It was just porn. And its place in the demon's shrine was no mystery to Alexander. It belonged among the religious artefacts no less than the music or the football scarves. It was ritual: purposeful activity unconnected to animal needs. And it was just like a demon to make the connection without discrimination: non-judgmentalism as a kind of insult to humanity. The remaining question was why the demon had assembled the shrine, rendered the insult. Was it a message to the world? A message to Alexander? Or was it simply part of the demon's own private devotions to his evil master? Alexander had no idea.

Some time before, the unit had dealt with a case of 'occult pornography'. It was a faintly ridiculous thing – people in robes fornicating on a church altar – brought to their attention only because the female star had been duped into taking part, not realising she was being filmed. She had been seduced into the act itself, not because the men involved were attractive or charming – they were neither – but because of her own fascination with the idea of sexual submission. She had not known until the last minute that she would submit, would take part in the ritual. And had it not been filmed, maybe she could have told herself it never happened. It was just a stupid fantasy.

Alexander remembered her sympathetically, the unwitting porn star. That tormenting question – why is she doing this? – did not arise in the same way in her case, because she had not known she was making pornography. Admittedly there was the question of why she had taken part at all in the perverted ritual, but she owned that question and had made no excuses for herself. People do all kinds of strange and appalling things when they are not paying attention to themselves. They forget that what goes on in their own heads is not insulated from the world.

None other than Satan had once asked Alexander, 'What do people who don't believe in sin tell themselves when they have sinful thoughts and desires?'

They had been talking about sex, so Alexander responded defensively: 'Maybe that they're not sinful, but perfectly healthy and natural.'

'Healthy and natural?' the Accuser had retorted. 'You know I can read your mind, right?'

That little suggestion had put Alexander's heart in his throat, preventing him from giving an answer.

'I'm kidding,' the Archfiend had said, 'But you know who *can* read your mind?'

Alexander had scoffed: 'I'm sure God's got more important things to worry about'.

Satan's surprisingly ranty answer to that now came back to him with force: 'Really? Your Supreme Creator – omnipotent, omniscient, omnipresent – do you think he has to prioritise his schedule? You'll be telling me next you're no "God botherer"! I'm sick of hearing that one. And believe me: I hear it a lot.'

Perhaps, Alexander thought, he should have reflected at the time that when the Devil himself is shocked at your impiety, you might want to take stock of your life. But only now, having visited Hell several times, did it occur to him – fleetingly – to consider whether he did actually believe in God. And like déjà vu, the question was gone almost as soon as he was aware of it.

That night he had a dream inspired by the pornographic film from the demon's shrine. It was the same scene, but as if the scales had fallen from his eyes. What he saw now seemed to have very little to do with sex. The woman's cheekiness was gone, as if having evaporated, as cheek always eventually does when it is not acknowledged. The men surrounded her like rutting bulls, their kisses were like the slavering of animals. They incessantly buffeted and groped her, tore what remained of her clothes, spat in her face. They laid their hands on her, and took her, one or more holding her hands or feet while the others did their work. 'Fuck her! Fuck her!' they whooped, almost chanting. In their arms, her body fell limp like a ragdoll, and her limbs dripped pathetically when dropped, except when she was in danger of collapsing altogether, and she used an arm or a leg to right herself, acting hard to maintain the semblance of passivity. The men looked at her with amused contempt as they sealed her ruin, glancing at one another and shaking their heads in sarcastic disgust. When they had finished, they threw a scarlet cloak over her shoulders, and put a plastic tiara on her head. 'Look at the princess,' they laughed, 'the special, precious princess!'

One of them peed in a champagne glass and offered it to her, but she brushed it aside as the camera zoomed in and she delivered her only line: 'My God, my God, why hast thou forsaken me?' As the men clapped and cheered, she began to laugh, looking to them for the recognition that might restore her cheek.

Alexander was stunned. He did not laugh, did not cheer. He did not have to. He felt himself complicit in the evil; it was his dream, after all. And instantly he found himself back at the author's side in Hell.

Having previously been anxious to talk to the author about pornography, he now wanted to talk about anything else. He felt dirty, contaminated by what he had seen – worse, what he had dreamt – and disinclined to think about it at all. Fortunately, there was a welcome distraction in front of them.

The monster from the deep had partly beached itself at the end of the channel just in front of them, where the bloody river rushed over the precipice to wherever the beast had come from. It had the head of a kind old man, but a bear-like torso dressed in a sort of tie-dye shirt and ornate waistcoat, after which its body continued like a serpent's, coiling into the abyss.

The author said he had to speak to the monster, and suggested Alexander go and see a final type of sinners found in this place before they descended to the next level. So Alexander wandered over to where several sinners sprawled miserably on the burning ground not far from the edge, their slouched demeanour only making their attempts to beat off the flames more laborious than they needed to be. And there were always more flames, causing them to howl pathetically. The futility of the whole thing made Alexander think of dogs chasing their own tails.

He didn't recognise any of them, but they wore T-shirts emblazoned with various logos and acronyms. Businesses, brands, consultancies, or enterprises that were at once all and none of the above. Between screams of pain, they muttered meaningless slogans that he soon realised they were reading from one another's T-shirts – engaging in discourse that was entirely self-generated and apparently self-sufficient.

Now one of them spoke to Alexander. 'What are you doing in our little cul-de-sac? Jog on. And since you're still breathing, you can let it be known that we are soon expecting the illustrious company of your leading "new economy" pioneers.' He paused to scream as he brushed fresh flames from his T-shirt, before adding, 'My colleagues are particularly excited about something called "social media". You probably haven't heard of it yet,' he sneered, and then stuck out his tongue like a cow licking its nose.

Alexander wondered what they had done in life. How had they related to the real world? How had they made a living?

CHAPTER 12: RENT

Then Alexander noticed another group of sinners sprawled out like the first in an agonised frenzy on the hot sand. Instead of T-shirts, though, they were dressed like cavaliers in wigs and fancy coats – tattered and singed by the flames, of course, but there was a grubbiness in their bearing that seemed less accidental. As he approached, one of them looked up, almost as if he'd been expecting someone. He was an old man, who welcomed Alexander even as he fought a losing battle to douse the flames that engulfed him. He introduced himself as Dougal MacCallum.

Dougal said he was here with his master – he pointed him out amid the fiery throng – having followed him in life through good and ill, thick and thin, pool and stream, as he would explain. He said his master had been a certain Sir Robert Redgauntlet, a laird in the Southern Uplands of Scotland, and a Tory in the old-fashioned sense. He had been notorious for his part in the Civil Wars, and especially their bloody aftermath. Under Charles II and his brother James VII, Redgauntlet was charged with hunting down recusant Whigs and Covenanters, a task to which he took with great enthusiasm. He and his cronies rampaged through the countryside with bugle and bloodhound, challenging poor hill folk to 'tak the test' of loyalty to the king. Failing this test meant death. Sir Robert was consequently hated and feared, so much so that there were rumours he was in league with Satan himself. People said he was invulnerable, bullet proof, that on steep hillsides his horse turned mid-gallop into a giant hare, the better to hunt down his prey. The best anyone would say of him was, 'Deil scowp wi' Redgauntlet!'

Indeed. But what was he doing *here*, Alexander wanted to know? Why not simmering in the river of boiling blood above, with the other tyrants and murderers?

'Let me tell you a story,' Dougal said by way of an answer, and without ceasing to struggle with the fires of Hell, duly recounted the following tale.

Now, in his bloody pomp, Sir Robert had grown rich on 'fines' extracted from his victims, and that wealth had bought the loyalty of the lackeys and troopers who rode with him. They would drink themselves blind to his health, and usually at his own expense. But some were more reluctant participants in the persecutions, and rode with Redgauntlet because in those days you had to be on one side or the other, and they had not the temperament to be Whigs. One such was Steenie Steenson, a tenant farmer on the most pleasant part of Redgauntlet's land, a place called Primrose Knowe. Steenie was a revelling, rollicking lad, and a fine piper, renowned for his mastery of such favourites as 'Hoopers and Girders' and 'Jockie Lattin'. He had the finest finger for the backlilt between Berwick and Carlisle. Merry-making, rather than blood-letting, was his kind of mischief – though he may have been forced to engage in both – but the laird enjoyed his playing, and often asked him to come to Redgauntlet Castle when they were at their merriment. Dougal was especially fond of the pipes, and made sure to keep Steenie in his master's good graces.

Then came the Glorious Revolution, which threatened to reverse Sir Robert's fortunes. With William and Mary installed on the throne in London, the Whigs crowed that they would have their revenge on their former persecutors, and Redgauntlet in particular. But as it turned out, too many powerful men were compromised by similar deeds for their to be a proper reckoning, and the matter was smoothed over, leaving Sir Robert free to hunt foxes instead of Covenanters. His revels were as loud and his hall as well-lit as ever, but his cellar and larder were no longer stocked at the expense of non-conformists. Consequently, he turned to his tenants, raising their rents and collecting them mercilessly, so that on rent day they feared his wrath nearly as much as his previous victims had done. Some even whispered once more that he was the Devil incarnate.

Steenie was not good with money. After the rent hike, he had one payment deferred thanks to sweet talk and sweeter piping, but soon he was two payments behind, and the ground officer advised him to come with the rent in full on the appointed day, or disappear for good. It was sore work for Steenie to find the money, but he was a popular lad, and finally scraped it together. In fact, Dougal had heard most of it came from a neighbour called Laurie Lapraik. Laurie was as shrewd as he was wealthy, and could be Whig or Tory, saint or sinner, depending which way the wind blew. But he also liked a good tune, and more than that, he was happy to have Steenie's livestock at Primrose Knowe as security for the loan. So off Steenie trotted to the castle with a heavy purse and a light heart.

Dougal had been glad to see him, and after some delay – since Sir Robert had a fit of gout and did not rise until after noon – he led him into the great oak parlour, confiding that the laird was as keen to keep piper Steenie on his land as he was to have his rent. Sir Robert sat alone, except for his pet ape, a notoriously badly behaved creature that had the run of the castle, and got up to all kinds of mischief biting and pinching people, especially before major turbulence –whether meteorological or political. The ill-favoured jackanape was called Major Weir, after the celebrated Covenanter who had been executed after confessing in old age to a lifetime of secret warlockry in the service of the Devil. Finding himself alone for the first time with the laird, the Major and Dougal, Steenie had been visibly ill at ease, and as Dougal conceded, who could have blamed him?

Sir Robert was slumped on his grand armchair in a grand velvet gown, his feet on a grand pouffe. He suffered from kidney stones as well as gout, and it showed on his face. Major Weir sat across from him in a red laced coat and the laird's wig on his head. The ape completed his pastiche of the man by girning hideously in imitation of Sir Robert's agony. They must have seemed a fearsome couple to someone unused to their company. The laird's leather riding coat hung on a hook on the wall behind him, and his broadsword and pistols were also close at hand. He was in the habit of keeping his weapons ready, and Dougal was responsible for ensuring a horse was saddled and ready at every hour of the day and night. This went back to the days when Redgauntlet would loup on horseback whenever he caught wind of dissenting hill folk. Some said he maintained the habit of readiness for fear of revenge attacks, but he was not a fearful man.

On a table next to his armchair was the laird's rental book, a great black thing with brass clasps. A slim volume of pornographic verse – Sir Robert's second favourite reading material – served as a bookmark, keeping the place where it was recorded that the Goodman of Primrose Knowe was behind with his mails and duties. Sir Robert gave Steenie a look he had perfected for these occasions, fit to wither a man's heart in his very chest. He had a way of bending his brows so a deep-dinted horseshoe shape appeared on his forehead, as if stamped there by Satan himself, and it was said that when the mark appeared, he could read men's minds.

'Are ye come lighted-handed, ye son of a toom whistle? Zounds if you are!'

Steenie bowed courteously, and placed the bag of money on the table with a dash, all but exclaiming, 'Ta da!'

The laird grabbed it in a flash. 'Is it all here, Steenie, man?'

'Your honour will find it right,' said Steenie.

'Here, Dougal,' said the laird, 'gie Steenie a tass of brandy downstairs, till I count the siller and write the receipt.'

But they were barely out of the room when Sir Robert gave out a yell that shook the castle's foundations. Dougal ran back in and was soon joined by panicked liverymen responding to their master's repeated howls. He called for cold water for his feet and wine to cool his throat, yelling about Hell, Hell, Hell and its flames. They brought him in a tub of cold water, but when he plunged in his swollen feet, he howled even more, crying out that it was boiling, and Dougal had to concede that it did seem to be bubbling like a witch's cauldron. And when Sir Robert had doused his throat, he threw the cup furiously at Dougal's head, protesting it was not burgundy but blood! It was only the next day that this too was confirmed when the lass had to wash clotted blood off the carpet. All the while, Major Weir jibbered and cried as if mocking his master in his agony. In the hirdy-girdie, Dougal forgot all about Steenie, but he must have fled – with neither his money nor his receipt – before the laird let out one final, deep-drawn, shivering groan. And died.

Redgauntlet's son and heir came from Edinburgh to settle his father's affairs. The young laird, now Sir John, had never got on with his father. He was a lawyer who – Dougal had foreseen on his arrival in Hell – would later sit in the last Scots Parliament and vote for the Union. Nobody knew whether he was motivated more by the promise of English gold in his own pocket or simply the opportunity to spite his dead father – the Union being a Whiggish enterprise and hated by Tories of that time. Anyway, despite Sir John's better manners, some who had to deal with him would come to miss Sir Robert.

As for Dougal, he did not weep for his late master, but went about the house in a state of numbness as he organised the grand funeral. Each day, he felt worse and worse as night approached, and was always the last to his bed, which was in a little turret opposite the parlour where Sir Robert now lay in state. Indeed, that was the cause of his sickness and foreboding. Each night, he heard the laird's silver whistle calling him, as it had when he was alive and wanted help turning over in bed. But now Dougal did not dare answer the call, could not bear to think what it meant. Finally, though, his conscience got the better of him; his conscience, that is, being in thrall to his dead master. The night before the funeral, he asked his fellow servant Hutcheon to sit with him in his room. After stiffening his resolve with a tass of brandy, he told auld Hutcheon what he had heard, and explained that, 'Though death breaks service, it shall never break my service to Sir Robert; and I will answer his next whistle, so be you will stand by me, Hutcheon'.

Hutcheon was not enamoured of the plan, but as Dougal had known would be the case, he found himself unable to let down an old comrade he had stood with in battle and broil. So the two old codgers sat sipping brandy as they waited. Hutcheon wanted to read from his Bible, but Dougal would have none of it, preferring some old poetry.

Midnight came, and the castle was as quiet as a grave. Then, sure enough, the whistle sounded as sharp and shrill as if blown by Sir Robert in rude health. The two old servants looked at one another. Then up they got and tottered into the parlour. And there on the laird's coffin stood the Devil himself, summoning Dougal to his fate. Instantly, he dropped dead, and had been here in Hell ever since. In death as in life, he served Sir Robert Redgauntlet and his cronies, and was punished along with them, not for the persecutions, but for what had been documented in that great black book.

Before Alexander could enquire further, Dougal said it was not the end of his story. At some point between his arrival and Alexander's visit – he had no sense of the time – Sir Robert had been visited by Steenie Steenson, who, like Alexander, had been very much alive. Dougal had welcomed him as he had always done at Redgauntlet Castle, and told him how much Sir Robert had been missing him and his pipes. Steenie, not realising quite where he was, had been amazed to find Dougal seemingly alive, having clearly heard report of his demise. But Dougal had played down the mystery, instead simply warning Steenie to take nothing from anyone in this place – not food nor drink nor silver – except the receipt for which he had surely come. Or been sent. Steenie had said was not sure how he had got there, but he did want his receipt.

Dougal hesitated and looked at Alexander. 'What do you see?' he asked, glancing at his company of sinners.

Alexander described what he saw: tattered cavaliers sprawled on the ground and struggling vainly both to fight off flames and to protect themselves from the burning hot sand. 'Seems fair,' Dougal said, brushing the flames from his own arms. 'But this is not what Steenie saw.'

Steenie had arrived at what appeared to be Redgauntlet Castle itself. Dougal knew it because the moment the living man had arrived, he too had felt himself to be in the familiar surroundings of the laird's home. Not that there had been any relief from the flames of Hell. But somehow, the whole company of cavaliers had been simultaneously burning in Hell as Alexander saw them now and raising Hell as they had so often done in life. There was much singing of obscene songs, birling of burgundy and altogether unconscionable talk. So Steenie had entered Sir Robert's hall to find him carousing with his cronies as of old, but forewarned by Dougal not to take anything at face value.

And Dougal had to admit that even what Steenie saw must have been terrifying for the man. He would have known most of those assembled, having piped for them in Redgauntlet's hall many a time when they were alive. Indeed, in some circles, their miserable deaths were as infamous as their wicked lives. There was fierce Middleton, who had died in agony after falling down some stairs: his first tumble had broken his arm, while at the next the broken bone had pierced his side. The crafty Lauderdale had grown so fat in old age that he finally exploded on the toilet, blasting his insides downwards along with his soul. Bonshaw's demise had been similarly scatological: after a drunken falling out, one of his own men had run him through while he relieved himself on a dunghill, at the very spot where he had cruelly bound the Covenanter Cargill a year before. Bloody Mackenzie had retired to London after the persecutions, and died a mysterious death with blood gushing from his every orifice. And finally Claverhouse was killed by his own manservant, who, having resolved to rid the world of his evil master, and knowing he was invulnerable to lead, had fashioned a bullet from a silver button on the monster's own coat, and shot him through the heart with it.

Dougal pointed Claverhouse out to Alexander, sitting apart from the others and watching their torment haughtily. His long, curly locks were on fire, and he struggled to fight off the flames while keeping one arm over his puncture. The others cried out wildly in pain, and Dougal reported that even Steenie had heard their screams amid their merriment in that Hellish shadow of Redgauntlet Castle, and seen their smiles contort from time to time into the horrible expressions seen by Alexander. The detective would find it hard to distinguish the guests from the catering staff, but Steenie had seen the cavaliers waited on by the same servants and troopers who had done their cruel bidding in life. The Lang Lad of the Netherton was there, along with the bishop's summoner who had been known as the Deil's Rattlebag. Worst of all were the wicked guardsmen in their laced coats, who in life had shed blood like water, pandering slavishly to their rich masters and driving them to worse: grinding the poor to powder when the rich had broken them to fragments.

When he had spied Steenie, Sir Robert Redgauntlet had called to him with a voice like thunder. His guest found the laird much as he had on Earth, ensconced on his throne with his feet up and his weapons at hand. Even the cushion for his ape lay at his side, and Steenie would have heard the guests speculating as they still did about when Major Weir would be joining them. But Sir Robert had more pressing business: 'Weel, piper, hae ye settled wi' my son for the year's rent?'

Steenie just about found the breath to explain that Sir John was demanding his father's receipt, and Sir Robert did not dispute that it was owed, but did request a tune on the pipes before handing it over, specifically 'Weel hoddled, Luckie'.

It was a tune Steenie had played before at Redgauntlet Castle, having learned it from a warlock who had heard it at a sabbat. But he was not fond of it, and now looked like he'd rather do anything else than play it. He hadn't his pipes anyway, he explained, so could not oblige. Unperturbed, Sir Robert bade

Dougal bring the pipes he'd been keeping for Steenie. Dougal brought Steenie a magnificent pair of pipes, but gave him a nudge as he offered them, causing him to look closely and notice that the chanter was made of steel, and heated to a white heat. So he excused himself again, explaining that he was quite overwhelmed by the circumstances, and had barely the wind to fill the bag. Sir Robert answered that all Steenie needed was food and drink, and they had plenty of both.

'It's ill speaking between a full man and one fasting,' he added, which, Dougal explained to Alexander, was a probably half-conscious reference to the murder of MacLellan of Bombie in 1452. The bloody Earl of Douglas had taken MacLellan prisoner over a political disagreement, and when the king's messenger arrived with orders to release him, Douglas insisted on feeding the messenger before even hearing him out. Of course, he killed MacLellan while the messenger ate. Steenie must have suspected similar mischief in the guise of hospitality, because he not only refused food and drink as Dougal had advised, but spoke up like a man. He said he was there neither to eat nor drink, nor to play the minstrel, but simply for what was his by right. He wanted to know what had happened to the money he had brought, and to get his receipt. And emboldened by his own righteous words, he even charged Sir Robert 'for conscience-sake' to deal fairly with him. Just as Dougal's conscience had bade him serve his evil master even in death, Redgauntlet surely had a code of his own, if not tied to virtue, then some simulacrum thereof.

Sir Robert gnashed his teeth and laughed at this, but he produced the receipt from his wallet and handed it to Steenie: 'There is your receipt, ye pitiful cur; and for the money, my dog-whelp of a son may go look for it in the Cat's Cradle.' (Dougal explained that this was a derelict turret in the castle.)

Steenie took the receipt gratefully and made to leave, but 'Not so fast!' Sir Robert stopped him, calling him a 'sack-doudling son of a whore' and insisting that he should return in exactly one year to pay homage to his laird, since, 'Here we do nothing for nothing'.

Steenie's newfound courage did not fail him, however. Dougal had not been able to make out his words, but whatever he had said with such conviction, it was the last anyone there had heard of him. In an instant, he had disappeared, along with the shadow of Redgauntlet Castle. Ever since, Dougal, Sir Robert and his cavaliers had been burning on the hot sand just as Alexander had found them.

The detective was intrigued, and confused. This would take some digesting, and he sensed that Dougal MacCallum had little more light to shed on his situation. In any case, he was worried the author might be growing impatient. So he returned to the precipice, where the author was indeed preparing to move on. He had mounted the monster's rump, where bear met serpent, apparently intending to ride it down the bloody waterfall to the next level. 'You took your time,' he said, before adding, 'I hope you're feeling brave. Climb on in front of me, so at least I can protect you from the beast's tail.'

Alexander was not feeling brave. The thought of climbing onto this Hellish thing to descend yet further into the pit filled him with sheer dread and despair. But he did not want to appear cowardly in front of the author, so he took his place and was glad to be able to close his eyes without it being noticed. And he was reassured beyond words when the author put both arms around him and promised everything would be OK.

'Steady now,' the author told the monster. 'Take us down in a wide, slow spiral, and remember the extra weight you're carrying. Let's go.'

At that, the beast backed tentatively away from the edge of the bloody waterfall until its weight was supported only by its own hideous strength. Then it arced its torso downwards, curling its tail above, so it could begin swimming downwards through the blood and air in a spiral as instructed. But if it was taking pains to swim gently, Alexander did not feel the benefit of it. His eyes clasped shut, he could only feel the bloody wind on his face, but that was enough. His gut told him all was lost. He felt like Icarus at the moment his wings failed him. That sinking feeling when you know you've really fucked up this time.

CHAPTER 13: A MAD DANCE

Alexander had never decided to divorce Laura. He had experienced his divorce as something that happened to him. Indeed, it was Laura who had first initiated their separation and then asked to make it official. But it had not really felt like something she had done to him either. After all, he had let her down. That was how he had always rationalised it. He had failed at marriage; they had failed at marriage, but he had left it to Laura to administer the last rites. Only now it occurred to him that it had not been like that at all.

He had wilfully neglected his marriage, if not his wife. Because while he had always made a point of being good to Laura – in his own terms, at least – he had never truly decided to treat her as his wife, his partner in life. He had rubbed along with her as if that would be enough. Buying a home together, having a baby, taking an interest in one another's careers. Or not so much the last, since he had known no more about nursing than she had known about police work. But the career thing was too much of a cliché, an excuse. The job costs marriages, everyone said. But people said all kinds of stupid things. It was Alexander who had chosen to treat his career as his own inviolable sphere of autonomy, graciously allowing Laura the same leeway in hers. As if their marriage ended at the front door. That now seemed to him worse than a mistake. It had been sabotage.

Alexander thought now of his marriage as if remembering a dream. He was not even sure if he recognised himself as the protagonist of that dream. He did have fond memories of the happy times, but those times had always come as a surprise, somehow. He had never made any particular effort to be happily married to Laura, not so much believing such things are meant to be spontaneous as considering it beneath him to aspire to happiness, even for his wife. So it was not surprising that things had turned out the way they had. Not miserable, exactly, not bitterly acrimonious, but unsatisfactory all round. Alexander had never looked forward to going home. Shift work had not helped, of course. But he thought of those evenings when he could have come home to his wife. He thought of the evening he had spent in Ayr, drinking with Johnny Souter and eyeing up the barmaid while Laura sat at home with the baby. And then that other stuff he'd seen at Alloway Kirk. He thought of how he'd narrowly escaped at the cost of his Rangers hat, but without reckoning with his defining moral flaw, his lack of care for his own trajectory in life.

It now seemed to him that it was his wanton, deliberate carelessness that had done for his marriage. He had not failed Laura so much as thrown her away. Not that there was any going back. She was remarried, happily as far as he knew, with another child by her husband. And now Alexander had Karen. He asked himself if he were making the same mistakes again. It did not seem so, and not just because he and Karen were not married, though their failure even to discuss moving in together – and what it might take to make that succeed – did ring a bell. But there had never been any question of siloing off his career from their relationship. Alexander's and Karen's shared working life was the foundation of their relationship. Maybe it was time to build something more substantial on that foundation.

Alexander found himself at his desk, coming to with a start from his reverie about marriage. And now he was mentally at work, the salience of the incident at Alloway Kirk seemed different, more prosaic. He was now ready to acknowledge that he had in fact experienced something not only unmistakably occult, but blatantly and terrifyingly supernatural. He would no longer deny it. He still felt his conversations with the Devil were plausibly deniable – perhaps they had been no more than internal dialogues with a theatrical flourish – but that night in Ayrshire had been different. There had been nothing whimsical about his long journey home after escaping with his life.

And now Alexander realised something else about his last visit to Hell. According to the tale told by Dougal MacCallum, Alexander was not the only person to have visited while still alive, and departed perhaps in the same condition. There had been Steenie Steenson, sometime in the late 17th century. Alexander consulted the parish records for Steenson's part of the world and duly found that someone of that name had indeed lived well into the 18th century. Delving deeper, he found this Steenie had been involved in a legal dispute with one Laurie Lapraik over certain property at Primrose Knowe, presumably in connection with the loan Steenie had secured to pay Redgauntlet. Alexander could find no more than a passing mention of this in the records, but by following every lead he could find, he did come across a remarkable story about Lapraik. There was far more detail about this case, because it had come to the attention of a chronicler who seemed to share Alexander's professional interest in occult matters. It had begun innocuously enough, though, with another dispute Lapraik had been involved in some years after the one with Steenson. This dispute was with a Tam Dale, this time over the wardenship of the Bass Rock in the Firth of Forth off North Berwick.

The Bass was by then uninhabited, but had a castle that had been used as a prison for Covenanters and other dissidents during the persecutions. The matter arose when the rock came into the possession of the judge Sir Hew Dalrymple and he sought to recruit a former soldier from the garrison to manage the rock's affairs on his behalf. He needed someone who knew the Bass and its assets – mostly sheep and gannets, which were harvested for food – and who was suitably responsible. Both Lapraik, now known as Tod Lapraik on account of his fox-like wiles, and this Tam Dale, seemed to fit the bill on paper. But the decision apparently came down to character.

Tam Dale had once been a typical young soldier, who enjoyed a lass and a glass and took little thought of anything else. But one day a Covenanter being held on the Bass, who was regarded by some as a prophet, had heard him blaspheming as he frequently did in those days, and warned him with such conviction that he saw 'the deil at his oxter' that Tam had flung down his pike instantly and resigned from the garrison, returning to North Berwick where he had settled down with a good woman and led a respectable life ever since. For his part, Tod Lapraik had served at the garrison till the end. Since then, he had lived elsewhere for a time – of course, Alexander knew he'd lived on Redgauntlet's lands to the west – but was now back in North Berwick and a weaver by trade. He was better known as a wheeler dealer, however, and in addition had a somewhat sinister reputation; more than once he had been found seemingly in a trance at his loom, even as he worked the shuttle, with his eyes shut and a creepy smile on his fat face that made anyone who saw it shudder.

Perhaps unsurprisingly, it was Tam Dale who got the job, but not before an ill-tempered encounter between the two of them when Tam went to talk the matter over with Lapraik and found him in one of his trances. When the appointment was announced, Lapraik said he hoped Tam would get what was due to him on the Bass.

Well, when the time had come to harvest the young gannets, Tam took to the cliff face as he had done since his boyhood, with four strong lads holding his line above and moving it as he directed. But then something uncanny happened. He was experienced enough to know that the birds did not attack people, even in defence of their young, so when a large gannet began pecking at the line above him, he was spooked as well as afraid.

The more he shooed the creature, the more deliberately it wrought at the line, using its beak to rub the soft rope against a jag in the rock. Tam signalled to the lads to pull him up before it was too late, but the gannet seemed to understand about signals too, and let go of the rope, spread its wings and, with a squawk, took a turn in the air before diving straight at Tam. Luckily, Tam had a knife on him, and the flash of its blade seemed to deter the uncanny bird, which squawked again and flew off around the cliff.

When the lads pulled Tam to the top of the cliff, they found he had passed out from fright, but after a dram of brandy, he sat upright and ordered one of them to run ahead and secure their boat, seemingly convinced that otherwise the gannet would set it adrift to leave them stranded. Then he told the others there would be no more harvesting, that they were all to get 'aff frae this craig o' Sawtan' forthwith. So they did, but by the time they made it to the mainland, Tam was in a crying fever, which kept him bed-ridden for the rest of the summer.

Apparently, Tam was visited more than once by none other than Tod Lapraik, and each time the fever had worsened, but eventually Tam recovered. If that had been that, the story might never have survived. But there was more. By the time Tam recovered from his fever, it was the season to catch whiting, and he went fishing with his lads. They had a good haul, which brought them close to the Bass along with another boat belonging to a Sandie Fletcher, who pointed to something on the rock that looked very much like a person. This seemed all but impossible, as nobody had been back on the Bass since they had fled weeks before. They brought the boats closer together to steady them, and Tam took out his telescope to investigate. It was indeed a person, in a patch of green down from the old chapel, all on his tod, but lowping and jigging and dancing like a daft bint at a wedding.

Tam identified the figure as Tod indeed, and passed the telescope to Sandie, who soon concurred. But Tam was unsure if the likeness were real. Sandie was convinced the thing was evil either way, and took out a fowling piece he always carried, resolved on shooting at it. Tam cautioned him to hold fire, reminding him that he'd been up before the Procurator Fiscal before for being hasty with his gun. He suggested instead that as he had the faster boat, he should head back to North Berwick, while Sandie and his crew kept an eye on the apparition. If Tam did not find Tod Lapraik at home, he'd come back and they'd both go to the Bass and have a chat with him there. If he did find him, he'd run up the flag at the harbour to let Sandie know he should shoot at the unnatural thing on the Bass. Then Tam gave Sandie a silver slug to add to his lead shot, just in case, and set off.

The witnesses' descriptions of the apparition of Tod Lapraik dancing on the rock all focused on the incongruousness of the spectacle. Yes, young girls could go like that all night, but they were fuelled by merry company and egged on by admiring lads. This thing was in perfect isolation. Dancing queens had rollicking tunes to move to. It had nothing but the indifferent skirling of the gannets. They had youth and energy and supple limbs. It was the image of a fat old man. It was ridiculous. And yet, there it was, dancing and spinning and screeching with sheer joy.

As Alexander read, he thought first of the witches and warlocks at Alloway Kirk, but they at least had music and company for their debauchery. Then he thought of the Minotaur in Hell, alone in desolation, skipping and hopping and raving to no purpose. And he thought of his own words to the author: 'What blind cupidity, what driving frenzy, spurs us on in our short lives, only to offer us up to ravenous eternity?'

Well, Sandie and his men duly saw the flag go up at the harbour. He raised his gun, took careful aim and pulled the trigger. The bang from the boat was answered by a woeful screech from the Bass, and the fishermen rubbed their eyes as they looked from the rock to one another and back again. Tod Lapraik's apparition was nowhere to be seen. The sun glinted and the wind blew, and the patch of green where the thing had been dancing was bare.

Sandie and his men made for the harbour in silence, and arrived to find a crowd gathered waiting for them. They soon learned that many of those gathered had gone with the agitated Tam to Lapraik's house, and found him in one of his trances, and then waited there anxiously as a lad ran to the harbour to run up the flag. Then, after an uncomfortable wait, all of a sudden, Tod Lapraik had leapt up with a terrible scream and fallen dead onto his loom. When his body was examined, not one piece of lead shot could be found. But a single wound had led into his heart, where Tam's silver slug had lain, still hot to the touch.

In normal terms, the story would have been easy to dismiss. It was a three-centuries old tale put together by a credulous chronicler from sources that amounted to little more than rumour and hearsay. And yet, Alexander suspected it was all true. After all, he had not doubted what he had been told by Dougal MacCallum. If he could visit Hell, why not Steenie Steenson? And if Steenie Steenson's landlord could appear to him in Hell as if entertaining in his castle, why could not Tod Lapraik make a Hellish apparition on the Bass Rock while working his loom at home?

It seemed all but certain that Lapraik would have gone straight to Hell itself when he was killed. But, not having encountered him there, Alexander did not know what his defining sin might be. He did know he had perhaps tried to murder Tam Dale in the guise of a gannet, but that seemed too obvious and banal, surely secondary to a more profound sin. Alexander also knew Lapraik had lent money to Steenie Steenson and got into a dispute over it. Usury? Or something more like fraud? As far as he could tell, Redgauntlet and his cavaliers were in Hell for living off spuriously inflated rents extracted from his tenants. Perhaps the weaver's other business interests amounted to something similar. But of course the most compelling part of the story was the mad dancing.

And then something seemingly quite unrelated dawned on Alexander. The girl who'd written that essay had missed the point of Holocaust denial. The Holocaust is not simply indefensible: it was never *meant* as a plan to be defended, only as a deed to be done as if without noticing. It was the removal of a problem – the Jews as the enemies of the people – that had been created from nothing and now had to be returned to nothing. Holocaust denial was an attempt to complete the erasure of its victims. And it was all the more perverse because the Nazis had been defeated and their crimes exposed. Holocaust denial was the wilful pursuit of an evil all the more pure for being a lost cause. It was a kind of mad dance. 'Almost more evil than the Holocaust itself,' Alexander's thought continued, but that was ridiculous. He dismissed it.

Karen appeared, or rather DC Smith, since she bore case files. The team was making progress on a couple of relatively straightforward cases that happily had little to do with anything genuinely occult, seemingly supernatural or even particularly morally troubling. Alexander spent the next couple of days immersed in those cases with his colleagues. He did not think about Hell. Nor, though, did he think about his life with Karen beyond work, and what he intended to do about it.

Karen was still pregnant, of course, and perhaps the hormones affected her mood. Anyway, after another failed attempt to bring it up with Alexander, this time over a specially planned dinner, she snapped. It was possibly deserved, as he was being less than receptive, but still, he was shocked when she hissed at him: 'Go to Hell!'

CHAPTER 14: MALEBOLGE

There is a place in Hell called Malebolge. It is made of stone the dull grey colour of iron, and takes the form of a gigantic cone contracting as it descends to a deep pit in the centre. The cone is made up of ten massive concentric rings, each tighter than the last until the pit itself, which we shall come to in due course, and each ring is grooved to form a circular valley – or pouch, since Malebolge means 'evil pouches' – going round the cone. A series of radial bridges run from the outer edge and over each valley to the centre.

Having descended through the bloody waterfall, Alexander and the author were deposited by the monster at the top of Malebolge, from where they could see down into the first valley as they walked around the edge. Below them, naked sinners circled either clockwise or anti-clockwise around the valley, on either side of a chain of metal barriers. Alexander was reminded of the hellish throng and the remarkably similar metal barriers used for crowd control during the millennium Hogmanay celebrations. Only, here, the trudging sinners were being beaten by horned demons with great whips.

Alexander thought he recognised one of the sinners approaching below, and stopped for a better look. The author gestured his consent for Alexander to walk back a little to keep pace with the sinner, who was trying to hide his face as he passed. 'I know you,' Alexander shouted, 'you're Benedict Riever.' Riever had been a prominent Edinburgh barrister. 'But what did you do to end up here?'

'It pains me to say it, but since you ask, I persuaded my sister to use her feminine wiles to advance my career. And now I sup with the common pimps I once prosecuted. Though there are more than a few lawyers here too, mostly from the city where you'll have had your tea.'

At that, a demon lashed him with his scourge and snarled, 'Move it, ruffian! There are no women for you to cash in on here.'

The author led Alexander on along the edge until they came to the bridge that arched over the valley. As they crossed it, the author told Alexander to take advantage of the view, as they could now see those sinners who had been trudging with their backs to them. He pointed out one in particular, a tall man with an aristocratic bearing, and told Alexander it was Jason, of Jason and the Argonauts fame. But the exploits that had landed him here were more personal: all his life, he had left behind him a trail of disappointed women. He misused his heroic charisma to seduce them with the promise of love, before knocking them up and abandoning them. The author explained that the others walking with Jason were guilty of similar deceits, and most lacked even his flawed nobility.

The one with the professorial bearing was Humbert Humbert, inventor and tormentor of 'Lolita'. Alexander had already seen child abusers boiling in the bloody river above. Humbert was being punished for a more particular sin. The author explained that the harm he had caused arose from a kind of fraud, specifically self-deceit. Unwilling to acknowledge his own sinful lust, he had projected it onto its objects, designating those pubescent girls who stirred his interest as 'demoniac nymphets'. He had then lived out that fraud by playing the victim to their predatory ways. There was nothing nymphic about the demons that now exerted power over him, nothing erotic about his torment.

Alexander and the author continued over the bridge to the inside edge of the valley, which was lower than the outside edge and also served as the top edge of the next valley below. They could hear sinners beneath them, whimpering, grunting and beating themselves, but this valley was so deep that they could only see to the bottom by continuing over the own bridge and looking directly down. This was no bad thing, given that the valley's banks were encrusted with a stinking mould. From the bridge they could see sinners immersed in what, judging from the smell, could only be human excrement.

Alexander set his gaze on a particularly filthy individual who seemed to take umbrage at the attention. 'What you looking at?' he shouted.

'If I'm not mistaken I've seen you before. With cleaner hair.'

'You're full of compliments,' said the sinner. 'And it's flattery that's brought me here. People used to say I was a brownnoser. I took that as a compliment too.'

Alexander shuddered at the literalness of the man's punishment, but before he could ask if it was not a little harsh, the author pointed out another sinner. 'You see that dishevelled bag lady scratching herself and doing squats in the shit? That's a prostitute who was notorious for convincing her customers she loved them. But now we've seen and smelled enough of this place.'

Indeed, Alexander now found himself in the office, awaking suddenly from a daydream inspired by his most recent visit to Hell. In it, he had been beating up a pimp he had in fact arrested several times earlier in his career. He had always hated pimps more than other criminals, and he did not pretend, to himself at least, that the feeling was entirely wholesome. It was tinged with a nagging, horrified fascination with the power they seemed to exert over their women. Alexander's fascination was not born of sexual jealously, at least not entirely, so much as tragic disappointment. He did not want what pimps had, but felt the loss of what they destroyed by having it, even if the loss was not his own. Of course, he understood that prostitutes made choices in the context of privation, drug addiction and violence. But he knew that these pressures were not always experienced as such. That some pimps succeeded in producing an emotional bond even as they coined their women. It was indeed a sickening fraud.

In fact, it now occurred to him that prostitution was all about fraud, about a pretence that what is happening is something other than what is really happening. He remembered how a prostitute had once explained it to him.

'In my experience, there's two kinds of customer. I call them the sad and the bad. The sad ones kid themselves you fancy them, and they lap it up if you moan and all that. Sometimes there's kisses hello and goodbye, and I think some of them even fantasise that you're their girlfriend. The bad ones are under no such illusions. They just like the idea that they've paid for you and you have to do what they want. They enjoy the feeling of control, and if you let them see it, they enjoy your humiliation.'

'So do you prefer the sad ones?'

'Oh, no, the bad ones. Much less work. You just switch off, almost like being raped.'

Alexander felt he should cry when he remembered that, but his pity was complicated by anger and other, darker feelings. He despised prostitutes almost as much as he hated pimps.

Alexander mentioned his daydream when he next saw Dr Bakshi, but in recounting it, he focused less on his violence towards the pimp than on his bewilderment about prostitution, which he now described as women being paid to pretend not to notice they are being raped.

'That's not how most people would describe it,' Dr Bakshi observed, rising to the bait.

'No, it's not. But it seems to me a better description than "selling sex".'

He went on to explain his theory that the whole business of prostitution is a kind of fraud, a pretence that sex is something that can be bought and sold. In fact, he insisted, it is *impossible* to pay for sex as most people understand and value it, because at the very least that involves the other person volunteering his or her time. You can pay someone to go through the motions, but that involves the pretence that what the client is getting is actual sex, that what the prostitute is selling is 'just sex', or both.

'Don't you think you're holding "actual sex" to an unrealistically high standard of authenticity?'

'What do you mean?'

'Don't you think even perfectly normal sex involves a degree of pretence?'

Alexander resisted 'speak for yourself' and even a more self-deprecating quip, and simply repeated, 'What do you mean?'

Dr Bakshi sighed. 'When people volunteer their time, as you put it, it's not always because they, strictly speaking, "enjoy" the activity in question. Is it?'

'Indeed not.'

A listening silence.

'But it would be odd to volunteer for something you didn't enjoy unless you at least believed in the cause it served,' Alexander said as he processed the thought. 'In fact, the most obvious reason for "faking it" would be to please or just to spend time with someone you liked. That doesn't seem to me such a bad reason for having sex.'

Then he thought of Karen, who had once told him about her early sexual experiences – not really enjoying it, but going along with it because that was what you did. She had supposed it was a gender thing – the boys had seemed enthusiastic but selfish and clumsy – but Alexander could not be sure, as he'd never had sex as a teenager. Maybe boys were ambivalent too. Maybe everyone was going through the motions. But what did it matter? Why should he defend teenage sex? He was the father of a daughter, after all. But these still private thoughts were interrupted by Dr Bakshi.

'What about having sex to please someone, not so much because you like them, as because you feel you need to please them, or because you want something from them? Like sleeping with the boss?'

Dr Bakshi did not know Alexander was sleeping with a junior colleague; it was not the sort of thing he shared with her. In any case, he was pretty sure Karen liked him, unless she were psychopathically devious, and to no obvious end. 'Would you describe that as "perfectly normal sex"?' he asked Dr Bakshi.

'I believe it's well within the range of normal human behaviour. Yes.'

Alexander was reminded that he was speaking to a woman of science, not a moralist. But the mention of 'sleeping with the boss' also reminded him that it was he, as Karen's boss, who would be considered to be in the wrong should the matter come to light. Especially if it came to light because it ended badly. The assumption was that such a relationship was, or at least could be, an abuse of power on his part. Of course, it was no such thing. And nor did he think he was being manipulated by Karen. Their relationship was not merely normal; as far as he was concerned it was moral.

He thought again of Karen's teenage experiences; normal, no doubt, but moral? It was surely a grey area. He knew young people were taught in sex education these days that peer pressure was a kind of abuse. He had even read an academic paper that suggested a married woman who does not feel like having sex but does it anyway because she feels it's her duty is in fact a victim of rape. Uncoupled from its traditional opposition to violent coercion, the notion of consent pitted free will against itself.

'I still think there's such a thing as "actual" sex', he told Dr Bakshi, 'and that it involves actual sexual desire on both sides, whatever else is going on. And if there isn't actual sexual desire on both sides, it isn't actual sex'.

'You don't think there's such a thing as *dutiful* sex?' she asked, as if she'd been reading his mind.

'I suppose there is,' he said, 'but then whether it's actual sex or not depends on the nature of the duty.'

'Meaning?'

'There's surely a difference between a loving wife's desire to make her husband happy – and vice versa – and a sense of obligation based on debt or blackmail of some kind.'

'Is there?'

'Yes. In fact, a desire born of uncoerced will is more authentic than a merely physical desire.'

'But now you're talking about a desire to please someone else, not *sexual* desire.'

'It seems pretty sexual to me.'

'Fake it till you make it?'

'I don't see that it's fake.'

'Isn't *genuine* sexual desire something that drives us to do things even *against* our conscious will?'

Alexander was caught between a sigh and a smirk. He recognised the truth in what Dr Bakshi said, and it was another reason the concept of consent was so slippery. Some people enjoy certain things sexually that they'd rather not put into words, let alone agree to in legally airtight terms.

'Who's to say which is more genuine? We all have conflicting desires. Surely it's up to us how we resolve them. And unless coercion is involved, it's what we do that ultimately reveals what we want.'

Except now he remembered that he had left his wife without ever really intending to. He had allowed himself to be thrown out, and made no serious effort at reconciliation with Laura, even when he had missed her terribly. Even when he had missed married sex, which sometimes did begin with a sense of duty on one or both sides, but rarely ended that way. As he still told Morgan when she didn't want to go to school, 'You'll like it when you get there'.

'Don't you think that's very naive, the idea that what we do reveals what we want?' Dr Bakshi asked. 'Don't you think we often do what we think we are *supposed* to want? What is expected of us? Isn't it easier to dutifully play a role than to assert what we really want?'

Now he thought of arranged marriage, but was afraid to bring it up for fear of offending Dr Bakshi; whatever her own circumstances, she might think he'd only thought of it because of her ethnicity. Anyway, in its most coercive form, arranged marriage was the paradigm of an unfree choice – a woman forced into a loveless marriage, who yields to her husband's sexual advances because she feels she has no choice. But it seemed to Alexander that role-playing was not always about avoiding self-assertion. What about a woman who actually enjoys being led by a man because she finds it sexy? Maybe she doesn't want to be a sassy feminist who owns her own sexual desire and demands sex on her own terms. Maybe she prefers to retain plausible deniability when it comes to her own lustful feelings and preferences. Maybe she feels more comfortable being passive and as demure as circumstances allow while her man has his wicked way with her. Karen was not like that. But if she had been, who would Alexander have been to judge?

He speculated that Dr Bakshi was the sort of person for whom frustrated desires were the only authentic ones, unrequited love the only kind that counts; everything else a disappointment. 'I think it would be better if people put their duty before their immediate desires more often,' he told her.

CHAPTER 15: PLAYING WITH MAGIC

Alexander had once known a gifted amateur magician called Simon, who had seen an old man perform tricks the like of which he had never seen, and fallen so much under his spell that he had offered to pay to be let in on the secret. The old man had been offended by Simon's lack of respect for what he himself apparently believed to be real magic, and he cursed Simon, who might or might not have ended up in the third pocket of Malebolge.

Alexander now found himself with the author on the bridge overlooking that valley. Looking down, he could see that the valley sides and floor were perforated with holes the size of manhole covers. Indeed, from each one protruded the feet and legs of a sinner who was evidently within. The soles of their feet were on fire, and they wriggled their legs violently, presumably in a vain attempt to put out the fire, but the flames merely danced all the merrier.

Alexander pointed to one who wriggled more wildly than the others, and whose flames burned redder. 'Who is that one?' he asked the author, who responded by offering to carry him down the steep slope for a closer look.

When he was put down next to the flaming sinner, Alexander called out, 'Can you hear me, in there?' He felt oddly like a priest new to the confession box and uncertain if it was 'working'.

'Is that you standing there already?' came a voice. 'Is that you standing there already? I wasn't expecting you for years. Have you already driven Rangers into liquidation?'

At the author's prompting, Alexander made clear he wasn't who the sinner thought he was, mindful of what he had learned about the damned seeing beyond the present and into the future. Rangers in liquidation? Someone was about to earn a place in Hell all right.

The sinner twisted his feet in frustration and shouted, 'Then what do you want from me?'

Before Alexander could answer, he went on, 'Since you care enough to have come down here, let me tell you that in life I wore a great mantle. And instead of doing my duty I made a fortune out of it, leading to my misfortune down here. Beneath my head, driven into the rock, are others who sought elevated positions for personal gain or out of vanity, wreaking havoc in the process, like the bastard I mistook you for. When he comes he'll take my place and push us all further into the crack. And he won't be the last. There are worse to come: lawyers who hate justice, scholars who hate knowledge, artists who hate beauty. They are like overgrown children playing at adult life, as I did, with no understanding of the responsibility that comes with it.'

It occurred to Alexander to doubt himself. Who doesn't sometimes feel like an overgrown child? He would not have made it to DCI without some degree of childlike ambition, vanity indeed, to supplement his grown-up vocation. Material greed was not his vice, but he was greedy for something more than justice. He took some consolation from the thought that others had done far more damage than he; time-servers, careerists, he had even known of blatantly corrupt senior officers for whom police work had been a game, and who had indeed wrought havoc. No doubt the same was true in other professions. He looked around him at the dozens of other flaming legs, whose bodies evidently drove others like pegs, deep into the rock. Careerism was no doubt as old as the oldest profession. And he was not sure that he was entirely innocent of it.

Without further discussion, the author picked Alexander up again and carried him back up to the bridge, which they continued along until they were looking down on the fourth valley. He looked down to see weeping sinners traipsing along in familiar misery, but their particular punishment was a new and stranger in its way than any yet told in this story. Their necks had been unnaturally twisted so their faces were turned behind them – reminding Alexander of *The Exorcist* – forcing them to walk backwards.

Perhaps these sinners' lamentation was infectious, but in particular it was the sight of their tears dripping down their backs and into the clefts of their buttocks, making a mockery of the human body, it seemed, that made Alexander himself begin to cry, holding onto the bridge for moral support. Certainly, none was forthcoming from the author, who rebuked him: 'Don't be such a fool. There's no point feeling sorry for the dead. And it's not right to get upset about just punishment.'

He told Alexander to look up and come to his senses and see who was coming now. A bearded figure, his beard of course trailing down his back rather than his chest. 'Nostradamus,' the author revealed, 'who spent his life trying to predict the future, and is now cursed with retrospect.' Nostradamus was followed, or preceded, by a tall, perhaps once-handsome man in a turban topped with a crown, all the wrong way round of course. 'King Saul,' said the author, 'who went so far as to banish mediums and necromancers from ancient Israel, only to seek one out in desperation when his luck ran out. Not that it did him any good.'

Then came Tiresias, the ancient Theban seer who was turned into a woman when he interfered with a pair of copulating snakes, and spent seven years in that condition before doing the same trick in reverse. According to legend, he had later been asked to resolve a dispute between Jupiter and Juno over which sex got more out of intercourse. Juno then blinded him as punishment for revealing the truth, and Jupiter gave him the power of clairvoyance as a sort of compensation. Not, again, that it had done him any good in the long term.

The author explained that clairvoyance was a mug's game, unless you were already dead, like the partially future-sighted sinners they had encountered above. Because as long as you are still breathing – as long as you acknowledge that you're still breathing – the future is not fixed, but still to be determined. Because you can shape it yourself, or at least try. 'If you can fill the unforgiving minute' he began, and Alexander joined him, 'with sixty seconds' worth of distance run...' They looked at one another for a second and thought better of continuing.

The point was made. Clairvoyance is inhuman, not because it is a superpower, but because it short-circuits human subjectivity. It rests on the illusion that we can know the end of our story before we have lived it. It measures distance run in metres rather than seconds. It awards placings based on perceived ability rather than the race itself. And of course, when people get ideas into their heads about what's 'meant to be,' all Hell breaks loose.

At the shriek of an invisible owl, the author pointed to another figure approaching retrospectively. A woman this time, with great, ginger braids trailing down her front-facing back; her woman's breasts could not be seen. 'Lady Macbeth,' explained the author, 'who was so captivated by the prophecy that her husband would be king, that she sought to help fate on its way.'

'But didn't she do that by colluding in *murder*?' asked Alexander.

'You're still not clear why fraud might be considered *worse* than murder, then?'

'I don't even see why this is a case of fraud.'

'Well, they weren't exactly candid about the deed,' the author replied, exasperated. 'This isn't going to work if you keep thinking in terms of criminal charges.'

Alexander held up his hands in submission, and the author continued: 'Fortune telling is always fraudulent because it tells of fortunes that haven't been made. There are no facts about the future, after all. Any grain of truth is always burnished with lies, distorted to suit what the listener wants to hear. And those like Lady Macbeth, who orient their lives towards fraudulent ends, become frauds themselves. Their other crimes, even hypothetical ones like dashing out the brains of a baby, are in pursuit of what they believe is their due, as if they have some kind of cosmic licence. That's why augury is inextricable from sorcery, the attempt to defraud the fraud by changing the result.'

Now the author pointed to a skinny figure he said was another fellow countryman, Michael Scot, a formidable intellectual by all accounts, who got ideas well above his station. Scot had put himself at the service of powerful men in medieval Europe, promising them secret short cuts to success. These were practical men, men who delivered the goods, and expected the same from those they dealt with. Scot, and others like him, convinced these men that to achieve their ambitions they needed to go beyond merely economic transactions. The author explained that sorcery is not just an alternative to honest toil, but its very opposite. That's why so much of it makes no sense. It begins with the kind of comically wilful senselessness that seems innocent to the innocent – take that fellow over there dancing like a lunatic with neither music nor company – and it advances into a shockingly evil lunge for the depths of depravity, thought to bring forth an answer of some kind from hidden powers. Its practitioners come to understand, consciously or unconsciously, that sorcery always means conjuring with evil, supping on horrors.

Karen was sitting at home looking at the anti-abortion leaflets she'd been given outside the clinic. She was unmoved by the pictures of fetuses (she knew what a fetus looked like) or the warning that she'd become suicidally regretful if she had the abortion (she was in the process of making a considered decision she'd know she could live with). Her attention was more taken by particularly garish leaflet that claimed abortion was a modern form of child sacrifice. That got her attention. But she found it less than convincing. She, at least, had no desire to sacrifice anything, to give anything up. Indeed, she wanted *not* to sacrifice her own freedom. She wanted not to be pregnant. Never to have been pregnant.

No, she thought to herself. Comparing abortion to child sacrifice was a rubbish argument. If abortion was wrong, it was not wrong for that reason. If the leaflets had accused her of being *selfish*, that would have hit harder. That was the argument she was still having with herself.

Karen imagined having a child, being its mother. She supposed it would not be that bad. The practicalities would take care of themselves, at least in the sense that she'd have no choice but to take care of them. She had noticed that nobody ever really seemed to regret having children, though they regularly joked about it. But she was also aware that she would never really know unless she took the leap and joined the mysterious cult of parenthood. And then it would be too late.

That was a terrible reason not to do something, of course. And now it occurred to her that she was simply afraid. Selfish and afraid. After all, the child would not regret having been born, even if it petulantly told her otherwise as a teenager. Karen believed that life was an intrinsic good, and although she had heard people say such things, she knew that whatever happened, she would never regret bringing a life into the world. It was just that it was not very convenient. It was not what she had wanted. But by now she had admitted to herself that she had not really known what she had wanted. As she weighed the prospect of a new life against her chagrin at being nudged by fate, she felt the special sting of a selfishness that was petty. Even as she tossed the stupid anti-abortion leaflets into the bin, she made a decision. She would have the baby.

CHAPTER 16: EVIL CLAWS

Morgan was determined to distinguish herself at the school sports day. Her teacher had told the class it was an opportunity for the children to make their parents proud, and Morgan liked the sound of that. The Easter egg controversy had cast a long shadow, she felt. Having weighed up the options, she had decided her best chance was in the 30 metres sprint, and she had begun training by running round the back court at home (Laura's home), measuring her times on her multi-functional digital watch, which also had a calculator and was waterproof to a depth of 50 metres. Fiddling with the watch at first added crucial seconds to her time, but she had developed a technique of reaching for her wrist as she approached the finish line and was now able to complete the operation seamlessly. She became obsessed with improving her record.

Laura told her that she and her father were already proud of her. What mattered was not a particular time, but just doing her best. Morgan wasn't buying it. What if her best was not good enough? It was not that she was deluded. She was not the fastest runner in the class; even among the girls, she was not tall enough to compete with a couple of outliers. But she had been gripped by the idea that she was competing with herself, and she was determined to beat herself, which meant doing better than her best. That would give her parents something to be proud of. Simply running quite fast while straining her face like some of her classmates did would not.

Sports day came and Morgan broke her record. She also came second, beating all the girls and all but the fastest boy. It was a triumph. But as she collected her prize, she was disconsolate. She should have come first.

Alexander and the author continued along the bridge to look down on the fifth Hellish valley, talking about something else as they walked. The valley beneath them was pitch black. Indeed, it was filled with boiling pitch, which bubbled and lapped both banks. Alexander was still taking in the scene when the author grabbed him and rushed him to the end of the bridge and off it onto the top of the far bank. Alexander turned to see what the danger might be, only to shrink back all the more when he saw it: a black demon was racing along the bridge towards them.

It was a fierce and sour-faced thing, whose pace was quickened by wide wings spreading from his shoulders. And on those shoulders he carried a sinner, much as a butcher might carry a carcass. When he reached the centre of the bridge he shouted down into the valley, 'Hey, Evil Claws! Another careerist politician for you. Put him under while I go back to Brussels for some more jobbers who won't take no for an answer.' With that, he pitched the sinner into the pitch, turned round and sped off like a German Shepherd.

Having splashed into the pitch, the sinner bobbed back up, but not for long. From under the bridge, a group of similarly winged demons – presumably the 'Evil Claws' – shouted to him, 'There's no gravy for you here, just pitch. So get back under unless you want to feel our hooks!' Then they pierced him anyway, with more than a hundred pricks from their long hooks. 'You do your jobbery in there if you can,' they added, poking away like cooks keeping a piece of meat from floating in a stew.

Then the author asked Alexander to stay crouched out of sight, and told him not to worry about him with the demons; he'd seen worse. But as soon as the author revealed himself to the demons below, they rushed from under the bridge like hungry dogs, only armed with hooks on long poles. The sight of these beasts armed with weapons now made Alexander think of the shock of seeing gorillas on horseback in *Planet of the Apes*.

'Don't try anything,' the author called down to them. 'At least let me talk to one of you before you think of hooking me.'

'You go, Evil Tail,' they shouted, and Evil Tail advanced up the valley towards the author, muttering that this would not take long. The author responded with disdain, asking Evil Tail if he thought he'd wandered this far into Hell on a lucky streak. The demon saw the sense in that, and dropped his hook pole despondently. 'Better not,' he shouted to his comrades.

At that, the author summoned Alexander from his hiding place, and as the detective emerged, the demons pressed forward with such fresh malice he feared they would disregard Evil Tail's advice. He remembered taking part in a dawn raid some years before, and being struck by the look of panic on the faces of the suspects confronted with overwhelming police force. Now he knew how they had felt. He moved as close as possible to the author, without taking his eyes off the demons, though he wished he could. They had lowered their hook poles, but kept muttering about giving Alexander 'just a little nick on the rump'.

Their spokesman Evil Tail shut them up, before explaining to the author that it would be impossible for the visitors to proceed over the next pouch by the same bridge, since the next section had been damaged beyond repair in some sort of accident a couple of thousand years ago. He said they could walk a little further round this valley instead to where they would find another bridge that was intact over the next pouch. He even offered to send some of his demons as an escort, assuring the author that they would absolutely not be treacherous in any way, before calling out their names, 'Pouncer, Stomper and you, Barker! Curler, you're in charge. And take Bleeder, Breather, Porker, Scratcher, Babbler and my mental Blazer! Now, escort our dear friends nice and safely to the unbroken path over to the next valley.'

Alexander was not at all happy about this, and begged the author to refuse the escort, since, after all, he was supposed to know the way himself. 'Just look at their faces!' he added. 'They're up to no good.'

'Don't worry,' the author replied, and nodded towards the boiling pitch. 'Those faces are for the paying guests' sakes, not ours.'

Their demon escort prepared to depart, then, but first they saluted their captain Evil Tail with a chorus of raspberries. He responded by turning, bending over, and returning the fluttery fanfare from his arse.

And with that, they were off along the valley, their long hook poles on their shoulders like rifles. Alexander had seen his share of motley passing out parades, political demonstrations and Orange walks, but this was something special. There were no flutes, drums or bagpipes, but a bottle or two of Buckfast tonic wine would not have seemed out of place as the demonic wind band wended its ramshackle way along the edge of the boiling pitch. This was Hell, after all, and it would have been disconcerting to be accompanied by choirboys, but still.

Alexander turned his attention from their escort to the boiling pitch itself. Every so often one of the sinners emerged like an unhappy dolphin, seeking a flash of relief from its agony before arching back into the blackness. Others only dared to push their snouts above the boiling murk, like nervous frogs, but as Curler's patrol approached, they sank one by one beneath the surface, like snouty dominos. Only one sinner lingered too long, and was hooked by Scratcher, who hoisted him up above the pitch. The other demons shouted for Blazer to grab and flay the bounty.

Alexander had noted the names of the Evil Tails (and the

absence of a Rudolph), and how they seemed to relate to one another as people, but he was still more interested in the sinners. He asked the author if he could find out the identity of the one who was about to be flayed. The author duly called out to the sinner and asked what he was in for. Between screams, he said he'd been a prison officer, and had taken money from criminal gangs to smuggle contraband into the prison: 'hot stuff' was his eternal reward now he was the one doing porridge. Only now he had yet more cosmic backhanders to collect: Porker leapt and tore into him with his great tusks. This little prison mole had fallen among wicked cats. Then Curler grabbed him jealously and told the others to stand back while he skewered him, pausing only to ask the author if he had any more questions for his victim before the next demon had his fun.

'Do you know of any polis in there?' he asked.

'I was in there with a CID officer just now,' the prison officer answered, 'and for once I wish I still was.'

Then Bleeder shouted impatiently, 'That's enough of that'. He hooked the sinner's arm and tore off the forepart, while Breather swung at the legs. Their leader angrily snatched the body from their reach and gave them a look.

So the author continued interrogating the wretch, who was gazing in shock at his ruined limb: 'Who was that, then?'

'It was a DCI Gordon from the drugs squad, who let more criminals walk free than any defence advocate. And with him more dirty cops than I can list... especially if that thing is about to have my scalp!'

This time it was Babbler that the lieutenant had to fend off to let the sinner continue.

'If you want to talk to more polis, I can make them come out. But you'll have to get the Evil Claws to back off so they know it's safe. I'll just sit here and whistle: that's our sign for when one of us escapes for a while. That way you'll get at least seven for the price of one.'

Barker snorted at this: 'The devious bastard. It's just a ploy to escape back into the pitch.'

The devious bastard retorted: 'I'm a bastard right enough to be setting up my pals for you.'

But Pouncer could not resist, and challenged the sinner to try escaping if he dared. The Evil Claws would not wait on the bank, but would fly up and hide behind the ridge overlooking the next valley, ready to pounce on his friends when they appeared, or on him if he made a false move. But sure enough, as the demons took flight, led by the previously sceptical Barker, the homesick prison officer took his chance, planting his feet before launching himself towards the pitch.

The Evil Claws were furious. Pouncer swooped, shouting, 'You're *well* caught!' But his demonic wings were no match for the wings of abject terror, and the sinner plunged into the pitch, forcing Pouncer to swoop back upwards like an angry eagle deprived of its prey. Stomper transferred his rage from the corrupt prison officer to the unpaid agent of his escape, and launched himself at Pouncer. The two Evil Claws clutched one another like two sparrowhawks in want of a sparrow, and unable to maintain flight, sank as one into the boiling pitch. The heat soon dissolved their clinch, but their wings were too gunged up with pitch for either to escape. Curler marshalled the remaining Claws, four on each side of the pitch, and as they laboured to retrieve their sticky comrades with their hooks, Alexander and the author made a sharp exit.

Alexander later thought of the Evil Claws as he read Aesop's Fables to Morgan. In the fable of the frog and the mouse, the faithless frog volunteers to help the naive mouse cross a stream by swimming across with one leg each tied together for safety. But in the middle of the stream, the frog plunges beneath the surface to drown his passenger. The ensuing struggle then attracts the attention of a kite – which is a kind of bird, not a toy – and the kite swoops and devours the frog along with the mouse. Alexander was musing on whether the two demons were like the frog and the mouse, their struggle resulting in their mutual downfall, or whether the sinner was more like the frog, since after all his reward for 'tricking' the demonic mice was just more eternal torture in the pitch. Then again, perhaps Alexander and the author were a luckier version of the mouse, and the Evil Claws collectively the frog, making the kite the sinner, or perhaps Hell itself. Morgan was more interested in why the frog had wanted to drown the mouse.

'Why, Daddy? Why?'

Alexander had no idea.

At the time, escaping along the valley with the author, he had only been able to think of the inevitable fury of the Evil Claws, and the likelihood that they would try to take it out on their uninvited guests. The author had been of the same mind, and even as the winged demons sped towards them, he unceremoniously picked Alexander up like a panicked mother grabbing her baby, and leapt over the ridge into the next valley. The two slid down the steep bank like a double luge pair, at which point Alexander had passed out, awaking on his sofa at home just as Morgan's mother had arrived to drop her off.

'She wants you to read her some stories. Maybe some nice animal stories.'

CHAPTER 17: CONSEQUENCES

Morgan normally enjoyed Aesop's Fables, or at least what she took to be the idea of them. Her favourite was 'The Boy Who Cried Wolf', because it was so logical. The first time she'd heard it, she'd thought the villagers refused to come to the boy's help as a deliberate punishment for telling lies. When she realised they simply didn't believe him because of those lies, she fell about laughing. That was hilarious, she said, smitten. As a runner, though, she was confused by 'The Hare and the Tortoise', because the usual moral, that 'slow and steady wins the race,' is obviously not true unless the faster runner is very stupid. She just didn't understand why the hare would take a nap in the way she understood why the boy would cry wolf for a joke. So there was no comedy in the conclusion for her either. She would have beaten the tortoise, but she would have been undone by her own joke when it came to the wolf. Not that she said so, but that was what made the story so funny.

Anyway, this story about the frog and the mouse and the bird called a kite had her unsettled. It was neither funny nor stupid, just weird. Though it was a weirdness she had met before. Morgan's teacher had tried to use Aesop's Fables to teach something called consequences, but none of the consequences with which she threatened the class had anything like the comic brilliance of 'The Boy Who Cried Wolf'. They seemed entirely unconnected from the matter being punished. Just as weird and disturbing as kites swooping down from the sky. Fail to do your homework and you have to write lines as well. Talk in class and you have to stay in the classroom during the break. How were these consequences? Morgan understood punishment, but punishment was deliberately imposed by a grown-up; it was not a logical outcome of behaving badly. And according to her Daddy's propaganda, it was supposed to stop you doing things with harmful consequences like burning your hand, getting fat or growing up to be stupid. So why did her teacher insist on dressing up punishment as nothing more than consequences? It made Morgan think of the old game of hitting a younger child with their own hand and asking, 'Why are you hitting yourself?'

Alexander came to back in Hell at the author's side. He looked up the bank they had just descended, to see the Evil Claws hovering hatefully at the top. But clearly they were stuck there: they belonged to the fifth valley, and could descend no further. So Alexander turned his attention to the sixth.

The sinners here marched wearily in hooded robes whose gorgeously colourful exteriors belied their evident heaviness. From the sinners' freighted bearing and crushed expressions, it was clear that the robes were a leaden torture device decorated with heavy irony. Alexander and the author wandered alongside the sinners a while, but could not comfortably walk slowly enough to 'keep down' with them, so they might as well have been inspecting stationary ranks of brightly arrayed knights in shining armour.

Alexander asked the author if he recognised anyone, but before he could answer, one of the sinners called out, 'Wait! Stop walking so fast! We want to talk.'

The author asked Alexander to stop and wait, as two sinners struggled through the sparkling crowd towards them. When they caught up, Alexander continued walking at their own pace, as they eyed him wordlessly until one said to the other, 'That one seems to be breathing. But even if they're dead, what right do they have to go about without heavy stoles?'

The other asked Alexander directly, 'Who might you be, to be wandering among the party of hypocrites? I hope not one so grand as to refuse to identify yourself?'

Alexander replied that he was a living man as he appeared to be, and a policeman, since they asked. 'But who are you?' he went on, 'And what kind of hypocrisy earned you such a pretty punishment?'

The first hypocrite replied that they had been politicians, as if that were sufficient explanation. The second added, as if trying to savour the poetry of it, that they were now crushed by the weight of their own promises. Alexander was appalled by their glibness, but before he could give them a piece of his mind, he saw something shocking.

A sinner was pinned to the ground in front of them with his arms outstretched, so the others in heavy stoles trampled over him one by one. 'He was a religious leader,' one of the politicians explained. 'All hypocrites if you ask me. His friends have the same fate further on.'

The author also seemed shocked and unsettled by this latest spectacle, as if half-reminded of something he could not quite put his finger on. But then he was brought back to the situation, and asked the politicians, 'If I'm allowed to ask, do you happen to know a way on to the next valley, without the need for a demonic escort?'

'Not a problem,' said one. 'Just ahead, there's a bridge that runs through all the valleys of Malebolge. It's broken in ours, but the rubble makes a gentle slope you should be able to climb up from here. I only wish we could do the same'.

The author looked outraged as he realised Evil Tail had lied about there being an intact bridge over the sixth pouch: 'That demon lied to my face!'

The politician commiserated, 'Well, you know they say the Devil is the father of lies.'

The author grunted and stormed off, free now from the need to keep pace with the sinners, and Alexander trotted dutifully after him.

They had escaped the Evil Claws, but the incident rattled Alexander. He wondered if the author actually knew what he was doing, if he could actually keep them both safe from the demons. His own loss of faith made him think of Morgan's expression when she had been a baby and he'd made to leave and she'd thought he wouldn't come back. Utter despondency in the face of seeming catastrophe: laughable to an adult who knows everything is just fine. And sure enough, when they finally reached the broken bridge, the author turned to Alexander and smiled so winsomely, his confidence was instantly restored.

The author kicked at the base of rubble to make sure it wouldn't give, and then lifted Alexander onto the first decent-sized boulder, advising him to test the security of each new rock before advancing. It was hard going, even with the floatier author helping with the occasional shove from below. Certainly, it would have been impossible for the heavily-attired hypocrites to make any progress at all.

The rubble from the broken bridge did not continue all the way up the slope, but when they reached the top of the gentler incline it made, Alexander sat down to catch his breath. The author told him to get up and push on. 'You're not here to enjoy the view,' he said.

Alexander groaned and pushed on. The slope was much steeper above the rubble, and he struggled to make progress, but he chatted to the author as he climbed to make light of his labour. Then, as he finally reached the top and mounted the unbroken bridge that continued over the next valley, he heard a voice from below, perhaps responding to his own. He could not make it out, but it sounded angry.

Looking down he saw only darkness, so he asked the author if they could continue across the bridge and climb a little way down the next bank for a closer look.

'That's more like it,' said the author.

Once across the bridge, they began climbing down the opposite bank, and soon Alexander could see that the entire base of the valley was writing with serpents. Think *Raiders of the Lost Ark*. Approaching closer, but not too close, he realised there were sinners amid the reptilian kaleidoscope - naked, terrified sinners with nowhere to run and nowhere to hide. Their hands were bound behind them with yet more snakes, which also slithered gropingly between their legs. Then a large serpent hurled itself at a sinner just beneath Alexander's and the author's perch on the safety of the bank. As it landed on his chest, it plunged its fangs into his neck at the shoulder. He instantly caught fire and was consumed in a flash. But his ashes had no sooner drifted to the ground than they swirled together to reform the very same sinner, a most unfortunate phoenix who now gazed about him like someone stunned by an unexpected punch, frozen in trauma and only gradually re-registering his Hellish situation.

The author asked him who he was, and he introduced himself as Fat Fucci, a nickname he'd earned by selling fake Gucci handbags. Paisley town centre had been his patch. Alexander vaguely knew him as a notorious thug, and wondered out loud why he was here rather than up in the bloody river with the other violent sinners.

Fucci answered directly: 'I wish I was. I hate snakes. But I'm here because I'm a thief. I had a heart attack and died while trying to slither out of a warehouse with a load of genuine Gucci stuff. Is that ironic or what?'

Alexander was not sure, but he was sure that filching fashion was not the worst thing this guy had done, and was about to ask the author to explain when Fucci interrupted, 'Rangers fan?'

Alexander didn't bother to ask how he knew.

'Youse are finished,' he said. 'I'll tell you that just to spite you.' Then, lest Alexander should take him for a Celtic fan, he did a little dance and made obscene gestures as he sang to the tune of 'The Red Flag': 'Hallo, hallo, how do you do? We hate the boys in royal blue, we hate the boys in emerald green, so fuck the Pope and fuck the Queen!'

The snakes must have disapproved, as they promptly silenced him, one strangling him at the neck and another binding his arms to his sides. Unable to express any further obscenities, he simply slithered off into the general chaos of snakes and naked sinners.

Now, from around the valley, a Hell's Angel screeched past their perch in pursuit of Fucci, shouting, 'Where is that poisonous bastard?' He was quite a sight, as both he and his motorbike were crawling with snakes, and a little dragon was even perched on his shoulders, its wings spread wide, breathing fire at every sinner they passed.

The author explained that this was Cacus, a notorious killer like his brothers up in the seventh circle, but like Fucci, he was here because he was also a thief, and a sneaky one at that. But before he could say any more someone shouted, 'Who are you?'

Three sinners were standing below them, seemingly curious about the visitors, but from their ongoing conversation, they seemed just as interested in one of their own, who was apparently missing.

Just then a six-legged serpent approached, and leapt at one of the sinners in a terrifying kiss, just like the face-hugging creature in the *Alien* films, except that it embraced the sinner's whole body, its two upper pairs of legs securing his torso and arms, and the bottom pair flat against his thighs, while it flipped its tail between his legs to clamp him tight, and sank its fangs into his face. Slowly, serpent and sinner seemed to fuse together like hot wax dummies, till it was not clear which was which. The other thieves gasped in horror as they could no longer tell what belonged to whom – something they'd struggled with in life, after all. There was soon just one head with two faces, or rather a single face with two owners. Arms and legs, belly and chest were similarly merged, the two bodies now wholly one, though neither wholly sinner nor serpent but something unspeakably gross, which now slunk off.

Before Alexander and the author could take it in, another little serpent darted furiously onto the scene. It hurled itself at one of the remaining two sinners, biting his belly button before falling to the ground, stretched backwards out in front of the thief like a right-angled mirror image. The thief stared dumbly at the serpent, and yawned as if nothing had happened. The serpent simply returned his gaze before emitting a cloud of smoke from its mouth, just as another cloud emerged from the sinner's punctured navel, and the two merged into a single almighty fug.

Alexander had seen both versions of *The Fly* and read Kafka's *Metamorphosis*. He was dimly aware of classical tales involving transmutation. But none of that had prepared him for what happened now. As the sinner and the serpent gazed at one another through the fog, the latter's tail split into a fork while the former's legs closed tight until you couldn't see the join. The serpent's scaly skin softened while the thief's hardened. Then his arms receded into his armpits as the serpent's four stumpy feet were transformed, the upper pair stretching out to become a man's arms, and the lower pair twisting together to form his manhood. The author and Alexander winced as the sinner's own member split down the middle to form two little legs. Amid the smoke they could just discern that his skin was turning serpent-green while the thing on the ground took on his previous complexion. He went bald, the thing sprouted hair; it stood up, he fell to the earth. Only their dead eyes remained constant, fixed on one another as they swapped forms. The flesh on the standing thing's face tightened, the slack forming ears as the soft centre formed a nose and lips. The crawling thing's nose lengthened like Pinocchio's, but he was no longer any kind of boy. His ears retracted like a snail's tentacles, and his lying tongue became forked just as the other's forked tongue fused together, so as the smoke subsided he was able to curse the serpent that now slithered away.

Only one of the original three sinners remained unchanged, though of course Alexander had no reason to believe there had been anything original about them. Their punishment gave new meaning to 'identity theft'. Who knew how many times their identities had changed hands, or little stumps, or whatever? He had always thought there was something poetic about thieves having their stolen goods stolen again in turn. And here that poetry would be recited for eternity.

But now Alexander remembered the time he had been caught stealing. In his early teens, he and some friends had stolen sweets from the local shop, just for kicks; they were not short of sweets or the money to buy them. When the shopkeeper confronted them, Alexander had insisted he had brought his Mars bar into the shop with him. He had summoned up genuine outrage, imagining not only that he could convince the shopkeeper that the Mars bar was his, but that he could actually make it so. He felt ashamed now, not so much of having stolen, as of having lied to himself like that. He had not stolen for decades now, but one way or another, he lied to himself every day. He thought again of Morgan and the Easter eggs, and it pained him to think that his daughter had inherited one of his worst traits.

CHAPTER 18: SUCK IT AND SEE

The evening, Alexander got drunk alone. He thought back to Dr Bakshi's question, his own question. Was drinking a joy to him or an exercise in self-pity? Right now, it was closer to the latter. At times like this, he did not even expect alcohol to make him feel better, though he sort of pretended to believe it would. It was easier that way. It meant he didn't have to think about it. And speaking of self-deception, he wondered if the author had really believed Evil Tail about the bridge. After all, Alexander had made his own doubts clear. Why would you trust a demon? He swirled his whisky knowingly. The demon drink.

What had the author been so afraid of that he preferred to go along with a troop of demons clearly intent on mischief than to refuse the escort? Alexander suspected he was simply afraid of confrontation. He had been less than impressive when confronting the demons at the gates of the citadel. It reminded Alexander of his own shortcomings as a father, the times he let a lie slip because it was easier than challenging his daughter. The Devil was the father of lies. He invited sinners like Alexander and the author – Morgan too, for that matter – to mix with his offspring, and too often they did so willingly, not because they were deceived but because they preferred lies to the truth, or because they feared the truth.

It should be easy, should it not, to reject something you know is untrue? Why get drunk when you know it's only going to make you feel worse? Why allow yourself to be led astray, putting yourself in danger even when you can see what's coming? Because it's easier than confronting the truth. Alexander had an idea what that meant in his own case, enough of an idea not to want to think about it. What was the author's excuse? Again, he found himself doubting whether his guide really knew what he was doing. The author seemed to be winging it, as if his own decisions did not matter, and true enough, it had been an *angelus ex machina* that had finally got them into the citadel the last time he'd been forced to confront demons. Then a panicked improvisation in the case of the Evil Claws, a literal leap into the dark

Never mind the author and *his* demons. Alexander knew his own lying demon was doing enough damage of its own, and not just to his liver. If he persisted like this, avoiding hard questions about his life by self-medicating, he would damage his soul. He would gradually become a lesser person, until there was nothing left. He recoiled from that thought, resolved to change, and fell into a drunken sleep.

Presently, Alexander found himself back in Hell, sober enough. The author led him away from the larcenous serpents and back up the rocky slope towards the next valley, half climbing, half crawling to make progress. From the summit, the view down to the other side was like a majestic cityscape at night: a thousand lights flickered prettily. On closer inspection, though, the lights were far from domestic. Each was an unguarded flame, floating slowly through the valley. But it would be indecent to wax lyrical about the beauty of the scene. And dangerous to be taken in by it. Alexander stepped onto the bridge over the valley for a better look, and almost fell over the side in his eagerness to take it all in.

The author explained that each flame contained a sinner's soul, which indeed fuelled the fire. Alexander had thought as much, but wanted to know about one flame in particular, which forked at the top, suggesting not one but two souls within. The author explained that these were the Greek heroes Ulysses and Diomedes, whose sins included the famous Trojan Horse deception, as well as a prior trick by means of which they had got Achilles to abandon his lover and join them in the Trojan War in the first place, and the looting of bounty from some Trojan temple or other. But Alexander was not satisfied. He wanted to understand why they were here, what made their dishonesty different or worse than that of the fraudulent sinners they had met until now.

He asked the author if they could wait till the twin flame came closer, and speak to the souls within. The author was pleased to agree, but told Alexander he would do the talking. 'They might not take you seriously,' he explained. Eventually, the flame approached and the author addressed it. 'Your names are not as well known above as they once were. Your stories are forgotten or distorted. If you talk to me, I'll retell your tragedy as best I can.'

The greater of the two horns of flame began to quiver, and formed a tongue to utter the words that now came forth from the fire. It was Ulysses, who told the author of his journey home from the Trojan War. How he had been lured from his course by the sorceress Circe, and how even having escaped her, he found himself unwilling to return to his home and his family. His epic adventures thus far had given him a lust for the knowledge that comes from experiencing extremes. He wanted to see the world, to see humanity at its best and its worst. He and his crew set off for the ends of the Earth.

Ulysses had hurled himself and his loyal men onto the open sea like a piece of driftwood tossed into the waves. Buffeted this way and that by the capricious sea, they gradually surveyed the coasts of Europe and Africa and the islands in between, and by the time they reached the rock that marked the boundary of the known world, they had become old men. But the hero was not ready to die. He rallied his men with the words,

'Brothers, you have sacrificed everything for this sunset. Our time is nearly over, so let us not waste it by refusing the final challenge. Think about your pedigree. You were not born to be cattle, but to be heroes, to know and to do what no man has known or done! To boldly go where no man has gone before!'

After that little oration, he could not have held them back if he had tried. They set their backs on the east and burst forth from the Mediterranean, the ship's oars like wings as it swept westward over the ocean, arcing steadily to the left until the sky turned upside down. After five moons, they spied a mountain in the distance, the biggest Ulysses had ever seen. They began to sing for joy, but their song soon turned into a lament. A storm arose from the mountain, smashed into their bow and formed a whirlpool. They span three times before the ship's poop rose up and prow shot down and they continued their valedictory voyage into the depths.

Having concluded his tale, Ulysses excused himself, leaving Alexander very confused. 'That's not the ending I remember,' he told the author. 'Wasn't he supposed to make it home to Penelope?'

'He was a great hero,' the author replied. 'Maybe he swam home.'

'Then why end the story there?'

'Because it explains why he's here.'

'Does it?' Alexander protested. 'The whole of Malebolge is supposed to be where people are punished for fraud. So far – as far as I can tell, that is – we've had pimps and seducers, prostitutes very broadly understood, careerists, fortune tellers, bribe takers and thieves. Is that right?'

'Pretty much.'

'And now explorers?'

'Come on, you can do better than that.'

Alexander reflected on what Ulysses had told them. He had effectively abandoned his family, it was true. And encouraged his men to do the same. Before that, he had been known for his trickery, but what was fraudulent about wanting to go to the ends of the Earth, to push the limits of human experience and knowledge? Should they also expect to find astronauts down here?

The author pointed to another flame, racing along at a gallop. He said it was the 3rd Earl of Lucan, who had ordered the charge of the light brigade, passing off mere magnificence as warfare. Then he asked Alexander if he played chess. He knew very well that he did, badly, because he had beaten him several times. Alexander got bored and took stupid risks. The author had tried to explain the difference between a bold move and a suicidal overreach disguised as a bold move. The former involved a careful appraisal of one's situation, an analysis of one's limitations as well as one's possibilities. The latter came of a glib 'suck it and see' attitude: not a genuine yearning for knowledge, but a lunge for experience, which is always a kind of death wish. That was Ulysses' fraud, one he had perhaps perpetrated against himself as much as his men.

Alexander was duly chastened, not only by the reminder of his lousiness at chess, but also because Ulysses' story now made him think of his own situation. The author had brought him here to seek knowledge, he supposed. All along he had been torn between grim fascination and detached bemusement. Was his attitude sufficiently earnest?

His thoughts were interrupted by a dull wheezing sound. A new flame approached, but the sinner within struggled to get his words out, like a schoolteacher made hoarse by a day of silencing children. Eventually he found his pitch, and having guessed that Alexander was a policeman, he introduced himself as a fellow officer, and asked how the profession fared. The author gestured for Alexander to go ahead and answer, and waited patiently as the two polis indulged in rueful shop talk until the sinner came to his own story.

He had been a lawyer before joining the police 'to make amends', but his superiors had valued his legal experience and knowledge more than he would have liked. Consequently, he had got caught up in an internal corruption scandal led by a chief constable who was more interested in that kind of thing than in catching criminals. The chief had asked him to take down a particular corrupt officer by any means necessary, and promised to cover his back, so he had persuaded the officer to confess and provide incriminating evidence by promising him immunity. That was a false promise, and when the case unravelled, it turned out the chief's promise to cover his back had been just as false. That had been the end of his career, and he supposed it was why he was here, though he still tied himself in knots internally debating the justice or injustice of it. No wonder he was hoarse.

Alexander sympathised to an extent, but he had never and would never do anything as unprofessional, not to mention illegal, as what his flaming fellow polis had done. He had enough ethical angst from doing his job properly. The Buchanan Street murder, for example. The case had not yet gone to trial, but was on track. The issue was no longer if *all* of the attackers were guilty of murder, but whether *any* had been fully responsible for his actions. Only one of the 14 had tried to hypnotise himself using the supposedly demonic website, while another two had dabbled in the wider hypnotism fad, but there was a theory that suggestion was contagious. Alexander still thought it extremely unlikely there would not be solid convictions, but he had to admit that this murder was unlike any he had investigated. He still did not understand why these young men had done it, and he could not feel the satisfaction he normally got from bringing criminals to justice.

Indeed, now he found himself far from the place of eternal justice, reviewing the case files at his desk. He was tempted just to let the case run its course – surely the convictions were safe? – but given what he had just seen and heard, this now seemed a dangerously irresponsible strategy. He would ignore his own reassurances, and force himself to run the permutations like a good chess player. Only police work seemed very unlike chess. Was anything in life like chess, apart from chess?

Starved of what facts there were until the case went to

trial, the media were going big on Glasgow's supposed gang culture. Footage had emerged of a gang initiation ceremony involving Masonic regalia, but this struck Alexander as more quaint than sinister. Glasgow gangs were typically very informal, territorial groupings of ne'er-do-wells, he reflected. The very idea of an initiation ceremony was pretty alien. Of course, these boys could have got carried away after seeing some film or other. According to legend, the famous Tongs of the 1960s had taken their name from a Hammer horror film about a Chinese sect, having charged out of the pictures shouting, 'We are the Tongs!' and 'Tongs ya bass!'. But, generally speaking, Glasgow neds were not known for appropriating ideas or practices from beyond the end of the road. The Masonic regalia probably belonged to someone's granddad, and dressing up was harmless enough. But in the current climate, it was always going to be read as occult.

Alexander could see the danger for the murder case. The occult was coming to be seen as an explanation of certain kinds of behaviour rather than a mere description. It was something that somehow infected people, a contagion, a virus. And those afflicted could hardly be held responsible for their actions. It was not that they were not feared, despised even. But like rabid animals, they were seen as beyond hope. Certainly that was the case when it came to the Buchanan Street murderers. There was much talk of throwing away the key. But Alexander was even more disturbed by the attitude of more compassionate observers. They insisted that occult violence was a public health problem. Prevention was better than cure. But cure was more appropriate than punishment. They talked about rehabilitation rather than retribution, but their understanding of rehabilitation was bereft of any moral content. It was all psychology. For Alexander, this vision was as hopeless as the first, because it refused to let the perpetrators own their crime. It made everything an accident, as if they could be cured and let go.

That evening, he had Morgan staying over. She said her homework was to flush matchsticks down the toilet and record whether they went clockwise or anticlockwise. He had his doubts, but he indulged her with a few spent matchsticks until she took the box and lit one when she thought he wasn't looking. As the flame hissed in the water and the stick span in the surf, he thought of Ulysses' ship in the whirlpool, but was distracted by the need to tell off his daughter. None of the matches had actually gone down, and the direction of the swirl had been indistinct anyway. Not only had she very naughtily lit a match, he accused, but the whole enterprise had been made up. It was not homework at all. Morgan shrugged: 'It's not my fault if your toilet doesn't work.'

He resisted the temptation to test that thesis with her head, but the rest of the evening did not go well. Father and daughter were out of harmony.

CHAPTER 19: CARNAGE

A thousand times a thousand words would not adequately paint the picture that lay before Alexander and the author as they looked down into the ninth pouch of Malebolge from its ridge. All the dead and maimed of both world wars assembled in a pit would not equal the foulness of it. The foulness here was about quality rather than quantity.

The first sinner to attract Alexander's particular attention was split down the middle like a haggis, his own offal dripping from its casing and raising a stink. He gawped back at Alexander and pulled his breast wide open like a flasher opening his raincoat. 'See how Uncle Joe is mangled!' he cried. 'And over there you'll see that splitter Trotsky, with an ice pick splitting his skull.'

Alexander and the author looked where Stalin pointed, but Trotsky was not in the picture.

The drawer of the Iron Curtain continued: 'And all the others you see trudging round this circle are charged with having sown discord and schism while they lived, leading others into error and division. So the demon back there carves us up with a vengeance, and we troop round until our wounds are healed and he carves us up all over again. But who are you to be sniffing around up there on the ridge? If you've been summoned below, you'd better report as ordered and answer for your crimes!'

The author intervened to explain that Alexander was neither dead nor under sentence, and that he himself had been charged with leading him through Hell to learn its secrets. At that, more than a hundred more trudging sinners stopped to look up in amazement. Stalin made to leave, but with one barely attached foot in the air, he paused to ask Alexander, 'If you're returning above, tell the Chechen Martyrs and their friends around the world they'll be joining me soon, but the demon back there will be the only one tearing hymens. Along with the rest of them!' With that, he finished his first step and was on his bloody way.

One of the other sinners who had stopped to look at Alexander had half his face sliced away. The detective half recognised him as Doper Pete, a notorious thug with paramilitary connections in Northern Ireland. Pete now began to speak directly from his ruptured windpipe, giving a nasty, rasping quality to his voice as he told his story, or rather the story he wanted this unsentenced visitor to convey to the world above.

He said he was expecting two acquaintances to join him, having foreseen a double mischief. Two leading members of some set of initials or other would be summoned from Belfast to a meeting in Glasgow, thoughtfully timed to coincide with an Old Firm game, to discuss a fictional arms shipment. Their host was a notoriously corrupt businessman. (In fact, he was the third Rimini brother, the one not included in Francesca's love triangle, but Pete could not have known that Alexander had met Francesca and Paolo above.) He was already reduced to one eye, so when he got here the slicing demon would have to use its imagination. Pete explained that he had booked his guests tickets on the Stranraer ferry bringing fans for the game, ostensibly so they could make a trip of it, but in fact he had conspired to have them thrown overboard.

It got better, Pete went on, with a glee that made blood

splutter violently from his windpipe. One of the two had got wind of the plan, but rather than tell his friend or even just back out on his own, he seized the opportunity to fake his own death along with the other guy's genuine demise. This was to allow him to settle numerous scores without fearing further retribution. Doper Pete was clearly impressed, but Alexander had heard enough.

He asked about another sinner who seemed to want to speak, but the one next to him opened his mouth to show that he had no tongue. 'This is Curio,' he explained, 'who egged Julius Caesar on to cross the Rubicon and march on Rome, assuring him that any delay would cost him his advantage. The result was civil war for the empire, and eternal surgery for poor Curio.'

From sordid squabbles between hard men to world historic events. Clearly, Hell was no respecter of scale.

Indeed, now another sinner stepped forward, brandishing bloody stumps where his hands had once been. Alexander recognised him as a petty criminal whose counsel ('in for a punch, in for a stab') had transformed a fight between football fans into a sectarian murder. But the detective's attention was then drawn abruptly to a sinner with a more severe amputation: his head. He carried it by the hair, and as he approached, he raised it higher even than its natural position, the better to address the visitors above, in verse.

'Behold the wretched punishment I bear,
Repaying the partisanship I did wear;
Through satire I sought vices to correct,
But vice my own intention did infect;
Against impious rebellion I did write,
But satire too inflames the bloody fight.'

Then the poet – clearly deprived in Hell of the talent he had enjoyed on Earth – withdrew, but Alexander could not seem to take his eyes off the general carnage. The author admonished him, pointing out that he had not lingered in previous valleys, but even as he followed his guide on to the next valley, Alexander explained that he had been transfixed by the sight of a former colleague.

'Don't let your mind linger on her,' said the author. 'You have other things to think about.'

Indeed, now they were standing over the tenth and final pouch of Malebolge. Alexander was struck by piercing cries from below, and then the stench, like rotting flesh. They climbed down a little, until Alexander could see sick sinners sprawled on the valley floor, draped over one another, or crawling painfully onwards, like plague victims on a road without recovery or even the release of death. The author led Alexander on till they saw two sinners sitting back to back, propped up against one another, both covered from head to toe in scabs, both furiously scratching, and in the process peeling off scabs like fish scales. But there were always more scabs.

The author asked them if they knew any police down here, since he was guiding a living detective through Hell, and he learned best from those sinners with whom he could identify. Immediately they broke from their position so each could face Alexander, while others within earshot also drew near. 'I was a detective,' said one. 'Murdered by a drug lord over a joke. But that's not why I'm here. I dabbled in the drug business myself, you see, but would you believe they sent me here for passing off legal substances as illegal ones?'

'Justice is a funny thing,' said Alexander.

'I'll second that,' said another scratching sinner. 'Do you recognise me, detective?'

Alexander did indeed recognise his old chemistry teacher, who had been sacked for using the school lab to counterfeit jewellery. Apparently he'd been very good at it, but had not even made money out of it. Just fooled his own wife.

Before Alexander could reply, two more sinners bolted onto the scene, seeming less like people than like wild pigs; indeed one of them sank its tusks into the teacher's neck before dragging him off. The corrupt detective explained that the monster was a notorious fraudster who had forged the will of her dead aunt with the connivance of her lawyer, awarding herself a rare sports car. Now the fraudster had no sense of her real self at all, and tore about in a mad rage, goring her fellow sinners.

'And who's the other one?' Alexander asked. 'Since it hasn't gored you, why not enlighten me?'

'That's Gunther,' said the lucky sinner, still scratching himself furiously. 'He's guilty of not seducing a woman. It's complicated.'

The author intervened to explain that, eternal damnation aside, Gunther had also been immortalised in Wagner's opera *Götterdämmerung*. He had colluded with the hero Siegfried (who was under the influence of a forgetfulness potion) to have the latter seduce his own betrothed while disguised as Gunther. Now it seemed Gunther had not only lost his own identity, but didn't get to do much goring of his own either.

'Very poetic,' said Alexander. 'But what did you mean when you said I learn best from sinners I identify with?'

'Well, don't you agree?' asked the author.

'But you mean other polis?'

'Sure, but not necessarily that. People here are not defined by their professions, are they? But their professions might have some bearing on what does define them.'

'They're defined by their sins.'

'Exactly. They *are* their sins.'

'And you want me to identify with those?'

'Don't you?'

Alexander thought first of the fellow detective in front of him. He had never been seriously tempted by corruption. But he had sympathised with the sinner's bemusement at his fate. Why was selling fake drugs worse than selling real ones? Why was it worse than his betrayal of his vocation as a polis? And given that any individual human being is guilty of numerous sins, who or what decided which defined them?

'We do,' said the author. 'When you went into the box in

the Hope, you were asked what you were in for, weren't you?'

'Yes, but the voice also said I wasn't supposed to be there. Here.'

'And that's why he had to ask. It's also why you're free to wander here. The dead are not asked, because they have already answered over the course of their lives. The sin that counts is the one they have chosen as their identity. So they are not free to wander, because in choosing their identity they have chosen their place.'

'But who decides which sins are worse?'

'It's not really about being worse. It's certainly not about the earthly consequences of sin. It's about the sinner. That's why I want you to identify with them, to understand them.'

Alexander understood that. After all, his own philosophy had always been that, far from the adage that to understand all is to forgive all, understanding is necessary for true condemnation; a crime that defies understanding defies condemnation. Perhaps if selling fake drugs seemed trivial to Alexander, it was because he had not thought it through; perhaps the corrupt officer's failure to see the justice of his situation was part of his sin, part of the identity he had chosen for himself.

Alexander was distracted from such thoughts by the sight of another sinner lying flat on the ground. Or not so flat, since he was grotesquely bloated, and craning his neck, open-mouthed, as if reaching for some unseen source of water.

'That's right,' he croaked, 'look at me. You, who somehow escape punishment, take in the fate of Adam McMaster. I had whatever I wanted while I lived, and now I crave just a drop of water.'

He went on to explain that he had been the tech brains behind a financial scam involving government gilt bonds, but he blamed three brothers from a company called Loch Lomond Finance, who he said had got him into it under false pretences. 'I'll tell you this,' he rasped, 'if I could just see them suffering down here, it would all be worthwhile, and despite my raging thirst I wouldn't trade the sight for Loch Lomond itself. One of them is already here somewhere if the crazy wretches who run about the place are to be believed. But what good does it do me, since I can barely move an inch?'

The mention of Loch Lomond in this context reminded Alexander of the story about American servicemen passing through Glasgow at the end of the Second World War, who hailed cabs and asked to be taken to Loch Lomond. Unscrupulous taxi drivers took them instead to a reservoir just outside the city and invited them to feast their eyes on that. He decided he ought to be more attentive to his own surroundings, so he asked McMaster, 'Who are the two sinners lying shivering by that great big belly of yours?'

'They've been there since I got here, and barely moved because of their crippling fever. The steam coming off them stinks. One is a woman who made a dozen false rape accusations. The other is a cop who bedded a string of women while undercover as an anarchist or some such, even had a family with one or two. Nasty piece of work.'

At that, one of the shivering figures struck out with his fist, landing a blow on the tech whizz's belly, which resounded like a drum.

McMaster struck back, hitting the other's face. 'I may be too bloated to move,' he said, 'but I have one arm free for the likes of you.'

'And a fat lot of good it did to save you from your fate,' came the reply, evidently from the undercover cop. 'All your mighty arm was good for above was tapping at your keyboard like the cash out button on a fruit machine.'

'Oh, very true, very true. But you weren't so forthcoming with the truth up above, were you?'

'Sure, I lied about my own identity, but you spawned lies by the million, defrauding more people than you ever knew'.

'That was nothing personal. The whole world knows what you did to those women, for shame.'

'He did it to me too!' chimed in the false rape accuser, but nobody believed her.

'You sound hoarse, McMaster,' the undercover cop replied bitterly. 'Why not have a nice, refreshing glass of water?'

'I'm not the only thirsty one,' came the reply. 'And are you warm enough with that stinking fever? Never mind the glass: you'd stick your head in a filthy toilet given the chance.'

This was all very entertaining, and Alexander was rapt, only missing a comfy chair and a tub of popcorn, when the author snapped, 'Are you enjoying yourself?' Alexander turned to him blazing with shame. Seeing himself through the author's eyes, he was disgusted. He did not want to be that man, gawping at Hell like it was reality TV. He'd have felt bad enough being caught watching reality TV. He wished he could think of something to say, some way to excuse himself, but his very mortification seemed to placate the author.

'It's good that you feel ashamed,' he told Alexander. 'It means there's hope.'

Alexander felt like someone waking at last from a bad dream, having pleaded in his terror for it to be a bad dream without knowing that it was.

'If we come across another scene like that, look to me,' the author said. 'The urge to take it in is not healthy.'

And now Alexander woke in bed, as if from a dream, but not in fact a nightmare. Instead he had the frustrating sense of having been shaken from the brink of enlightenment, as if he had been about to grasp something profound. Something about Hell, and at the same time something about the world of the living. He knew now that it was good to feel ashamed, to want to flee from himself. Somehow the author offered a means of escape. But now the author seemed just like a character in a dream, a dream Alexander felt he had now mostly forgotten, though its imagery lingered on his mind. He could not recover the true essence, the meaning of the dream that he had been about to grasp, so he sat up in bed and scratched.

He did recall the bare facts of what he had just seen in Hell. Indeed, two of the sinners he had encountered were known to him in real life. McMaster he did not know. His crime had been white collar, and of the old-fashioned acquisitive type that Alexander was rarely called to deal with. The others were more his style: sordid and unsettling.

The false rape accuser had died many years ago, but her case was notorious, not only because of the seriousness of her crime, but also because it was politically awkward. Historically, the police had too often disbelieved rape complainants, or failed to take their accusations seriously, especially if they knew their attacker or had been on a night out. Now the orthodoxy was that complainants must be believed. DCI Alexander had no problem with that: the default position was to believe someone reporting a burglary, despite the prevalence of insurance fraud. But he had seen enough of human deceit and criminality in all its variety to know nothing was impossible. A crime like this woman's was all the worse precisely because it cast doubt on the testimony of other women. He saw no virtue in pretending it never happened. And she had been convincing enough to have two men convicted of rape under the old dispensation, in the early 1970s, persuading the police and juries alike that a lady would never have willingly submitted to what she did, or in one case, it later transpired, merely proposed. Her motives were never satisfactorily explained.

The cop had been part of an undercover operation to investigate environmentalist protest groups during a weird moment in the 1990s when tree-huggers became identified as the post-Cold War enemies of the state. The protestors would camp out in woods on the site of proposed new roads, and chain themselves to trees and construction plant in a bid to prevent works going ahead, mostly unsuccessfully. It later emerged that their 'benders', or makeshift tents, had been infiltrated by undercover policemen, who took an interest in more than political strategy. While it was hard to believe that this had been decisive to the movement's failure, it certainly caused emotional carnage in the lives of the women who later discovered their dreadlocked exes had actually been cops (there didn't seem to be any cases of undercover WPCs).

This one's apparently accidental death shortly after his exposure had aroused much suspicion, but if anything it had probably been suicide. If so, his suicide was clearly a footnote to his defining sin, the deceitful affairs. It was an intriguing case, since of course it is an undercover policeman's job to deceive. It seemed the senior officers in charge of these operations had been deliberately vague about what was and was not permissible, but common sense insisted there was an ethical line between using deceitful means to detect and prevent crime – or even for the more dubious purposes of counter-subversion – and entering into an intimate relationship under a false identity. 'You think you know someone,' they say. But this was ridiculous.

Moreover, it had always been unclear whether this man and the others like him had thought of themselves as devoted secret agents, selflessly as much as ruthlessly seeking any advantage for their inquiries, or mere chancers, taking advantage of women as a perk of the job. Maybe they even developed genuine affection for the women. Alexander imagined it would have been harder not to. Arguably a 'real' element to these relationships would have made it worse on the women, though, spurring them on to expose their deepest feelings, their very lives, to an enemy. The whole thing was a mess, but a mess for which these policemen were undoubtedly culpable, whatever they felt about it. If this one had thought suicide was the easy way out, he knew better now.

CHAPTER 20: IMPOSTER SYNDROME

DCI Alexander was called to a meeting with the Chief Super, whose secretary said it was important, but unconnected to any case. That was all she could say. Alexander had the normal reaction of someone summoned by their boss: mild panic as he considered possible accusations and prepared his defence. But when he arrived in the Chief Super's office, it was the boss who seemed cagey, or more so than usual.

'It's about your counselling,' he said when Alexander had settled in his seat.

Alexander wondered if he'd had a bad report card, but then he remembered his sessions were supposed to be confidential. He was not being 'assessed' but 'helped'. And he trusted Dr Bakshi to play by the rules of her own profession if nothing else. 'Oh,' he said.

The Chief Super stood up and turned to the window behind his desk. It was like something out of a film. He turned back to Alexander with his hands clasped in front of him. 'There's no easy way to say this.'

Dr Bakshi was dead? 'Sir?'

'Your counsellor, Dr Bakshi...'

Alexander felt a wave of grief rise through his shock.

'Well, it turns out she's not what she seemed.'

Not dead, then? Alexander held his silence.

'I'm afraid the service has been taken in along with Dr Bakshi's other clients.'

The Chief Super was on the defensive; that was why he seemed so cagey. But more importantly...

'What are you saying?'

'Dr Bakshi is a fraud. She's not qualified to practise as a counsellor. I'm sorry, but we contracted her services in good faith, and she had all the right certification, professional recommendations even. She conned everyone.'

'Right,' Alexander said, still processing what this meant for him. He'd rather have done that without the Chief Super staring at him. 'I understand that. Nobody's fault.' Then with a little laugh, 'I'm not going to sue!'

The Chief Super bellowed. What would Dr Bakshi have made of that?

'I understand this must be very disturbing news for you,' he told Alexander, sounding more comfortably scripted now. He explained that Dr Bakshi would be prosecuted for fraud and that a properly accredited counsellor was now available to help Alexander and her other former patients work through their inevitable trauma. Alexander had not thought of himself as a patient, but never mind. He took the number and thanked the Chief Super and made his excuses and left. This would indeed take some processing, with or without professional help.

Karen had suffered on and off from imposter syndrome since joining the police. It was hard to say why. It was not that she felt out of place as a woman – though sometimes she did, just a bit. She had several female colleagues, and, after all, Jackie Reid off *Taggart* had been a role model to them all for years. Nor had she been unusual in having a university degree and seeing her time in uniform as a sort of purgatory to be endured on the way to becoming a detective. That was true of several of her cohort, and indeed had been true of Alexander, for what that was worth. She did not even have Alexander's social awkwardness. For the most part, she was confident in her abilities, at ease among her colleagues and the public, and most importantly, sure of her vocation. But still, she lived in fear of being exposed, found out. And it was not that she felt unfit, so much as unworthy. Her very qualifications felt like subterfuge. How devious of her to have all her paperwork in order, to have a demonstrable aptitude forsooth! Just the sort of trick you would expect from a sneaky fake. An unworthy interloper.

Nor was it that she considered her colleagues especially virtuous. Often the best polis in her eyes were the most obviously flawed human beings: callous, cynical, borderline racist and misogynist, but somehow not only good at the job, but in tune with it. Meant for it. Karen did not feel she was meant for the job.

Often, she was not at all sure she was meant for this world. And not because she was too good for it, not that at all. The world was so strange, so improbable. It was not that she belonged somewhere better, just somewhere more like home. Sometimes Karen felt like Dorothy in *The Wizard of Oz*. As if the story of which she thought she was part were actually a dream within a dream, a plot device, an artifice. Often she was reminded of her childhood interest in acting, and felt as if she had followed that vocation after all. And now her character was pregnant. Dorothy the pregnant detective. How could she have a baby on the Yellow Brick Road? Where was Kansas anyway?

Having decided to have the baby, Karen had been to see her GP for advice about next steps. Appointments, tests, scans. She had been thrown somehow by the realisation that she could still change her mind if something were wrong, or even if not. Her inner decision had not removed the option of an abortion. And nor had she told Alexander she was having his baby. In fact, it seemed, she had not decided at all. And now she had to consider the possibility that their baby could have Down's syndrome or much worse. That was not the new life she had reconciled herself to, even begun to look forward to. So even as a biologically-certified prospective mother, she was a fake.

'I'm pregnant,' she told Alexander eventually.

'What? With a baby?'

She just looked at him.

'Right, of course. A baby.' He was on the spot now. 'Is that good?'

'I thought we should talk about it.'

'Of course.'

'Look, I'm sorry. I wanted to come to you with a decision, but I can't seem to make one on my own. So I'm going to need your input. If that's all right with you?'

'Of course.'

'Please stop saying "of course". There's nothing "of course" about it.'

'No. Well, do you want to have a baby?'

'I'm asking *you* if *you* want to have a baby. With *me*.'

DCI Alexander had the faintest inkling that this conversation was about more than an unintended pregnancy. He sat down. 'I never really intended to have a baby with Laura.'

This was unexpected, but Karen rolled with it. 'You're not telling me it came as a surprise?'

'No, of course not. I knew it was what Laura wanted, and I was fine with that. It just wasn't my idea.'

Suddenly Karen went from cold to furious, and Alexander realised he was getting this conversation all wrong. Thinking out loud was not helping. 'What am I thinking?' he said. 'Come here.'

They embraced.

The conversation then continued more constructively, if not conclusively. They agreed to sleep on the matter, but together now. After all, they joked, sleeping together was how Karen had got pregnant in the first place. It was not a good joke, but it lifted the atmosphere between them, and they were able to talk more easily about life and their lives.

Karen told Alexander how motherhood had gone from being something expected but deferred in her youth to something she did not think about as she pursued her career to something she now had no choice but to think about. And to talk about. Alexander told her how Laura had made the fact of fatherhood relatively easy for him; he had not particularly had to think about it until he had been presented with his bundle of joy. The trials of fatherhood were not existential. Or they hadn't been the first time.

They were both conscious that they could have led other lives, other careers. Loved other people, even. Karen said it was funny to think how different either of them might have been if they had ended up with someone else, belonged to a different story. Not just how their *lives* would have been different, but how *they* would have been different as part of someone else's life – perhaps even someone they had known, someone who still thought about them, but imagining them as someone else. Had he ever thought about that?

'I don't think I'm anyone's "one that got away",' Alexander said.

'Oh, I bet you are! You're just the type.'

'No, I really never had that many relationships.'

'But OTGAs aren't necessarily about relationships.'

'Otgas?'

'Ones That Got Away.'

She had a word for this?

'No, an OTGA is more like someone you flirted with or had an unsuccessful date with, but who you never really got to know. That's why you can indulge the fantasy that if only things had worked out differently, you could have been fabulously happy together.'

'Do you have someone like that?'

'Don't be ridiculous. I'm just explaining what it means.'

Alexander growled. Who did she think she was, having an inner life of her own? 'And what do you mean I'm just the type?'

'I mean all interesting and mysterious. Until you get to know you, of course.'

They exchanged sarcastic faces.

Because here they were, after all, not with anyone else, but with one another. And pondering parenthood. Alexander knew that if they were going to do it, he would have to commit to Karen in a way he had never committed to Laura, despite having married her. He would have to let Karen in. But into what exactly? She was already as much a part of his working life as she could be. DS Smith was all but indispensable to DCI Alexander. She had been at the core of the occult crimes unit since its inception, and had lived its ups and downs at his side. She knew how he liked to work, how he struggled with the ambiguities of the unit's remit and the expectations of his superiors, not to mention the media. And she was on his side every step of the way. A sympathetic observer might even have been moved to opine that she would have followed him to Hell and back. But of course, his visits to Hell had been either solo or accompanied only by the author.

The author knew Alexander, if not exactly in a professional capacity, still primarily as a police detective. He had even introduced him as such to the damned. But he had also told him he would never understand Hell as long as he thought like a policeman levelling criminal charges. It was not DCI Alexander who was being asked to explore and understand the place, but the other Alexander, the one with a soul of his own. And that was the Alexander who now needed to reach a new accommodation with Karen. Did that include talking to her about Hell?

In fact, he missed talking to Dr Bakshi. Not that he had ever discussed Hell with his apparently fake psychotherapist, but of course he had brought up some of the thoughts that had been inspired by his visits there. It was good to talk to someone who was not part of his life in any capacity, let alone a worryingly undetermined one. He called the new counsellor's office and made an appointment. It might be fun, he thought.

In fact, when the appointment came, just seconds after

the receptionist sent him in to the consulting room, he was racing down the stairs and out of the building. The new, fully-accredited, genuine counsellor was the very same demon from whom Alexander had fled the hospital.

CHAPTER 21: THE FACE OF EVIL

Alexander's colleague DC McGrain had been looking into the demonic website that had supposedly inspired the Buchanan Street murderers. It was no longer online, but had been registered to a company that operated numerous porn sites, all legal and none particularly 'occulty' as far as McGrain could tell. For his part, Alexander now found it impossible to look at even the most innocuous pornography without seeing it as demonic. The company said the demonic hypnosis site had been a 'novelty service' that it had withdrawn after complaints that it was in bad taste. The developer responsible was no longer with them, and McGrain had not so far been able to track him down. The site had not come up in any other inquiries.

McGrain did have something, though. A picture of the supposed demon, which they had never seen till now as it had not shown up in cached versions of the defunct website. McGrain had recovered it from a laptop belonging to the school where the matter had first come to light. Someone had apparently saved it deliberately. McGrain was in a state of agitation when he showed it to Alexander, laughing nervously as he asked if the demon looked familiar. Alexander glanced at it and froze, struggling to compose himself. He was looking at a still image of his own face. More particularly, at his own face as he had seen it in his bathroom mirror when he was being tormented by his demons, smirking maliciously at him. He looked at McGrain, trying to replicate his nervous smile rather than the demon's grimace. 'It looks a bit like me, huh?'

McGrain exhaled. 'I'm not sure whether to be relieved or even more worried. But I thought you might say that, and I think I'm even more worried.'

Alexander understood. 'You see yourself?'

McGrain nodded.

They both looked again at the picture, then at one another. Neither looked well.

'Karen,' Alexander called to DS Smith, who was a couple of desks away. 'Come and look at this.'

She came over and looked at the picture. 'Is this some kind of joke?' Her voice dried up on 'joke'.

'I'm afraid not,' both men said at once.

Alexander began mumbling about the possibility that hypnotic suggestion could somehow be embedded in an image, even as he began inwardly processing what this meant. If this were in fact a supernatural emanation from Hell, it was the first time to Alexander's knowledge that anyone other than him had been privy to such a thing on Earth. Given that this image had apparently been accessed by pupils at a school connected with both the Buchanan Street murder and the Holocaust essay, this opened the possibility that both were in some sense the work of the Devil. Who knew, perhaps even the wider epidemic of misbehaviour in schools too? On the other hand, the face of the demon suggested something at once more prosaic and more disturbing. Was this another demonic joke?

Karen interrupted his thoughts. 'Do we know if the kids saw themselves too?'

'No one has said as much,' said McGrain. 'I suppose we can ask?'

The two kids they knew for sure had viewed the site were the boy and girl respectively charged with murder and disgraced by the Holocaust essay. The girl's brother was also charged with the murder, but there was no evidence that he had viewed the site. Access to the boy who had done would be complicated by the ongoing case, so Alexander resolved to speak to the girl, along with Karen, who knew the case best though she had not actually interviewed the girl. They approached her through the school, though she was no longer enrolled there, and she agreed to meet them in the Mitchell Library, where she had been continuing her studies in exile.

'I'm not a racist,' was the first thing she said.

'We know,' Karen said, though she had no idea. 'That's not what we want to talk to you about.'

'It's about a website you looked at,' Alexander continued. He had the image on a laptop, but was less interested in what she might see now than in what she had seen then. 'Do you remember looking at a site that claimed to channel the power of a demon?'

Her sudden pallor told them that she did. 'I've looked at lots of websites,' she said. 'Most of them are pretty stupid.'

'Sure,' Karen said. 'But this one got to you, didn't it?'

The girl looked afraid. She was going to need some encouragement.

'You're not in trouble,' Karen said. 'That website has upset plenty of other people. We just want to know if you saw the same thing they did.'

It was the closest she could get to a nudge without putting ideas in the girl's head.

'Have *you* looked at it?' she demanded.

Karen and Alexander exchanged looks.

'OK, fine,' the girl said, 'It was *myself*. The "demon" had my face. Is that what you want me to say?'

'It's a scary trick, isn't it?' Karen said.

'Oh, it's a trick, is it? Is that what Agent Mulder thinks too?' she asked, looking at Alexander.

Alexander winced. Since the occult crimes unit had been established, he had been at pains to avoid comparisons with *The X-Files*. But in this case, he did not want to make the girl feel stupid for believing something uncanny might be at play. He did not want to shut her up.

'It would be very helpful if you could tell us what you saw, in as much detail as you can,' he told her. 'Don't worry how daft it sounds.'

She looked thoughtful for a moment, as if on the brink of divulging thoughts she had been harbouring for some time but had never dared to express. Then another expression took over her face, just for a second – a scowl, a glimmer of meanness, even – before the thoughtful look returned with a hint of melancholy, and then faded to indifference. 'I don't see what I can add, really. It looked like me, and I didn't like it, so I switched it off. I even unplugged the computer at the mains, just in case,' she laughed.

Alexander and Karen smiled at that. In a witness in court, it would have been what an advocate they both knew called 'relatable'. And, after all, they had got what they had come for. The girl had confirmed that she'd seen what they had seen. Whether it was a trick as Karen assumed or something truly demonic as Alexander feared, it was real, not merely a figment of the collective imagination of three overworked occult crimes detectives.

In fact, though, the girl had been harbouring thoughts she would have liked to share. Only she had learned to be cautious about oversharing. That was what she had told herself, with a certain bitterness that helped gloss over the fact that her motivation for writing the Holocaust essay had been less than innocent, if not wicked in quite the way it had been taken. Actually, the thoughts she would have liked to share were about just that: bitterness. It was what she had seen in the demon, in her own face. And even as she recognised it as who she was, she hated it. The particular expression she had seen in her demonic face was one she associated with the way she felt when she argued with her mother. It was a complaining expression, a blaming expression, a grumbling, moody, disavowing expression. Teenage in the worst possible way. It screamed, 'It's not fair' without any willingness to take responsibility for so much as thinking about what fairness meant. The girl hated herself when she argued with her mother, and yet found herself spiralling deeper and deeper into the self that she hated. But she didn't know these detectives and thought better of baring her soul for their amusement.

'Are you talking to my brother?' she asked instead.

The detectives exchanged looks again.

'Did your brother look at the website?' asked DS Smith.

'Is it a porn site?' came the sarcastic reply.

'We know one of the other boys involved in his case did. Your classmate.'

'"*Involved in his case*"?'

Karen just raised her eyebrows, inviting the girl to bring on the cheek.

'They can all go to Hell as far as I'm concerned.'

'Then why did you ask about your brother?'

'I don't know. Because he actually *killed* someone?'

'Why do you think he did that?' Karen asked, reasoning that they had nothing to lose with the girl.

'*Why*? As if there's a *reason* for mindless violence. Murders like that don't happen for a reason. They happen when people stop bothering with reasons.'

This sounded rehearsed, and Karen wondered if there would be more, but the girl checked herself again. She wanted to say there had been something in the air at the time of the murder. Nobody had failed to make the connection with the epidemic of bad behaviour in schools, notwithstanding the monumental leap to murder. If anything it was a logical progression. Why not? The same spirit that moved a young child to lie beyond all reason, even when that lie had been exposed beyond all doubt, could just as easily move an older boy to pursue a chase beyond all purpose, to see it through to the bloody end. The knife went in. In fact, the common factor was not really an animating spirit so much as an absence of the ordinary restraint that under normal circumstances put a stop to such nonsense. It was as if someone had somehow suspended the simple worldliness that kept people from behaving stupidly and destructively unless they really put their minds to it. But she did not say any of that. She didn't suppose it was the sort of thing the detectives would be interested in.

In her own case, she supposed it was indicative of her more cerebral character that her reckless nonsense had taken the form of a history essay. But of course she could not be sure that had anything to do with whatever was in the air. Maybe she was just obnoxious. Her visit to the demonic website had not felt particularly decisive either. She had already mostly written the offending essay. Perhaps she would not have submitted it; she'd been unsure of that when she was writing it, and perhaps the thought that she might not submit it had given her a certain freedom. The freedom to run with an idea. To the bloody end. But submitting the essay had itself been a logical progression. The knife went in. The website could have done no more than spur her on. It had planted nothing in the girl's mind that had not been there already, including the desire to visit it in the first place.

Of course, she had not believed a website could really channel the power of a demon. She did not believe in demons. But she'd been curious. She had wondered what would happen, how the site would deliver on its outrageous claim. She'd expected to be disappointed, and was half-braced for a practical joke – a crap-looking cartoon demon that would lull the viewer into a false sense of security and then go, 'Boo!' In the event, the shock had been of a different order, the joke more profound. Instead of a demon entering into her, she had been confronted with her demonic self. Not possessed by something else, but all too much herself. But she didn't say any of that to the detectives.

They thanked her for her time and left her to her studies. Outside the library they looked at one another as any two colleagues might after a meeting: 'Well? What do you think?'

Alexander shrugged.

Karen was a bit crestfallen. She had hoped talking to the girl would somehow help make sense of what they had all seen. Instead, the surly teenager had seemed weirdly resigned to the uncanniness of it all. That was not an attitude Karen could share.

CHAPTER 22: THE LITTLE BITCH

There had been a time when Karen had been more carefree. She had tried not to take life, or herself, too seriously – at least, that was what she would have told you if you'd asked. It was how she felt she ought to be. But early in her career, something happened that changed her mind, made her more self-aware and even slightly afraid of herself. In a way it had been the making of her, but not entirely in a good way.

When Karen first qualified as a PC, she had been friendly with a female senior officer who took a shine to her during her training and became a kind of informal mentor. They occasionally spent time together away from work, and talked about life as well as policing, as much as the two things could be separated. Superintendent Moore had recently married a famous and not-long divorced crime writer, Des Duke, and the joke was that she'd wooed him with war stories from her years as a polis. Colleagues looked forward to recognising themselves in his future books. Karen read his entire back catalogue in anticipation. She also met him in person a number of times at Moore's house, along with the Super's other young protégé, PC Michelle Cass. She and Karen were also on reasonably friendly terms. But then Michelle got drunk at a work function and disgraced herself by getting into a shoving match with a waitress. This reflected badly on Moore, who duly turned frosty towards her. Such was the lie of the land when another function came up, and a very sober Michelle approached Des, who had arrived before his wife, in hope of securing his intercession.

To this day, what happened next often played on Karen's mind. Something had happened inside when she had walked into the pub with Moore, and noticed Michelle making her excuses and shuttling away from Des when she saw them coming.

'What the...?' Karen said, half-spontaneously.

'What?' said Moore.

'Oh, nothing.'

'Was that Michelle talking to Des?'

'Was it? No, I'm sure she'd have stayed to say hello when she saw us coming.'

But when they greeted Des, he confirmed that it had been Michelle, and freely admitted her purpose. In fact, he began beseeching Moore to forgive the poor girl, suggesting they have her over for dinner to clear the air. Moore agreed – 'Anything for a quiet life' – and Des went back to mingling, never one to waste an hour or two in a room full of polis.

'Did they know each other before you were married?' Karen asked, knowing perfectly well that they had, since Des was an old friend of Michelle's parents.

'Well, yes,' Moore said. 'She was even our wee go-between for a while.' And then, after an awkward pause, 'Why do you ask?'

'No reason.'

'What's on your mind?'

'Nothing. I just didn't realise they were that close.'

'Close? Och, I wouldn't say that. Maybe she's a bit of a groupie. There's no harm in that.'

'Of course not. It's hard not to be a bit star struck! I suppose you'll get used to it.'

'Anyway, she's your pal, is she not?'

'Oh, totally. Michelle's great.'

'Is there something you're not telling me?' Moore laughed, all but spelling out the question in the air, the better to dispel it. Karen's laugh sounded even more forced, the more so because she did not intend it to.

'Look, I'm not worried in the slightest,' the Super said. 'But if there's something on your mind, spit it out. I'm not having you harbour some daft suspicion on my behalf.'

'Oh, but you're right,' Karen said, 'daft flights of fancy are all I've got. I'd blame the job, but *you've* done well enough without thinking the worst of people. Only now you must be thinking the worst of *me*. I should keep my stupid mouth shut.'

'You've barely said anything,' Superintendent Moore pointed out. 'You're just being weird.'

'Sorry,' Karen said, 'it's harder to do anything about that.'

The Super laughed.

'But you're right. It's my own problem,' Karen went on. 'The green-eyed monster, you know? It's been a self-fulfilling prophesy for me more than once.'

This was not true. Karen had never lost a man because of her jealousy, but with one university boyfriend she had imagined that she might, and not even by making rash accusations, but just by thinking them. It had become a kind of superstition. If she imagined him with some other girl, he'd end up with her right enough. It was a script she had imagined for their relationship, though not one they had lived out. Maybe she should have been a frustrated playwright rather than a frustrated actress.

'Och,' said the Super, 'You can't live like that. You either trust someone or you don't. And if you don't, that's the end of it as far as I'm concerned.'

'Very sensible,' said Karen. 'You can't just assume Des would do to you what he did to his ex-wife.'

Or maybe Karen did not say that. At least, she did not get a slap. But she definitely thought it. She wondered if Moore could tell. In any case, the super looked ready to end this conversation with her awkward rookie friend and mingle with her peers. Karen made to leave, but then hesitated with a confidential air.

'Sorry to burden you with my own nonsense. You should definitely have Michelle round for dinner, and you'll see for yourself how harmless she is. I'll leave you in peace now.'

The Super gave her an indulgent look, and Karen departed to do her own mingling. But she was troubled by the advice she had just given. Why should Michelle seem any more harmless over dinner than she had done before Karen had inadvertently planted the deed of doubt in the Super's mind? She could not help smiling, slightly shocked at herself, as it occurred to her that, if the seed had taken, just about anything Michelle did or said now would only add to the super's suspicions.

She forgot the little matter as she enjoyed the rest of the evening, but as she was leaving the pub, alone, she noticed something on the carpet by the bar. It was a pen, a fancy one, and she recognised it as one the Super had bought for Des. He'd probably used it to sign an autograph and then dropped it. She picked it up. Des and the Super had left already. She slipped it into her pocket so she could return it at the next opportunity. Alternatively, of course, she could plant it on Michelle. Ha-ha! She smiled again, enjoying imagining herself as a wicked schemer. She may have been a little drunk.

Karen was taken aback the very next day when Superintendent Moore asked her to join her for a coffee. 'It's not right just to drop hints if you know something, or think you do.'

'What do you mean?'

Moore looked at Karen to establish that she knew exactly what she meant. And then she unburdened herself. She said that even if Des were having an affair, at least she'd been able to sleep until last night when she'd seen the way Karen saw PC Cass with her husband. She said she would rather suffer a broken heart and public humiliation knowing for sure than be haunted by suspicion like this. She would have been happier if Des had worked his way through every rookie officer who would have him, if only she'd known nothing about it. Then she got a bit hysterical. She said her life was over, her career meant nothing. How could she take herself seriously as a polis when she couldn't even see the crime being committed in front of her nose?

Karen did not know what to say. She could hardly believe

this was her own doing, and asked if something else had happened to shake the Super's confidence in her husband.

'So there *is* something!'

'What? No. I mean, I don't know.'

Superintendent Moore gave her a murderous look. 'You made this happen,' it said. 'Don't play dumb now.'

Karen was in deep. Too deep to extricate herself from this madness? 'Oh, God,' she said, 'how is this happening? This isn't fair...' Only maybe she didn't say that. Maybe she said something else.

Then the Super almost whispered, 'I want proof'.

'How did I get into this?'

Another look.

'Listen, if I had proof I'd tell you. I should never have said anything... I mean, what did I even say?'

The look was still there.

'What kind of proof do you need? I'm pretty sure there isn't going to be a sex tape.'

The Super winced.

Karen felt for her, but more urgently felt the need to move the conversation on, one way or another. 'You know, maybe the reason I reacted the way I did is that there is something...'

A really intense look now.

'..but it doesn't mean anything. I mean it's not about Des, just Michelle.' Karen took a breath. 'Look, you said yourself she's a bit of a groupie. She was always into Des' books, and she just really liked the fact that she knew a famous writer.'

'And?'

'Well, it's just that we sometimes shared a room during training, and... Honestly, I'm really ashamed to say I once picked up her journal.'

'And?'

'Well, she'd written these wee stories... involving Des.'

A different kind of look this time.

'Oh, just schoolgirl stuff, you know?' Karen laughed spontaneously, the memory taking her back to when none of this mattered and it had been hilarious. In fact, it was perhaps with just a bit too much glee that she added, 'Well, quite *racy* schoolgirl stuff, actually... But, you know, it was all in her head!'

'The little bitch!'

'No, it was sheer fantasy! I should never have read them, and they're the only reason anything else even occurred to me!'

'I have to get back to work,' the Super said, and left.

'Fuck,' said Karen.

She took Des' pen from her pocket and wondered if planting it on Michelle could have made things any worse. She laughed again, partly at the memory of Michelle's dirty stories and partly at herself. At the situation. Whatever. She rehearsed all that she'd said about this imaginary affair between Des and Michelle. Had she really, single-handedly turned Superintendent Moore into a sexually jealous lunatic? She could not remember exactly what she had said at every turn, but even if she'd set out to drive the super insane, how was that even in her power? Karen did not understand what had just happened. She wondered what an impartial observer might have made of it, how they might have judged her part in it.

Her own judgement on herself hardened two days later when she learned Superintendent Moore had strangled Des in his bed before stabbing herself to death.

There was no question of Karen bearing any legal responsibility for what happened. The very enormity of Moore's crime made anything anyone might have *said* to her to 'precipitate' it seem trivial. It was not as if Karen had given the name and address of a suspect to the parents of a murdered child. Whether or not Des had been having an affair, there was no mitigating his murder, so even a malicious rumour monger could bear no responsibility for such an extreme response. The question did not even come up in the police investigation, or indeed in the media frenzy that inevitably followed the murder of a famous crime writer by his senior police officer wife. The headlines! And yet Karen was plagued by the question of whether 'malicious rumour monger' was in fact an apt description of her part in the drama. After all, the thought had crossed her mind more than once. She had briefly enjoyed the idea that she was getting under the Super's skin, and then over coffee it had almost seemed easier to play the scheming bitch than to back out of it. After Moore's murder-suicide, the thought of those brief exchanges made Karen ill, and she was bed-ridden for days, muttering to herself in a semi-conscious state. When she returned to work, she learned that PC Cass had resigned, and she never heard from her again.

Naturally enough, this episode had stayed with Karen, but never had it loomed so large as now. It had come to mind immediately when she saw the picture of the internet demon, because the Karen she saw reflected in that image was precisely the Karen she had imagined enjoying herself as she manipulated Superintendent Moore into doubting her husband. And now, every time she looked in the mirror, there she was again. The little bitch.

CHAPTER 23: IMMORTAL HORRORS

Morgan was agitated about something that had happened at school. Evidently the teacher had said something about the children wanting to 'have their cake and eat it'.

'What's the point of having a cake if you don't eat it?' she wanted to know.

Alexander had to concede it was a good question. 'It's an expression,' he said, as if that explained anything. Then he added, 'I suppose the idea is more like wanting to eat your cake and then *still* have it.'

'Oh,' Morgan said. 'But surely you'd want to eat it eventually? Otherwise, what's the point?' It was still a good question.

'What was the teacher actually talking about?' Alexander asked.

'Homework Club.'

It transpired that the school had set up an after school club where children could do their homework for an hour in their classroom, rather than taking it home. But some of them had been messing about instead of getting on with it.

'Right,' Alexander said, after a moment's thought, 'so the cake is having the rest of the evening off. But if you waste your time in Homework Club, that's like eating the cake and still expecting to have it when you get home. And you can't, because you still have your homework to do. See?'

'Hmm, but even if you do your work in Homework Club, you still eat the cake when you get home, don't you?'

'Well, yes, if you have any sense,' Alexander agreed, quite pleased with his daughter. 'It's a silly expression, really. What about you? Do you get your work done in Homework Club?' he asked Morgan.

'Most of it,' she said. 'I mean, I'm not that obsessed with cake, to be honest.'

Alexander liked that, but it took him by surprise. Not that it was so strange not to be obsessed with cake, even for a child. But Morgan understood perfectly well they weren't talking about cake, or even free time. She was expressing her feelings about the abstract notion of reward. Putting it firmly in its place. He looked at his daughter as if at a stranger. She was a strange little person.

Speaking of those, he decided he was ready to talk to Karen about everything. Encountering the demon counsellor had convinced him once and for all that psychotherapy was not for him. Finally he saw that he did not 'need to talk' in the therapeutic sense; he needed to talk to Karen. He took her out to a new wine bar to show serious intent. Only what to bring up first: their possible impending parenthood, or Alexander's visits to Hell?

In the event, Alexander did not have to decide. 'I don't want to have the baby,' Karen told him.

'Right.'

She explained as best she could how she'd come to this decision. Telling Alexander she was pregnant had been an important step. It had made it more real, more urgent. And she just didn't feel ready to be a mother. Oh, probably no one ever does, but that's no reason to have a baby. She was close to tears. Alexander put his arm round her protectively. She breathed, straightened, calmed down. She took a sip of wine and smiled inwardly at the thought that she could do so without fear of judgement now she was no longer 'expecting'. Then she looked at Alexander and smiled outwardly. 'Was there something else you wanted to talk about?

The timing seemed wrong, to say the least, but Alexander had also come to a decision.

'I've been having supernatural experiences,' he said. 'For a while now. I've been visiting Hell.'

She pulled away from him. 'What are you talking about?'

'I mean it. I know it sounds mad, but it's not the first time I've experienced something like this. At the very least, I'm having visions. But I think it's more than that. I believe it's real.'

'Hell?'

'Yes.'

She was scanning his face furiously, trying to detect signs that this was a joke. 'Does this have something to do with that picture? The demon's face?' She was poised between wanting him to say yes – preferring supernatural sense to no sense at all – and wanting the whole thing to be a joke. She was poised between wanting to believe him and wanting to kill him.

'I think it might. I'd better tell you the whole story,' he said, and sipped his wine in preparation.

He told Karen how the author had contacted him with what he said was a tip. Karen knew of the author, but hadn't met him or read anything by him. Alexander explained that he hadn't mentioned the approach at the time because he hadn't known how seriously to take it; he didn't mention the mysterious woman. He told her how he had followed the author's instructions to go to this strange pub and order a particular whisky, and how drinking it had transported him to Hell.

He told her about the bloodless sinners too dull to be allowed into Hell proper, and how he had descended via the toilet-cum-confession box to where the lustful dead were blown by the mad wind. He told her how he'd returned to Earth and said nothing to her because it all seemed so insane, but how he'd then been sent more whisky and drunk it under the flyover to find himself surrounded by the gluttonous dead being tormented by wild dogs in the hail. And how he'd later found himself in a Hellish nightclub where dead money grubbers on roller skates had given new meaning to the circulation of currency. She did not smile at his joke.

He told her how he had proceeded to the canal, where he had found a filthy bog strewn with the wrathful dead, going at each other furiously amid acid bubbles sent up by the sullen dead below them. Then he explained how he'd found himself worrying when he returned to the world of the living that the strange behaviour of the schoolchildren and their teachers was in some way Infernally influenced. He added that the author had later assured him this was not the case.

'Where is this author friend of yours?' Karen demanded.

'I'm coming to that,' he said.

He told her how he had returned to the canal and been ferried by the late Sergeant McGinty to the Hellish citadel, how he had phoned the author when the terrifying demons had refused to let him in, and how a mysterious figure had eventually shown up seemingly from another dimension to open the gates for him. Then he had met the author, amid the flaming tombs of the heretics, and the author had been his guide for the rest of his visits to Hell.

'So there is such a thing as heresy?' Karen asked.

'Yes. Yes, very much so, it seems,' Alexander said, hesitating as he framed this thoughts. 'Only it's not so much error that's the issue as intransigence. The dead heretics are eternal prisoners of their own stubborn intellectual attachments.'

'But as opposed to what? The one true religion?'

'Well, just the truth, I think. Religion hasn't really come into this,' he added, to Karen's obvious bemusement, before remembering it was not quite true anyway. The demon's multifaith shrine had appeared on Earth, not in Hell, but the pornographic film it contained had seemingly served as an illustration of the third kind of violence punished in Hell, and in some sinister way, that certainly had something to do with religion.

But he was getting ahead of himself. He tried to explain

to Karen that heresy was more intellectual than religious in character. It clicked for her when he described it as a kind of vanity. She got that all right. He tried not to seem too pleased with himself, then, and decided to leave Aristotle out of his explanation of what had come next. He told her how the author had explained the difference between sins of excess and sins of deliberate malice, how those guilty of the former were given over for eternity to their self-defeating passions, and how the rest of Hell was divided between different forms of the latter: violence, fraud and especially treachery.

He told Karen how he and the author had dodged the Minotaur and tussled with Hell's Angels before encountering the dead who had been guilty of violence against others, suffering eternal justice in the river of boiling blood. Hitler, child abusers, all good. But after crossing the river, he told her, he'd got the call about the Buchanan Street murder, and been transported back to Earth to deal with it.

'Are you sure it wasn't the other way round?' she asked. 'You didn't dream about a bloody river full of murderers *after* taking on the case?'

'No,' he said. His visits to Hell were nothing like dreams. And he didn't have the order wrong: if anything, he'd been afraid the murder had been a case of Hell spilling over into the real world as a result of his visits, but again he'd been assured that was impossible. Anyway, murders were not such a rarity in their line of work, even if this one had been especially gruesome and weird. The question that had troubled him was whether the killers now deserved Hell. Had they transformed themselves in an instant into eternal peers of Hitler and co? Was there any hope for them?

Karen ordered another bottle of wine.

Alexander told her about the forest of the suicides, those guilty of violence against themselves. That visit had happened immediately after he was attacked in the bar, he noted. He hadn't told her his attacker had been a demon, of course, and decided not to complicate the story with that detail now. He did stress that the inanimate suicides were joined by other sinners who had merely squandered their lives away through drink, drugs or other self-destructive occupations. That had struck him as intuitively right. Addiction was often described as a kind of Hell in its own right, a foretaste perhaps, almost as if people chose Hell for themselves before even dying.

And that brought him to the burning sands where sinners were punished for the third kind of violence, or what the author had described as the deliberate perversion of morality and disdain for natural goodness. He told Karen how he had met his old tutor, and how Dr Brown had warned him to guard his innocence. Dr Brown and his colleagues had apparently been guilty of deliberate moral transgression disguised as intellectual curiosity. It was, after all, possible to be too clever for your own good. Then Alexander had encountered the Marquis de Sade and his friends, whose transgressions were of a similar kind if rather more obvious. But things had been made even more obvious for Alexander back on Earth.

Karen knew about the shrine, of course, but again, Alexander had not told her about the demon part. Telling her about the pornography was if anything even more awkward, but he felt it was an indispensable part of the story. So he explained how had watched the video, and how it had occurred to him that it was indeed a kind of religious artefact: ritualistic, liturgical, creepy. Then he told Karen how he had reimagined it in a dream, more explicitly as a pastiche of the Crucifixion, and how he had landed straight back in Hell. He wondered if that was because he had found within himself that same deliberate perversity that was punished on the burning sand.

'Wait,' Karen said, demurring to comment on the content of Alexander's dream. 'You were taken there just by your thoughts this time?'

He explained that after the first few times drinking the whisky, the transitions between Hell and Earth had been more fluid. The author had explained that since Hell was not a geographical location on Earth or in it, there were no physical portals in or out of it. Alexander's entrances, from his first via the Hope to the one through that dream, had been specially arranged for him somehow. The author had said something about how he'd wanted Alexander to return to Earth at more or less regular intervals, giving him time to reflect on what he had seen, and think about it in terms of his own life.

'And what, repent?' Karen asked.

Now she'd said it, it seemed obvious. 'Something like that, I suppose.' But he didn't want to lose his train of thought.

It occurred to him now that maybe his transitions from Earth to Hell were more important than he had realised: but more than that, each sinner's own transition was far more significant than the progress Alexander was making through Hell itself. After all, the damned made the journey only once, and saw only that part of Hell to which they'd been damned. His own visits were taking him through the whole of Hell apparently for the purposes of education, or perhaps as Karen suggested, something a little more like exhortation. But what he was being invited to understand, and what he was now trying to explain to Karen, was not some hierarchy of sin, but how sinful human beings consigned themselves to an eternity in a particular place in Hell through their deeds – and thoughts, dreams? – on Earth. How, as the author had told him, they chose their Hellish identities in the course of their lives. How they faced immortal consequences.

He told her how on his next visit, he'd seen what he'd taken to be business consultants or some such, before encountering Dougal MacCallum and the cavaliers, all burning on the hot sand. Then he told her the story of Steenie Steenson, who like Alexander had been allowed to visit Hell and return to Earth, though he could not say why. He did know that Sir Robert Redgauntlet and his cronies were in Hell not for persecuting and murdering religious dissidents, for which they'd have boiled in the river of blood, but for living off the fines they'd taken from their victims, along with the rents from Redgauntlet's own tenants. This was another form of the third kind of violence, so the victimisation of others was not the point. It had more to do with the cavaliers' evident disdain for actual hard work, their attempt (successful while it lasted) to live by gaming the system, albeit very crudely. He supposed the T-shirted business people had done the same thing by more sophisticated means.

'So, it's violence more in the sense of *violation*?' Karen said, suddenly grasping the idea. 'I mean, obviously in the case of the pornography. But your rent-seeking cavaliers too. I can see a sort of shamelessness in that way of life. A blatant violation of the natural order of things. It's cheating.'

Alexander nodded. It was much more like Karen than him to think in terms of a 'natural order of things', but he supposed she was right. And it occurred to him that such a natural order was more fundamental than the law. There was something peculiarly sordid about breaching it, violating it, *within* the law. He thought again of the pornography, how the girl's consent added to rather than subtracting from the horror.

'Very good,' he said. 'So that's violence.'

Then he told her how the author had summoned a monster to take them yet deeper into Hell, and how, as they had descended precipitously, he had felt like Icarus meeting with the consequences of his own folly.

'Did you ever talk to your therapist about this?' Karen asked, evidently having decided it all sounded a bit Freudian or whatever.

'Not really,' Alexander answered, choosing not to be annoyed by Karen's implied doubts about the reality of his experiences. 'Once or twice I brought stuff up obliquely, but never directly. Anyway,' he added mischievously, 'she wasn't a real therapist. Remember?'

He didn't mention how the Icarus experience had reminded him of his marriage, or how he had been reflecting ever since on the state of his life, including their relationship. They'd had the pregnancy talk, after all, and that at least seemed to be resolved.

'So,' he continued, 'there is a place in Hell called Malebolge.' He told her about how various kinds of fraud and malicious deceit were punished in the descending, concentric valleys that made up Malebolge. It the first valley, pimps and seducers trudged in both directions being whipped by demons. In the second, flatterers wallowed in their own filth. Then there were the irresponsible office holders, driven like pegs into the rock for putting vanity or personal gain before solemn duty. And in the next valley were the soothsayers and sorcerers, twisted arse about face in return for their effrontery. The valley after that had been the most frightening, not because the corrupt sinners were boiled in tar there, but because it was patrolled by the Evil Claws.

Alexander explained to Karen that the demons had insisted on escorting their visitors round the valley. He didn't mention his disappointment that the author had allowed this to happen, as it would have felt disloyal. But he told her how they'd met the corrupt prison officer, how he had tricked his torturers into letting him escape back into the tar, and how he and the author had taken the opportunity to make their own escape into the next valley.

'Escape?' Karen said, 'Do you think you were in actual danger?' Apparently she'd been disturbed by the switch from documentary to drama.

Alexander hesitated. 'Probably not. But I was afraid. And I think I was supposed to be.'

'Right.'

He continued. The next valley had contained the hypocrites, weighed down by dazzling but oppressively heavy robes. From there, Alexander and the author had climbed over the ridge to the valley of the thieves, writhing with snakes. He explained that the thieves themselves were intermittently reptilian, relentlessly metamorphosing so their very limbs were never their own for long.

The valley after that had been Alexander's favourite, though that was probably the wrong word. There they had met Ulysses in the form of a wandering flame, and he had shared the heroic yet mystifying tale of his demise in the Atlantic. And the author had tried to explain what the great hero was doing in Hell, sharing the valley among others with the 3rd Earl of Lucan, who had ordered the charge of the light brigade, if that helped.

Karen nodded non-committally.

In the next valley, they had been greeted by Stalin, who was violently split down his middle, and explained that he and the others there were damned as schismatics of one kind or another. He and his fellow trouble makers now suffered bodily and eternally the bloody division they had wrought in life.

In Malebolge's final valley, Alexander continued, counterfeiters and falsifiers dragged themselves agonisingly around, afflicted with some stinking pestilence that made them scratch themselves without rest. He skirted over the fact that the author had told him off for enjoying too much the reality TV-style trash talk between Adam McMaster and his friends. Suffice to say he had been reflecting ever since on what this all meant. But he was sure there would be more to see before it was over.

'You do intend to go back to Hell then?' It was hard to tell whether Karen's question was sincere, sarcastic or something more like a request. Alexander certainly detected an edge of some kind.

'As I say, it's not really been a conscious decision since the first couple of times. But I don't believe I've seen everything, and I'm assuming that's the idea.'

'So you want to see absolutely *all* of Hell before you consider repenting?'

They both laughed at that. And in an instant, this awkward conversation was over, and they continued their evening out as if it had never happened.

(It definitely did happen, though.)

CHAPTER 24: GIANTS

Having reached the bottom of the cone of Malebolge, Alexander and the author stood at the edge of the pit at its centre, the very bottom of Hell. The air was murky and the light dim, but a horn sounded deafeningly, drawing Alexander's gaze to what appeared to be one of several high towers in the murk.

'Is this another citadel?' he asked.

'No,' said the author. 'You'll be able to make them out better as we walk round.' But then he thought better of it, and stopped Alexander. 'Actually, I don't want you getting a fright, so you might as well know now that they're not towers but giants.'

'Giants?'

'Yes, giants. They stand in the pit up to their bellies, guarding the perimeter.'

Alexander looked again, inching forward along the edge of the pit. Then his previous misapprehension gave way to fear as he made out the massive upper bodies of the giants. He gazed up at the awful face of the giant closest to him, his monstrous shoulders, chest and arms, and reflected that creatures like this one would be formidable weapons of war if they existed on Earth. Giant battle elephants with both wits and purpose, and no little malice by the look of this one. Just then, the giant proved he was not dumb by bellowing words at the intruders, albeit incomprehensible words.

The author shouted back, 'Save it. Blow your horn if you must, but nobody understands a word you say.'

Then he turned to Alexander, 'Why do I bother? He can't understand me either.' He reassured Alexander that the giant was bound at the neck and could not harm them. He was Nimrod, who did once walk the Earth, in fact. He had been a man of renown in primeval days of yore. Larger than life in more ways than one. He had built the Tower of Babel as a monument to himself, and lost his fame in its aftermath when the ancient common tongue was lost, because now nobody could understand the stories about him.

Proceeding around the edge of the pit, Alexander and the author came to a second giant, much bigger than Nimrod, and fiercer too, straining furiously at the chains that coiled around him and strapped his giant arms to his giant body. 'That is Fafner,' said the author. 'He killed his brother Fasolt for a hoard of treasure, and then literally sat on it.'

'So, don't tell me,' Alexander said. 'I've got a feeling for this by now, and if I'm right the murder is less important than the greed that motivated it?'

'Yes and no. It depends what you mean by greed. You saw the gluttons much further up. They at least enjoyed their cake, or tried to. Fafner wanted to have his cake and *not* eat it. Is that greed?'

Cake again. 'I suppose he didn't want anyone else to eat it either?'

'Exactly. It's not so much greed as jealously, the jealousy of someone who can't have something or someone but doesn't want anyone else to have them either.'

'But he did have it, even if he didn't eat it. How do you eat treasure anyway?'

The author gave Alexander a look. 'You enjoy it,' he said. 'But enjoying treasure is not like eating food, or if it is, it's more like taking part in a feast than just ingesting calories. It generally involves sharing, one way or another: giving or receiving jewellery as a gift, displaying beautiful artefacts for people to admire. Just sitting on treasure misses the point entirely. It's insulting to the people who put their own creativity, imagination and industry into producing it.'

'You seem to have given this some thought,' Alexander observed.

'So should you,' the author told him. 'If you're really getting a feel for things, you'll begin to understand that sin is less about deeds than temperament. The giants are a lot like the sinners we saw above on the burning sand. They're perverse in their defiance, rebelling against their own good.'

Alexander would indeed have to think about that. He thought now of Sir Robert Redgauntlet and his cronies. They had feasted, all right, albeit at the expense of his tenants. Now, they feasted eternally, in flames. Of course, he intuited that there had always been something unwholesome about their feasting, not unlike the witches' dance he had witnessed on Earth. Both were somehow set against the rest of the world rather than in harmony with it. The cavaliers had relished their exploitation of the people, savoured it in every mouthful of burgundy. And the witches' dance was a celebration of all kinds of mischief. But this was neither the time nor the place to ponder further. Nimrod's horn was still echoing in Alexander's ears, and he was eager to move on.

'So how are we going to get past the giants and into the pit?' he asked the author. 'Is the Big Friendly Giant down here too?'

The author refused to take the bait. 'He's a bit further on. And you don't want to see him, because he's actually more frightening than this one.' At that, Fafner shook himself within his chains more violently than any earthquake, which had the author's desired effect of all but scaring the life out of Alexander.

'This is the one we want,' he continued, leading Alexander on to the next giant. He said it was Epistemon, tutor and friend to the celebrated giant Pantagruel. He had been beheaded by yet more giants, but his head had been stitched back on, after which he had fabricated a story about having been to Hell while he was dead. He told his companions it wasn't that bad. It was just that people had menial jobs beneath their station: for example, the great general Hannibal was a poulterer, and his nemesis Scipio Africanus some kind of pedlar. He said Hell was nothing to worry about, in perverse defiance of the truth. But the author did not labour the matter with the giant himself. Instead, he shouted: 'Epistemon, you're free to move around unlike the others, so why not be our bell boy and drop us down to the next level? This man will repay you by reminding the world of your name.'

Epistemon did not hesitate to reach out and take them in his giant hands. Then he tilted – reminding Alexander of how a junky on temazepam seemingly defies gravity by swaying perilously without actually falling over – and stooped, lowering his cargo gently. As he did so, he made eye contact with the detective, communicating a melancholy that chilled Alexander to the bone. Indeed, when the giant set them down on the floor of Hell, he realised that it was made not of fire, but of ice. Epistemon did not linger, but shot violently back up like a dozing drunk momentarily regaining his composure.

Presently, Karen did something similar. She had been dozing fully dressed on her bed, having returned from the abortion clinic earlier in the afternoon. She had been dreaming about something else entirely when it had suddenly come back to her. The abortion.

Having made the decision, she had quickly made the arrangements for a medical abortion, but there were two pills involved, two appointments. Now she was in between, in a kind of limbo. The counsellor had explained the process, but Karen had struggled to take it in, partly because she did not really want to know the details. Consequently, she was not completely sure if she was still 'pregnant' or not. She felt like she was carrying Schrödinger's cat. The second appointment could not come quickly enough.

In the meantime, she was still troubled by what Alexander had told her. She simultaneously took it for granted that he must be mentally ill and knew he was not. Or at least, that was not the issue. She had a nagging feeling that what he had described to her was in some sense profoundly true. Oh, it was metaphorical, no doubt – it was just like Alexander to experience a metaphor as if it were real life – but not simply a delusion or fantasy. Then Karen realised something else: she *wanted* it to be true. The idea of Hell as Alexander had described it resonated with something deep in her soul. The same thing that had made her want to be a polis. It occurred to her to feel guilty for wishing eternal damnation on anyone, but that was not a thought that resonated at all. What Alexander had described was not arbitrary or even cruel, but entirely just. She tried to imagine a corresponding Heaven, but for some reason she could not begin to do that.

Of course, Karen could hardly avoid putting the two things together, at least for cursory consideration. Her abortion and Hell. Even the most hair-raising of the anti-abortion leaflets – the one that compared abortion to child sacrifice – had not mentioned Hell. She did not suppose she would have found it any more persuasive if it had done. But, sure: some people considered abortion to be murder. Maybe she would go to Hell for it if Hell were real after all. But she did not seem to fear that nearly as much as she had feared that feeling of becoming ever more petty and selfish, the feeling that had made abortion a no-brainer before it became a dilemma.

She thought of what Alexander had said about sinners choosing their own Hellish identities, and places, in the course of their lives. If she allowed herself to become that petty, selfish Karen, she would be on the road to Hell sure enough. In fact, it had been that taste of Hell that had made her decide at one stage to have the baby, to open herself up to something unplanned and unwanted but potentially wonderful. It had felt good to make that decision, to leave behind the selfish, fearful Karen who had refused even to countenance motherhood, and whom she could not now help but picture as the demonic Karen from the website. But she also felt that decision had changed her, and she didn't actually have to have the baby – this baby, now – in order to grow as a person. She could live with herself.

She wanted to grow as a person, felt it was necessary, but she felt somehow blocked by her relationship with Alexander. Talking to him had been important. It had been a way of taking responsibility, facing up to reality. She had needed to speak to him, and not just about the pregnancy, as much as he had needed to speak to her. He had told her how it had been the exposure of Dr Bakshi, his false counsellor, that had made him realise it wasn't a disinterested interlocutor he needed anyway, but Karen herself. 'What a breakthrough!' she had managed not to say.

Karen had previously been curious about this therapist, perhaps a tiny bit jealous, and when Alexander had revealed she was a fraud, she had felt genuinely angry on his behalf. But Alexander did not believe the business with Dr Bakshi had anything to do with his visits to Hell. Just an ordinary case of... actually he wasn't sure. Dr Bakshi had been making a living out of it, but was probably a bit of a fantasist too. He had always described his sessions with her as 'jousts', which Karen had always considered a bit weird, but having reflected on it, he had assured her that he had said nothing to Dr Bakshi that would cause him embarrassment, and he had never mentioned Karen at all. That had been reassuring, if not flattering.

In any case, it was clear by now that Karen's real rival for access to Alexander's thoughts and feelings was not the therapist but the author. The author, who, for reasons unknown, had decided to take Alexander on a tour of Hell. At least she knew the author was a real person, and not a figment of Alexander's imagination. She'd seen his book at Alexander's place; it was reddish. So maybe it was all true. Maybe the author really was guiding Alexander through Hell just as he had told her.

Why? The obvious reason was to make him repent for his sins. And while Karen did not consider Alexander to be particularly sinful, she understood that was not the point. As

Alexander had described it, Hell was where sin came into its own, where hidden vices blossomed into grotesque caricatures. If that was where she ended up, Karen would look like the face from the demonic website, and suffer who knew what torments. Deserved torments. She shuddered. Maybe *she* needed to repent. But what did that even mean?

'I'm sorry,' she said out loud. But of course there was no one there to hear her.

She was not going to get back to sleep, she decided. She would go into work. Catch up. Maybe there would be good news for once.

CHAPTER 25: THE FLOOR OF HELL

There is nothing above to serve as a simile for Hell's floor of ice, which heaves under the weight of all the sins of the world, but makes no sound in reply. Those who suffer there would better have been born without the wits they misused to earn their places. But Alexander was still gazing up at Epistemon the giant, who had lifted the author and him down from above, until he heard a voice from below call out, 'Watch your feet! It's bad enough down here without you stomping our poor heads!'

He looked down and around him, to see that the ice preserved the suffering of innumerable freezing sinners, with just their heads emerging, and apparently not too numb to notice the inadvertent attentions of a policeman's boot. They made Alexander think of indulgent dads who let their kids bury them on the beach on holiday, except their faces were cast down dolefully and their teeth chattered from the cold. Then he noticed two heads so close together that their hair was intermingled. Alexander asked them who they were. As they turned to face him, tears streamed from their eyes and immediately froze, fusing the two men's cheeks and lips together. Clearly they were unhappy with such intimacy, because they began furiously headbutting one another.

Another head addressed Alexander without looking up. A woman's voice: 'What are you looking at? If you want to know who those two are, they're twin brothers who killed one another. You won't have heard of them, but believe you me, you'll find none worse down here. Not Mordred, who betrayed his own father King Arthur. Not that notorious gangster Jock Varda, who murdered half his own criminal gang. And not that one right in front of me, blocking my view. You'll have heard of her: Senga Vizard, who murdered her brother over their inheritance.' Alexander had indeed heard of Senga Vizard. Hasn't everyone? 'And to save you asking,' the head continued, 'I was Camisole Nutt. I murdered my cousin for reasons I won't go into. But that's nothing compared to what my Uncle Charlie will freeze for.'

Alexander and the author moved on to where countless teeth-chattering heads now showed their faces above the ice, almost turned blue by the cold. Alexander would not feel the cold again without thinking of this place. As they wandered, following a gradual slope towards the centre of Hell's floor, he inadvertently kicked one of the heads hard in the face.

'Ow!' it said. 'What did you do that for? Have you got some point to make? Else why pick on me?'

Alexander asked the author if it was all right to stop a moment to investigate. The author did not object. 'And who are you to be taking offence?' Alexander asked his victim.

'No, who are you to be wandering around down here, knocking people about?'

'Police,' Alexander said, from force of habit. 'But more to the point, I'm returning to the world, so if you play your cards right I can make you famous.'

'That's the last thing I want. Fuck off and leave me alone, since you have no idea how to ingratiate yourself down here.'

Alexander stooped to kneel on the ice and grabbed the sinner by the hair. 'Tell me your name or I'll leave you without a hair on your head!'

'Go ahead and pluck away. I'll tell you nothing even if you stamp on my head a thousand times!'

Alexander had already plucked a tuft of hair, and now twisted another handful until the sinner howled. Another protruding head called out in a woman's voice, 'What's the matter, Trapp? Do you have to howl now as well as chattering like the rest of us? What demon torments you?'

At that, DCI Demon relented. 'You don't have to tell me now,' Alexander said. Trapp had been a senior policeman who had tipped off a criminal gang about a raid, resulting in the killing of two officers and a civilian. He was universally hated by polis. 'I'll be happy to report your whereabouts,' Alexander told him.

'Say what you want,' Trapp retorted, 'But be sure to mention her too. She betrayed her country for cold, hard cash, and in doing so earned her cold, hard fate.'

'Which country was that?' Alexander asked, wondering if it mattered.

'Who cares? If it's our country you're interested in, over there is Robert the Bruce. Before making himself king, he murdered an ancestor of your author friend at a parley on holy ground.' Alexander looked at the author, who gave a sort of Gallic shrug. Trapp went on describing his other neighbours: another political schemer of some kind, a businesswoman who had ripped off her partner; the scale of the offence did not seem to be relevant. It was betrayal of one kind or another that had come to define each of these sinners.

Alexander had never thought of betrayal as the ultimate sin and had not got used to the idea since the author had tried to explain it. Now he worried that he had been missing something. The author had explained the logic, of course. Like all forms of fraud, betrayal was deliberate, calculated – a misuse of wits and reason – but more specifically, it was an abuse of particular trust. While common fraud preyed on naivety or a mere lack of vigilance – the possibility of deceit not occurring to the victim – betrayal went against an explicit belief that the traitor would not do such a thing, would not go against a principle held so deeply it was part of who they were. A mere fraud pretends to be someone else; a traitor pretends *not* to be who he *is*. The effect on any surviving victim was that much more existentially disorienting. It was brutal.

Alexander wondered if he had ever been guilty of betrayal. He was divorced, it was true, and thus had reneged on his wedding vows, but that had been mutual, and had thus not felt like betrayal. He was also conscious of having let down his daughter on occasion, or at least failed to live up to her unrealistic expectations of him. That did not feel like betrayal either, but he sensed that in Morgan's case the real betrayal would be to stop worrying about that sort of thing, to stop caring whether he was a good father. Traitors must begin by turning their backs on something essential about themselves, trading in something that others would not have imagined they could ever abandon. Alexander felt a chill as he reflected that this sounded like one definition of growing up – adapting to the real world, compromising, all that. Nobody's perfect. Certainly not Alexander. He was resigned to that. But what if that resignation itself were a betrayal?

He wandered on until his attention was drawn to two heads frozen together in the same hole, the one behind gnawing at the other's brains like a zombie, only with what appeared to be a certain deliberate animus. 'You really seem to hate that guy,' Alexander observed. 'If you tell us why, we'll share your story in the world above.'

The zombie raised his head from his greasy snack and wiped the slobber from his mouth on the hair of its container. And suddenly he was anything but a zombie. 'It's such a heart wrenching tale I can barely think of it without tearing up,' he said. 'But if you'll spread the infamy of this treacherous bastard, I'll fight my way through my tears.'

Alexander put on his best listening face.

'I don't know how you got down here, but I take it you're a polis. So if I tell you my name was Shug Wolf, and this is the Archbishop, you'll know he betrayed our conspiracy and murdered me. But when I tell you how he did the deed, then you'll understand everything.'

Alexander did indeed know the story of Shug Wolf and the Archbishop, both notorious gangsters who had been long-standing co-conspirators until the latter had capriciously betrayed the former. The Archbishop – not in fact an archbishop but a disgraced former priest – had seemingly disposed not only of Wolf, who was presumed murdered though the body had never been found, but also of his cubs, four sons who had disappeared at the same time as their father. Alexander could not deny his curiosity.

'Early that morning, I got a tip off that he was coming for me,' Wolf continued, 'so I decided to run for it with the boys. I knew he'd have airports covered, so we got in the Land Rover and headed for the Highlands to hide out. But he must have had us tracked, because we were intercepted on the way, I was knocked senseless and the next thing I knew I woke up with the boys in some kind of cave. Cold, damp and almost without light. They were asking for their breakfast, but all I had to give them was the sweets and crisps we'd packed for the journey. Was it mercy or cruelty that led the Archbishop to leave us those? I followed the light looking for a way out, but when I found it I knew we were doomed. There was a railing stuck fast into the rock, with its gate locked shut. It was an old mine, and now our dungeon.'

He looked plaintively at Alexander, 'You'd need a heart of stone not to feel for me when you imagine what went through my mind. If that won't make you cry, what will?'

Alexander looked back at him, but the tears would not come.

Wolf continued, 'The boys ate what we had while I shouted for help, but then I noticed something on the gate. It was a first communion pendant. The Archbishop loved mafia films and books, and this was straight out of Mario Puzo."

Alexander immediately understood. He'd seen the same films. A 'communion' was a murder where the body was never meant to be found. And more out of cruelty than worry about the police. The other kind of murder was a 'confirmation', where the body was left to be found by the authorities, leaving the victim's people in no doubt.

'Well,' Wolf went on, 'I knew then I could shout all I wanted. The Archbishop would have made sure there was no chance of anyone hearing. I looked at the boys, not knowing what to say, but wee Andy started crying just at the look on my face. I sat stunned for I don't know how long, and the boys alternated between panic and crying in a huddle. What could I do? Days passed. Starving, yearning for a simple sangwich. We even licked the walls for moisture.

Then, one morning a ray of light shone into our dungeon and onto the boys' faces. They looked like me, my boys. I just cracked, and bit my hands in frustration. But they thought it was from hunger, and would you believe it? They said I should eat them! Eat my own children! So I went quiet. I actually wished we could all just die in an instant. Then on about the fourth day, Gary fell at my feet and said, "Why don't you do something?" And then he died. Over the next couple of days, I watched the others die one after another. Or in the end I could only feel them with my hands, as I'd gone blind from darkness or starvation. Eventually, my hunger was worse than my grief.'

He paused for a second, an expression flashing over his face, before he sank his teeth back into the Archbishop's brains.

Alexander did not weep, but he felt for the boys if not their father. No doubt Wolf had earned his place in Hell through some treachery of his own, but it was the Archbishop's crime that had been laid before Alexander, and betrayal seemed the least of it. To murder innocent children in such a cruel way was unfathomable. He felt strangely relieved that the story had never got out and shamed the very nation that says sangwich. How could it have seemed just to the Archbishop to kill these boys over a collapse of trust in a criminal conspiracy? And why was he being punished in Hell for his own betrayal of his erstwhile partner, rather than for what he did to the boys?

He looked at the author, who reminded him that each

sinner's place in Hell was determined by his or her defining sin. The Archbishop might also have been a child murderer, but he had defined himself as a traitor. Perhaps it was the sin that had weighed heaviest on his own conscience, such as it was – the violation of a code with which he truly identified – but ultimately he had chosen to embrace his treason rather than to repent. So here he was. The author also pointed out that there seemed to be a certain poetic justice in the brain-eating thing. Anyway, he added, we all tolerate the starvation of children – but the Archbishop had done it out of malice towards their father.

'I guess,' Alexander said, but it was the author's mention of repentance that seized his imagination, something for him to chew on.

They set off again, and soon found that the heads emerging from the ice now had their faces cast upwards, so their frozen tears clogged their eyes completely, forming blinding goggles of ice. Alexander's own face was by now almost frozen, but not so much that he could not feel a mysterious breeze. 'What's that?' he asked the author, who told him he'd see soon enough. But before he did, one of the heads called out to them.

'Help for pity's sake! You must be as evil as me to be down here, but have pity and take the ice off my eyes so I can vent my sorrow before my tears freeze up again!'

The author answered, 'If you want this man's help, first tell him who you are. Then if he doesn't free your eyes, may he be consigned to the bottom of the ice.'

Alexander looked at the author with alarm, but the author gestured reassuringly. Or meant to.

The sinner announced that he was Walder Frey, who had invited his enemies to a wedding with the security of 'guest right', only to have them slaughtered. He had finally got his bloody comeuppance after being served a pie filled with the flesh of his own sons, a fate not entirely unlike that of Shug Wolf. Alexander had never heard of Walder Frey or either incident;

the author just shrugged apologetically, before asking the murderous host who else was around.

Walder Frey responded enthusiastically, keen to ingratiate himself with his soon-to-be benefactor. 'The Glencoe murderers are that way. And you must have heard of Chalky Gold? He's been over there for years now.'

Alexander had of course heard of Chalky Gold, but last he had heard the gangster was serving time in jail for the murder of his father-in-law at a Christmas party. He challenged Walder Frey: 'He can't have been here for years; you're lying.'

'No, even before his victim was being speared above by the Evil Claws for his own sins, Chalky was frozen into his place down here. If his body still walks the Earth, it's been taken over by a demon. Because the moment someone commits a betrayal of this gravity, the soul is cast down. But now I've fulfilled my side of the bargain,' Walder Frey continued, 'Now do as you promised and free my eyes of ice.'

Alexander looked at the author, who shook his head. 'You can't relieve his suffering. It would be bad manners down here.'

'But you said I if I didn't I should be consigned to the bottom of the ice?'

'And that's exactly where we're going.'

Alexander looked down at the solid ice. 'How?'

'You've already noticed the breeze. Can you tell where it's coming from yet?'

Alexander looked in the direction it seemed to be coming from, but it was now too murky to make anything out from where they stood. The author gestured to proceed, and they walked on till there were no longer heads protruding from the ice, just the eerie figures of bodies completely submerged. They were fixed in various positions, some vertical, some horizontal, others contorted or upside down, all plastic and stiff in their agony, lit terrifyingly not by light but by darkness visible.

When Alexander had got used to seeing by the dark, the author stood in front of him and told him to prepare himself. Then he stepped to one side to reveal what now stood behind him. Alexander reeled. He suddenly felt a powerful sense of reckoning, as if he were no longer in Hell as a visitor, but as one of the damned. Indeed, he stood as frozen as the sinners beneath his feet, unable to move or even utter a breath as he beheld what stood in front of him. It was the Devil. And no suave charmer, no heroic rebel, but the font of all grief and the terminus of all resentment, a vast monster whose very ugliness betrayed its former beauty. The Emperor of Hell stood surrounded by the ice up to his furry chest, which emerged from his prison like the torsos of the giants above, but immeasurably bigger. His head had not two but three faces, gazing ahead and to the sides.

Alexander felt sure that Satan would have recognised him at any point up till that very moment. They had met before, after all, and spoken many times. The Devil in human form, and Alexander secure in his old, Earthly life. Innocent of Hell and the true nature of his interlocutor. But now he was different, not part of the same story somehow. His panic subsided and he went back to being a visitor in Hell. He felt his shoulders relax as he exhaled and glanced at the author for further reassurance. 'He has no power over you now,' said the author.

Alexander looked again at the three faces of the Devil. The middle one was vermillion, the one to its right wheaten and that to its left the colour of bruised flesh. For each face, an enormous pair of wings emerged from Satan's shoulders, not feathered but leathery like a bat's wings. And now Alexander realised that these were the source of the breeze he had felt. The Evil One beat his six wings steadily, fanning the base of Hell to keep it frozen. From all six eyes issued bitter tears, merging on his three chins with bloody slobber from his three mouths, in each of which a sinner was being mangled as if caught in the jaws of a bin lorry compactor. The one in the middle had the worst of it, since he was in head first and the Devil clawed at his body like someone struggling drunkenly with a fried chicken wing. The heads of the other two hung loose from Satan's other sets of lips as he chewed, so the author could identify them for Alexander as Napoleon and Chairman Mao, each of whom had in his own way betrayed humanity and his own historic cause by embracing tyranny.

'And that's it, really,' he told Alexander. 'Let's go.'

He approached the Devil, and it dawned on Alexander that their journey 'to the bottom of the ice' was to continue via Satan himself. The author paused a short distance from the Beast, timing their leap to avoid being struck by the Devil's flapping wings. 'Hold on to me,' he said, and Alexander obliged. Then, as the wings arched upward away from them, he leapt, crashing into Satan's body and grabbing hold of his fur. 'Hold tight,' he uttered breathlessly, and began descending through the narrow gap between the ice and its captive. At the Devil's hips, the author twisted and seemed to change direction, so Alexander thought they were climbing back up. But when they emerged again from the hole, it was Satan's giant legs that protruded upwards, as if they had passed through the centre of the Earth to the other side, gravity reversed. The leg they clung to leaned close enough to the edge of the Devil's hole that they could clamber onto it like drunks collapsing onto a bar.

Indeed, now they were no longer in Hell, but in an Australian-themed pole-dancing bar. An exotic dancer clung upside down to her pole in front of them, kicking her legs in the air like the Devil's, before spinning back to her feet and taking a bow. 'G'day!' she said.

'This is ridiculous,' said Alexander.

The author could only apologise.

CHAPTER 26: A CHANGE OF DIRECTION

They wandered out of the bar into a crisp spring morning in Glasgow, the moon and even a few stars still visible in the sky above them. 'And what do you mean, "That's it, really"?' Alexander demanded. 'Are you going to explain why you've dragged me through Hell? And when do I get to meet this mysterious woman?'

The author shrugged. 'I never actually said you'd get to *meet* her.' He gestured towards a street bench and they both sat down. 'It came to me in a dream,' he continued. 'It was all a bit "meta", to be honest. I get them a lot.'

Alexander nodded indulgently, and the author continued: 'You've seen *Gregory's Girl*, right?'

'Yup.'

'Well, you know how Gregory gets a date with Dorothy, but then she sends a friend to say she's not coming?'

'Yes.'

'And then that friend takes him to get chips, and passes him on to another friend?'

'Margo, I believe'

'Whatever. Then she takes him to another accidental-on-purpose meeting with Clare Grogan, and the two of them hit it off and smooch and that's the end?'

'Yes, I am familiar with the plot of everyone's favourite 1980s Scottish coming-of-age romantic comedy. Where are you going with this?'

'Well, like I said, I had a dream, and it was a bit like that. A chain of commissions. And I was commissioned to guide you through Hell. I have no idea what's supposed to happen next.'

Alexander looked around theatrically in search of his next guide.

'Only,' the author added, 'I don't think you can go where she is, the one who commissioned me. I don't think you have the potential for it inside yourself like you do with Hell.'

Alexander shifted uncomfortably, and then asked, 'Can't you at least tell me *who* she is?'

The author shrugged again: 'She didn't give me her name, and I got the strong impression I was not supposed to speculate beyond what she told me, or to encourage you to speculate. But for what it's worth, in the dream at least, I'm pretty sure she was an angel.'

Sure, why not? 'But she said she knew me?'

'Your guardian angel?' the author suggested, seemingly having passed the point where he knew any more than Alexander. The stalemate was broken by Alexander's phone ringing. He answered it. A development in the murder case.

A confession. Or rather 14 confessions. Every single defendant in the case had changed his plea to guilty, without mitigation. Alexander told the author to keep his phone on: he wasn't finished with him yet, at least until he heard from Clare Grogan. But for now, he needed to know what the Hell was going on with this case. He set off for the office, leaving the author on the bench gazing idly at the moon.

Alexander was not shocked by the confessions. He lacked the confidence in his own understanding of the case to be shocked by anything about it. He had looked these boys in the eye and seen nothing like guilt or innocence. He had listened to their bewildered mutterings and got the impression that their own understanding of what they had done was no better than his. That was not so unusual, especially when it came to violent, impulsive crime. But typically it was possible to piece together what had happened from the physical evidence and witness statements. To come to an understanding not just of what had happened objectively, but of what the perpetrator of a crime had been thinking and feeling. Human nature was not that complicated most of the time. What had always disturbed Alexander about this case was that he had no idea what these boys had been thinking and feeling. Their crime did not make sense.

The one boy's sister had said the murder was the sort of thing that happens when people stop bothering with reasons. Like her, he did not doubt that it was connected somehow to the madness that had swept through the schools after Easter, and perhaps the demonic website too. Unlike her, he had also faced a demon in the flesh, and not just in Hell but here on Earth, up to some mischief with its shrine. He could not rule out direct demonic involvement in the murder, in all of it. Who was to say that demons were not routinely involved in crime? It was hard to know, precisely because human nature would give them so much to play with.

In any case, apparently the boys were no longer claiming to have been influenced by external forces of any kind. The hypnotism theory was dead. They were owning their crime. In fact, it transpired they had even apologised, all 14 of them. The Procurator Fiscal had never seen anything like it. There were no new facts in the case. The boys all maintained they had not known their victim, nor most of their fellow killers. But they had willingly joined the chase, deliberately reached for their knives, and when the blades 'went in' they had no one but themselves to blame. They were all guilty of murder. But now they willing to accept their punishment, or the consequences of their actions, as the Procurator Fiscal put it. Alexander, however, was now very conscious of the difference between the two things.

Earthly punishment was an artificial consequence of crime, externally and deliberately imposed by human institutions. At its noblest, it was an attempt to save the perpetrator from the natural consequences of his crime. It was supposed to stop his in his tracks, to turn him aside from the road to Hell. In remorsefully embracing their punishment, the Buchanan Street killers were almost rendering it unnecessary, but Alexander felt it was right that they should go to prison to make sure. The idea that they could ever really pay their debt to society was a polite fiction, but pay they must, if only for therapeutic reasons. How else would they process the enormity of what they had done? They wanted to pay something, needed to.

Alexander did not know what had made the boys turn back from Hell, but he felt thankful for it. Not just because it gave him a much-needed sense of closure on the case, but for humanity's sake. For Morgan's sake. For his own. If there was hope for everyone, no matter how serious their crime, then perhaps there was also hope for everyone however seemingly *trivial* their sin, dragging them almost imperceptibly in the same direction.

But now he thought with some urgency of Chalky Gold. Walder Frey had told him Gold was in Hell already, despite being very much alive, albeit in prison. Could it be that some crimes put their perpetrators beyond hope? That Hell came to them before their time? Reluctantly, Alexander resolved to visit Gold in prison at Shotts. Since Frey had said Gold's body would be possessed by a demon, he half expected to find the one he'd encountered first in hospital and then in the therapist's consulting room. No one else would be any the wiser that it was not Gold. But Alexander would know, whatever form it took. He thought also of Tod Lapraik, working his loom in a trance while his devilish doppelganger danced like a lunatic on the Bass Rock. Was Gold now frozen in Hell while the demon went through the motions of serving time on his behalf? Alexander supposed he was about to find out.

Gold agreed to the visit, though he had nothing to gain.

Alexander guessed he must have been curious. Or rather hoped that was it. If Gold really were a demon, his motivation for accepting would be more mischievous. In the event, Alexander found himself unafraid of the man, for man he was as far as Alexander could tell. Of course, he was also a murderer. And if Frey was to believed, Gold's cold blooded murder of his own father-in-law had already been established as his defining sin. He was already in Hell. So if the man in front of Alexander was not the demon he had feared, was he simply a less terrifying stand-in? Alexander scanned him carefully as he introduced himself. He didn't appear to be in any kind of trance or stupor. If he had, it would have been unremarkable enough in prison. Instead, he looked at Alexander with curiosity right enough.

'How can I help?' he asked.

'Your name has come up in connection with an inquiry,' Alexander told him.

Gold looked even more curious. 'You're the detective in charge of the Buchanan Street murder, aren't you?'

'Yes, I was. But that case is closed now, and that's not actually what I'm here about.'

'So...' Gold stopped when he realised Alexander was staring at the tattoo he had where his right hand met his wrist: 'ADELE'.

'What do you know about Adele McGlone?' the detective asked him abruptly, if not recklessly.

'Adele McGlone saved my soul,' he said.

Alexander was stunned. Adele McGlone, Leanne's older sister, also a murderer, and a fugitive. And perhaps an angel? Was Adele the mysterious woman who had summoned Alexander to Hell? Was Gold the next link in the chain?

'Tell me more,' he said, trying not to give anything away.

Gold told Alexander Adele had written to him through a prison pen pal scheme. Her letters had given him hope, allowed him to reconcile himself to his fate and even to feel remorse for his crimes. Alexander wondered how much if anything he knew about Adele's own crime. In any case, he was now much less interested in pursuing her as a suspect than in understanding what all this meant in terms of everlasting judgement and damnation. It did seem like good news.

'Well, technically, it wasn't Adele who saved my soul,' Gold seemed to think it was important to add, 'But she pointed me in the direction of the one who did.'

Ri-ight. A few weeks earlier, Alexander would have rolled his eyes, inwardly at least: 'Here we go...' He knew who Gold was talking about. But he was rapt. He said nothing, just looked at Gold expectantly.

'You don't need me to tell you, do you? The truth has been hidden in plain sight for nearly two thousand years now.'

Alexander tried to look receptive, as if waiting for a surprise.

'Read your Bible, man,' Gold said with an exasperated shrug.

Your Bible, not *the* Bible. Whether Gold knew it or not, it was quite true that Alexander both owned a Bible and was familiar with its contents. Whatever he was lacking, it was not that he did not know what the Bible said. He knew it much better than most. He knew it better than he knew 'his' classical mythology, though he thought of it in much the same way.

He had last picked up his Bible several months before. Jeremiah, the source cited by the Millennium Bug cult. 'If it's in here, it can be dismissed as superstition,' he had told himself and everyone else. And of course he had been right about the cult. There was no doubt that the Bible appealed to crazies, and that they used it in ways that could indeed be dismissed as superstitious. But then, as he had discussed with Dr Bakshi, Alexander was no stranger to superstition himself, and not because he gave too much credence to an ancient holy book, but because he had been tormented by demons. He could hardly dismiss the possibility that he was crazy, or at least profoundly disturbed. How else was he supposed to make sense of what had been happening to him? The Bible? Gold had not mentioned a particular passage or even theme for Alexander to read up on.

Nor had he suggested a new, clever way to decipher the text. It had not been an invitation to crack the da Vinci code. Hidden in plain sight, he had said. You don't need me to tell you. His intention had not been to reveal something new about the Bible, but to insist on something very old. That it was true.

Gold believed he had been saved from damnation by Jesus Christ, just as the Bible promised. In Hell itself, Alexander had been told Gold was beyond salvation, but then the denizens of Hell had been known to lie. It would hardly have been shocking after all he'd seen.

'Jesus Christ died for my sins,' Gold said. 'And for yours if you only believe it.'

Alexander looked around nervously. He did not want this conversation to be overheard by the prison officer at the door. Gold registered this and changed tack, 'You wanted to know about Adele McGlone. A few years ago, she began a prison ministry in America. Something in her past drove her to that, but you probably know more about it than I would.' He glanced curiously at Alexander, who maintained a poker face. 'Anyway, she must have had a patriotic streak, because she also took to writing to prisoners back home. Like me. So now I do my best to share the gospel with the other prisoners. With *mixed* results.' He gave Alexander a wry look. 'But, hey, I cast a demon out of a horribly-afflicted new arrival the other day. Which was nice.'

Alexander looked at him suspiciously, wondering if he was taking the piss. He seemed to be sincere. 'So you're an exorcist now?'

Chalky shook his head dismissively. 'There's no such thing. Of course, it wasn't *me* who did the casting out, not really. I just commanded the evil spirit to depart in the name of our Lord Jesus Christ. The humblest of Christians can do that. The humbler the better!' Alexander thought of Satan's contempt for 'accredited' exorcists, and wondered if the Lord of Darkness would indeed be more troubled by this tattooed murderer with a humble heart.

Chalky noticed again that Alexander was looking at his

tattoo. 'She's dead now, of course.' Alexander's shock must have shown on his face. 'I'm sorry. Did you know her *personally*?'

'Not really. I met her once. I know her sister.'

'Leanne?' Now Chalky seemed surprised. 'Adele told me she'd never get through to her sister on her own. A stubborn girl, apparently. She said she was making arrangements, though. That's all she said to me about Leanne. I wonder...'

'I should go,' Alexander said, standing up. 'You've been very helpful, so thank you for your... Thank you.'

'I'll pray for you,' Chalky said, smiling. Alexander smiled back politely and took his leave.

When the prison officer had escorted Alexander from the visiting room, he explained that the governor wanted a word before he left. 'Sure,' Alexander said, still preoccupied with what Chalky had told him. He followed the officer through a maze of corridors and security doors to the governor's office. The officer announced DCI Alexander and ushered him in, shutting the door behind him just as the detective recognised the governor: *he* was the demon Alexander had feared so much. The Hell beast sat behind the governor's desk with that same aura of malice, the same evil grin, and as Alexander scrambled with the door, the cruellest laugh he had ever heard on Earth or in Hell.

The door was unlocked, at least, and Alexander was able to make his escape to the corridor, unpursued. From there, he was guided out of the prison by the puzzled officer. His escape lasted only as long as the journey home, however. The demon governor was waiting for him when he got there. Sitting on his armchair and grinning at him.

'The dance is over,' it said, when Alexander looked bac in a panic towards the front door. 'No more running. This ti you're going nowhere except with me.'

Alexander was so terrified he could hardly speak barely managed to whisper, 'No'.

'You must know by now that Hell is not a place come and go from. It's a destination, and the only reas been able to see it before now is that it's your final de

Alexander felt as if the demon had just confirmed something he had always known, but then he thought of Chalky Gold and a waft of hope rose within him. 'You're lying,' he said.

'Oh, I lie all the time,' the demon admitted, 'but I'm not here to persuade you of anything. I'm here to take you to Hell, for good this time. You know you belong there anyway. You know *exactly* where you belong.'

Time stood still.

Alexander was not sure he *did* know where he belonged. Even assuming it was in Hell, he could see himself almost anywhere there. At least given time, he could imagine reducing himself to one of a multitude of sins. Heresy and self-destruction had both seemed likely contenders, but perhaps that was because in a perverse way they appealed to his vanity. He was uncomfortably aware that he was not above (or below) simple lust and gluttony. Or something like careerism for that matter. He was a sinner like any other. And perhaps worse in a less glamorous way: there was that nagging feeling that his whole life had in some way become a betrayal of who he was supposed to be.

At the same time, he resisted the notion that he belonged in Hell at all. It was so unfair. He acknowledged his sin, and even his *potential* for all-consuming wickedness, but surely he was not the finished article? He was not that bad; perhaps deserving of Purgatory at worst? But then everyone thinks that, and the convenience of Purgatory had always made it seem to Alexander much less plausible than Hell itself. Nothing he had seen in Hell had made the idea of a cosmic finishing school seem any more likely.

It had been the unreliable Walder Frey who had told Alexander that some sins are so heinous the sinner is cast straight down to Hell. He now knew this was false, but he should have realised before that it jarred with what he had already learned. Hell was not a place of punishment for particularly evil people.

It was indeed a destination, and you didn't so much earn your place as choose it. And even if you never got round to doing anything spectacularly heinous in life, death was the only vehicle required to get you where you'd have ended up given long enough to realise your potential. So even if the demon had no power to take Alexander before his time, what was to stop it simply murdering him? He'd end up in the same place.

Anyway, the author had said nothing about Purgatory, let alone Paradise - except to say that Alexander would not be visiting his angelic benefactor at home. The mysterious woman who might be the late Adele McGlone. But then Adele had been a murderess before becoming an angel, or whatever she was where he could not visit. And the equally homicidal Chalky Gold apparently believed he would be joining her there when his time came. The author had said Alexander did not have the potential for that place inside himself like he did with Hell. But presumably it had not been something inside that had made the difference for Adele or Chalky either. They'd been destined for Hell at least as surely as Alexander, except for what? He suspected it had little to do with their own efforts.

The author had presumably taken Alexander through Hell for a reason. And if not his own reason, then Adele's. And whatever the plan was, it surely did not involve Alexander being consigned to Hell on his own account before he'd even had time to digest what he'd seen. To understand what it meant. To convey that understanding to others, and one other in particular? In which case, he would need to live. Even more urgently, he would have to change his destination, as Adele and Chalky had done before him. He would have to become the person he had been supposed to be all along. He had, after all, been Christened as a baby.

Alexander returned to himself and faced the demon. It had risen from his armchair and now stood directly in front of him, ready to seize him. Alexander did not back away, but spoke as boldly as he could: 'I command you in the name of Jesus Christ, leave!'

'You don't believe in Jesus Christ,' the demon sneered in his face.

Alexander looked down: the demon had taken at least two steps back, and was now hovering at an ever-so-slightly unnatural angle to keep in Alexander's face. 'Your feet give me hope,' said the detective.

The demon followed his gaze downward and snarled before withdrawing. Then it spat a parting shot from the front door: 'I'll be back for you later.'

Alexander was not so sure.

ABOUT THE AUTHOR

Dolan Cummings

Dolan is a freelance writer and editor born in Glasgow and living in London. He writes speeches, articles and other copy for a variety of private and business clients. A selection of his own articles, reviews and essays can be found at dolancummings.com.

BOOKS BY THIS AUTHOR

That Existential Leap: A Crime Story

Part bildungsroman and part psychological thriller, That Existential Leap is a novel of ideas about the struggle for self-realisation and belonging in the postmodern West.

Printed in Great Britain
by Amazon